COLLIER SPYMASTERS SERIES

Consulting Editor: Saul A. Katz,
founder 999 Bookshop, New York City

The Whistle Blower by John Hale
The Third Truth by Michael Hastings
The Oxford Gambit by Joseph Hone
Exchange of Clowns by Theodore Wilden

D1431366

THE WHISTLE BLOWER

John Hale

COLLIER BOOKS
MACMILLAN PUBLISHING COMPANY
New York

Collier Books
Macmillan Publishing Company
866 Third Avenue, New York, NY 10022

Library of Congress Cataloging-in-Publication Data
Hale, John.
The whistle blower.
(Collier spymasters series)
I. Title.   II. Series.
PR6058.A438W5   1988   823'.914   88-16122
ISBN 0-02-028851-4

This is a work of historical fiction. Names, characters,
places, and incidents relating to non-historical figures are
either the product of the author's imagination or are used
fictitiously. Any resemblance of such non-historical
incidents or figures to actual events or persons, living or
dead, is entirely coincidental.

First Collier Books Edition 1988

10 9 8 7 6 5 4 3 2 1

Printed in the United States of America

For
Simon and Joanna
my dear children

PART ONE

ONE

1

Frank Jones was an ordinary man. When young he served in the Fleet Air Arm as a rating pilot. Because they would not make him an officer – which denied him the pay and privileges which an officer pilot received for doing the same job – he left the Service when he was thirty.

By that time he was married to Margery and had two small children, Bob and Helen.

In civilian life he learned about money by working for other people until Margery inherited five thousand pounds from a great-aunt in Dover. She gave it to him.

Frank started his own business believing that if you pick the right line and work your guts out you will win. That was in the 1960s when you could write your own cheque. He bought a two-storey house in Reading whose ground floor had been a failed corner shop. He converted it and sold office equipment. He also did printing, photocopying and employed a mechanic to deal with typewriters, dictaphones and calculators.

The house had a large basement for storage.

They lived on the first and second floor: sitting room and kitchen-dining room one flight up; three bedrooms and bathroom two flights up. After ten years they could afford central heating. He ran a tight ship.

Frank never flew again after leaving the Navy because it cost too much. For years he drove cheap old cars which he serviced himself. He cleared his overdraft. He did not join the Rotary Club. He paid his bills if not by return at the latest by the end of the month, even at the height of inflation in the 1970s. He did not try to make a friend of his bank manager.

At the age of fifty-four he looked seven years younger and could take all the stairs at a run without effort. His hair was still dark, he had his own teeth and he only needed glasses to read in a bad light.

There were things he missed which he never mentioned. Deep in him was the same bloody-minded streak which had flared long ago and lost him a commission when he faced the final selection board. With it was linked another feeling which had not been satisfied since the steam catapult slammed the aircraft forrard and he lifted her over the bow and nobody could touch him because he was airborne.

He loved his wife, voted Tory and was unable to express the pride he felt in his children.

That is how it stood until the house bell rang sharply on a fine Monday morning in June.

It was a quarter to nine. Anne, whom Frank employed to serve in the shop, type, photocopy and help with the printing, had probably forgotten her key. Frank had been in his office in the back room of the shop since seven-thirty. He left the quarterly VAT return and went through to the passage and opened the house door.

A policeman stood there. People were going by to work.

'Mr Jones?'

'Yes.'

'Can I come in a minute?'

'What for?'

'I've got a bit of bad news.'

The policeman had difficulty in passing Frank in the narrow hall. He then hesitated between Frank and the stairs.

Frank closed the door. The policeman started to speak and Frank said, 'Just a minute.'

He listened. If Margery had heard the bell she was not coming down.

'Right,' he said, 'just through there would you?'

They went into the back room of the shop and Frank stood between the man and the cash books and vouchers and calculator laid out on the table he used as a desk.

10

'What is it?'

'It's very bad news,' said the policeman, 'your son is dead.'

2

He had driven the route many times because Bob had gone to the University of Bristol. Today he saw nothing on the M4, nothing when he turned off at Intersection 15 to bypass Swindon driving north-west to Cheltenham.

What he saw was the face of the policeman and then the face of his wife screaming. In those seconds when she registered what had happened it was as if she turned at once into a deranged stranger.

He heard himself on the telephone to the doctor, to Margery's sister, Eileen, in Faversham. After that Anne arrived and opened the shop.

He sat with Margery and could not comfort her. The doctor like the policeman expressed sympathy without conviction.

As he drove his last conversation with Bob jumped into his head, was suppressed, came up again. Five weeks earlier he and Margery had visited Bob. It began like any ordinary visit with the Sunday papers strewn about and, through the open window, snatches of *The World This Weekend* on the Welsh woman's radio blasting next door.

What Bob said later in private to Frank had troubled him every day since. It went against everything Frank believed.

As the automatic pilot in him drove with precision and exactly up to the speed limit the realisation that it had been their final conversation filled him with anguish. He knew himself to have been obdurate, unsympathetic and worse, that afternoon.

Bob had Margery's deceptively gentle temperament. Only once or twice had Frank met another side to his nature and then they clashed head on: no compromise; no shouting; no passion on the surface; certainty. On these rare occasions, of which the Sunday visit was the last, Frank completely failed to recognise himself in his son.

Another, darker feeling kept trying to break through. Frank

held it off trying to be rational, to think straight, to reconstruct that day. He focused on the petrol gauge which was hovering over zero. Then it was through. He shouted aloud against the engine, 'How? How could he fall?' The Inspector on the phone said Bob fell from the roof. Frank saw them all out on the roof. He saw Bob smiling, pouring the cheap wine. He shouted, 'No.' He saw them in the moment before he had stepped out to join them.

3

The doorway was on the penultimate landing of the converted house. Mark, one of the two who shared it with Bob, had called out, 'Mind your head, Mr Jones.'

Frank said, 'Thank you' and wondered why Mark always seemed to invite the boot. As he stepped down on to the roof Frank had sniffed the air and thought for a second how good it would be to fly today, one of those rare West Country days when the light makes every building and stretch of water look like a Canaletto and the air is not sleepy from south-west winds. No sniff of the Atlantic this afternoon as Tiger, the ginger tom, strutted up to him and rubbed his leg. Tiger had a thick square head and what looked like a cubical body, balanced on four short legs. Frank scratched him behind the ears and thought, good job he's neutered or he'd spray me and I'd stink.

He wrinkled his eyes against the light. The roof was over the kitchen-dining room on the first floor which all three of them shared – Bob, Mark and the big girl, Rose.

Bob was pouring Margery a drink. He had put the bottles of cheap wine and the tumblers on the stained cane table. Frank half expected him to drop the glass or balance the bottle too near the edge of the table, which was rocky. Seeing him Bob said, 'Red or white, Dad?' as Margery, who was laughing at something, made a gesture with her hand at the backs of the other houses each with its flat roof. 'But it *is* lovely out here, Bob, even with the houses all round you don't *feel* overlooked the way we do at home.'

12

'Where is Rose?' asked Bob. 'Not clearing away or something is she – we've washed up.'

'She wants to take a photograph,' said Mark. 'Her parents phoned from Australia to say Happy Birthday and she said she would – '

Rose ducked through the doorway on to the roof with a camera saying, 'The light is wonderful, shall we have a colour-supp type group? The bottles, the old cane chair – ?'

'Tiger?' said Mark, picking him up. Tiger fondly dug his fore-claws into Mark's shoulder and dribbled on his collar.

'Look at him,' said Margery.

'Hideous,' laughed Bob. 'You didn't say, Dad?'

'Red, please.'

'Oh Bob, he isn't,' said Margery.

'That cat', replied Bob, handing a glass to Frank, 'is abnormal, not only does he regularly bite the hand that feeds him – he gets down there – ' he pointed, 'into the garden from the kitchen and then can't get back up – so he howls and howls – and who do you think is the lucky citizen who hears him at four in the morning? And eventually has to go down and let him in?'

Bob had never been conscious of his height, unlike Rose who tended to tuck her head down. In later life she would be humpbacked. Frank watched her as she arranged them for the photograph. Thirty today, big breasts, big hips, long legs but altogether unsexual. Moon face, long fair hair; business-like.

He wanted, as he so often did, to be away on his own. He dismissed the feeling and allowed himself to be placed on the outside of the group beside Margery who was still talking about how well the two young men had cooked the lunch. Frank knew she was uneasy and talking too much, unable just to be silent and let the day flow round her. And yet afterwards, he knew, she would say how wonderful it had been – and mean it. Who in this universe knew where to put himself when not actually at work or asleep? That one facing them with the camera saying, 'If you could all smile?' and smiling herself as she pressed the button – she knew.

In the car he said aloud, 'I never saw that photo – I must get that photo,' and then in his head the sentence tailed off because could he or Margery ever bear to look at it?

13

At the time he knew it would be sharp focused and well framed because Rose, he had noticed, was ostentatiously efficient. His conceit at that time, five weeks ago, made him believe that twelve naval years teaches you all you need to know about human beings.

The shutter clicked. They smiled. Bob was in the centre of the group.

4

A print of the photograph – with two others of different men – found its way into a file marked 'Dodgson'. The file was in a metal cabinet bolted to a wall in a room in Soho. The room had an alarm system fitted by a team from British Telecom who, like the rest of their department, had been positively vetted as well as signing the Official Secrets Act. The room was at the top of a building in a small court; its entrance had an opaque window with A. J. Ball Builder and Decorator painted on it. Inside, at the ground level, there was a short counter with a man sitting behind it, a strip light overhead and a door leading to stairs.

If an unexpected customer from a delicatessen or a film distributor's happened to come in to ask for a plumber to clear a blocked lavatory the man put them off. He had a list of alternative builders and decorators because A. J. Ball was booked solid, sorry squire, why don't you try . . .

A. J. Ball was not listed in the London directory but the team from British Telecom had put in two telephones, one down, one up. There had been a Mr Ball but he went into liquidation.

The ordinary police did not come round; they had been told to leave these premises to the Special Branch.

The man behind the counter was capable of dealing with any others, drunk or sober, who wandered in to see if A. J. Ball concealed hard-core porn movies or a massage parlour where you could, as they put it, buy relief.

Frank telephoned from the service station outside Cirencester where he filled up with petrol. Although his hand was steady he seemed to be trembling. There was a vibration in his chest, arms and hands. For the first time in years he wanted to smoke.

Before he left he had turned off the extension from the shop phone to the sitting room so that Margery would have no more shocks. Anne answered to say that Eileen had not arrived yet, but the pills had worked and Margery was asleep. There were no messages. Everything was all right, how was he? Fine.

He put down the phone. The box smelt of urine. Did anybody, ever, clean out public call-boxes?

The sun was out and when he got back into the car it was stuffy with the heat through the glass. He put a cassette into the slot and drove – listening for five minutes to Benny Goodman playing at the Maltings before he switched it off. Green country, grey Cotswold stone, the sun on his left hand through the passenger window and the sound of Bob's voice in his head.

They had lingered on the roof in the surprisingly warm late afternoon; the faint smell of other people's Sunday dinners – Frank never got into the habit of calling it Sunday lunch – had drifted away across the roofs of Cheltenham. Perhaps in the more elegant terraces they still called it Sunday luncheon? It was the sort of thing Margery made jokes about.

She was saying to Bob, 'But what *is* H and S?' and Bob was laughing his odd sort of coughing laugh which made other people laugh with him as he looked down at her through his big spectacles and said, 'Hammer and Sickle! Shortened to H and S. It's a phrase the raincoat men use about anything they think tends to sedition, didn't you know?'

'No, of course I didn't, and what are raincoat men?'

'Oh them! They're the ones who keep H and S files. They're ex-detective superintendents and the like and they wear boots and bowlers.'

'They don't, Bob.'

'Well no, Mum, perhaps they don't, but what they do is PV chaps like me – and indeed Mark and Rose.'

'He's talking about security, Margie,' said Frank, 'positive vetting.'

'It sounds like Crufts or something.'

'Oh you must have heard,' said Bob, 'they PV us regularly. In fact, dear mater – they are Pee Veeing me at this moment. It comes up five yearly and is known in the trade among us civil servants as the quinquennial review.'

Driving the car, watching the bends, Frank recollected the way Bob facetiously elongated the two consonants and knew that he did it because Margery worried about the state of the world, and particularly about her son being a Russian linguist. She had quietly and ineffectually opposed the idea from the beginning. Since the Dodgson case she had seemed more preoccupied than usual and changed the subject if it came up. She hated violence and feared death.

But what had he said? He, Frank, standing a little apart from the group, irrationally irritated for reasons he could not recall – what had he said to provoke that conversation? It began with something which made Bob turn sharply towards him and say with surprise, 'I'd never have thought of that, Dad – now that really is an H and S idea.'

It seemed vital to Frank that he get it all clear before he met the police at Cheltenham. The primitive, instant-reaction part of his mind knew that whatever he was going to do started with that day, Rose's birthday.

And then he remembered it clearly: first some conversation about the three of them – Bob, Mark and Rose – living under the same roof. Himself standing apart, bored, thinking it was the same with unmarried members of the Foreign Office and other government departments. He knew this from one of his London customers who had a son in the diplomatic service. He said without thinking and it came out sharply, 'You're all under the same roof because the powers that be prefer it, aren't you?' It seemed obvious.

Mark said at once, 'Oh I don't know about that.'

Overlapping Rose said, 'Good lord, no – '

There was silence while Bob looked at each of them. Then he laughed and said, 'Oh I see – to keep an eye on each other.'

Frank was astonished.

'Of course not – I didn't mean that, Bob.'

That was the moment when Bob looked straight at him and said, 'I'd never have thought of that, Dad – now that really is an H and S idea.'

Frank saw the moment complete. He had been standing against the low wall which divided them from the roof next door. Bob was near the unwalled edge opposite with the afternoon sun on his face. Tiger was picking his way fastidiously among the old sinks and urns full of plants and flowers which lined the edge behind Bob, and Rose was about to stop him digging a hole in one of them. Mark was red in the face and turning away towards the house. Margery, sensing something she could not understand, was wearing her brave smile, the one that sometimes preceded private tears.

Frank feeling responsible for the change in atmosphere said, 'I meant it must be easier to unwind after work with people who do the same sort of thing – '

'Oh, we don't talk shop,' said Mark.

'Of course we do,' said Rose, 'well sometimes.'

'Not supposed to,' said Mark, 'and certainly not supposed to mention we do, I should have thought.' He poured himself another glass of wine without offering it.

Bob went on as if no one had spoken, 'We are Pee Veed by IOs, Mother; an IO is not, as you might think, an Intelligence Officer, he is an Investigating Officer – and sometimes, if we look dodgy because someone who isn't us at all, but with the same name, turns up at a peace rally, the case is referred to an HEO Pee Vee Assessor – who is, in all his glory, a Higher Executive Officer Positive Vetting Assessor – I may set that to music.'

'I don't think we should talk about it,' said Frank.

'You are right,' smiled Bob, 'it is, after all, a method devised to let people like Dodgson get away with it for years.'

'That's not quite fair,' said Rose immediately. 'Dodgson was very clever and we're not the Soviet Union.'

Bob seemed to consider this. He wandered to the unwalled edge of the roof and looked down.

'Bob,' said Margery nervously.

'Hmmm.'

17

'Don't er — '

'I was thinking', said Bob, 'that I might arrange a cat-type ladder so that Tiger can make his way up on his own.'

'It's nearly thirty feet,' said Mark, not going too close to the edge.

As if it were part of the same thought Bob said, 'I went to look at Dodgson's house.'

Frank wondered for a moment if this was some new joke but Bob was no longer smiling. Mark looked at Rose who did not appear to have heard the remark.

TWO

1

For the first two weeks after his conviction Dodgson was lodged in the Segregation Block adjacent to A Wing. It could have been worse. It could have been Durham. It might yet be because they never left you long in one place. They moved you in secret from one maximum security prison to another. He looked forward to the Isle of Wight.

He had been conditioned to the idea that he would be isolated at first if caught; he had also been warned both in East Berlin and Vienna of the stages of interrogation.

What had not been anticipated by his controller was that he would be tried and sentenced *before* interrogation. A certain element of hope had been removed from the duel to come.

He had pleaded guilty without reservation. The instructions were always to do that in the United Kingdom: to plead guilty, to show remorse, to appear to co-operate and, essentially, to create an impression − according to your circumstances − either of character weakness which the cruel Soviets had exploited or of passionate idealism which the British with their ideas of fair play could grudgingly admire. Whichever way you did it you kept in mind that your last service, having been caught, was to make the worst publicity for your captors, driving the wedge as deeply as possible between them and the American imperialists.

They drummed into you that they looked after their own. In his case there was a special clause to this understanding. There was a false trail he had to lay when interrogated. A subtle manoeuvre and difficult to pull off. But he must do it and then they would get him out. Blake had got away from this very prison where he, Dodgson, sat in his 'greys' and waited for his interrogator.

Of course Blake was a long time ago and he had been a professional of quite another kind: the kind they make films about, men who live dangerously from their youth up, face death and torture, speak several languages and always, as in the apparent simplicity of his final act – the escape through the cell window – leave an air of mystery. Why had he been in that cell? Why had the bar been loose?

How different from himself, Dodgson, plump and round-faced, considering one of the consequences of the theory of quantum mechanics; a physicist's problem, really, it had fascinated him for years.

When they had first interviewed him at GCHQ Cheltenham he faced a ferocious mathematician who resembled a wolf in a wheelchair; this man set the problems, combinatorial problems, the manipulation of numbers, and then, as it were, at the subsequent interview played three-dimensional chess with him on a hot afternoon while two others watched him sweat. Long ago.

How many thousand brain cells had he shed in the natural wastage of the intervening years? How many codes encrypted and decrypted? What a wonderful game of bluff and double bluff and treble bluff. The Russians were the best at it in the world, the game of illusion. It was like the 'spontaneous' manoeuvres they played out before foreigners. Whole armies were taken from normal duties and rehearsed over the terrain for anything up to a year; hundreds of tanks were worn to scrap so that on the day, as they crossed impossible ground going into and under impassable rivers (whose beds had been lined with steel mesh to prevent the tank tracks bogging down to emerge magnificently on the other side, foreign observers would be stunned by the scale of it, the precision, the initiative of army commanders who had practised every move in every weather, faced every contingency, fifty times in secret.

Who would not be on the side of a people who thought like that? They were Elizabethan those Russians: they roared, they drank, they embraced, they wept and they sucked in the blacks the yellows the browns from all over the globe; even when those deluded idiots were in the very heartland itself, at the Patrice Lumumba University for example, or at the Bolshoi, others having been thrown out to give them a seat, they did not for a second suspect the tremendous and wonderful illusion, the game itself, the subtle reality hidden behind all that turgid stuff about Marx. Their problem – those myriad converts to the future – was that they had never read *Alice*.

Dodgson considered the notebook and biro they had permitted him. He could now put his whole mind to the problem of the behaviour of two infinitesimally small particles moving apart at great speed until separated by miles; his whole mind because he had peace of mind. Until the door closed on him and he was confined within a space five paces by three he did not know that all his life he had been looking forward to prison. He was free.

There is no connection between the two devices which will measure the particles, and it is arranged that no signals travelling at or below the speed of light may pass between them. And yet, against common sense, or to put it another way, against the scientifically accepted view of reality, when a measurement of some property of one of the particles is taken the other behaves as if it 'knows' and adjusts its state accordingly.

Trying to explain this to his son, who preferred cricket, Dodgson said it was like twins, separated at birth, one in Australia and one in England. You operate on the one in England to remove his appendix and at that moment in Australia the other one exhibits a fresh scar in his right groin.

Einstein described the effect as 'spooky action at a distance'.

And that, thought Dodgson waiting for interrogation, is a reality I understand. So did one of the two men discussing him in another part of the prison that day.

2

'I would prefer to deal with him off the premises.'

'The commissioners won't have it,' said the official who resented the other man's air of bored detachment. Without

21

appearing to have heard what the official said, the man, in his precise and irritating Morningside accent, said, 'It is good of you to offer a protective room but we do not use force – '

The official took his pipe from his mouth but was given no chance to reply.

' – there are grapevines in these places, we would not relish headlines in the *Guardian* about the use of a padded cell, nor odious comparisons between ourselves and the Lubianka . . . you do follow?'

Outside one of the special watch cells they were passing the signal arm went up. Inside a prisoner began an epileptic fit. A prison officer strolled towards it, looked in and then dealt methodically with the heavy lock mechanism.

The official, who spent part of his life measuring the appearances of men against their crimes, studied the other man who had paused to watch.

Bony, no meat on him, looking older than his age; a long face with the skin pale and tight over the skull; the eyes dark and opaque behind the spectacles, no hint of the thoughts in the expression. A grey suit, old enough to have turn-ups on the trousers, excellent cloth you could hardly drive a nail through . . . and a showy tie, dull orange . . . there was a hint of red in the hair giving the impression of a damped down fire. Black shoes, no toecaps, well polished, old like the suit, probably handmade. A slightly hunched attitude of attention, like a stork, or the way a man hunched and leaned to listen to an argument and hitch a gown. White hands, long fingers, no rings. The head would look formidable and eighteenth century under a wig.

The official was sceptical of any correlation between appearance and profession except in the crudest cases involving violence – but he thought he knew a lawyer when he saw one. Barrister? No, being Scots it would be an advocate. So this was to be the Interrogator.

A second warder joined the first and disappeared into the special watch cell. The official measured the advocate against the plump and apparently docile Dodgson as he had last seen him, preoccupied with quantum physics, in the segregation unit above them at the north end.

The advocate was looking at him. The official was disconcerted. The advocate seemed for a moment to take in the rough

22

walls, the flaking paint, the smell which suggested a distant but vast urinal. The faintest expression of distaste passed over his face and was gone.

'You see', he said softly, 'we're having no more outcry of any kind over Mr Dodgson. We shall require a cover so that when he leaves his cell, daily, possibly for weeks, it will seem a normal event, as if he were going, shall we say, to the tailor's shop. I suggest you let it be known that he has cancer and is going to the hospital next door for radium treatment and chemotherapy, something like that. I can promise you that he, himself, will not contribute to any grapevine.'

'There are', said the official, 'some old storerooms. Terrible state, they'd have to be cleared, cleaned, painted ... '

'Simply submit a budget, it will be dealt with. Shall we look at them? I want him to be comfortable.'

'Comfortable!'

'Oh yes,' said the advocate, 'definitely comfortable.'

3

Flecker turned left past the Queens Theatre into Wardour Street. He disliked Soho and regretted they had set up shop there. He walked briskly for five minutes sometimes seeing himself reflected in shop windows. Did he look like an actor? Lord once told him that he had recruited him because he looked like an actor. Not a hero, not a leading man, but one of those deceptive, middle-aged actors who never stop working: they play bank managers, insurance brokers, confidence men, unspecified civil servants – capable of being either cosy or sinister, of suggesting either integrity or sexual deviation; having the sort of face that becomes one thing with a military moustache and quite another with mutton chop whiskers.

He did not look like the actors appearing at the Queens Theatre, that was certain. Their photographs depressed him each time he saw them.

He pushed open the door of A. J. Ball Builder and Decorator. The man behind the counter was reading the *Sun*. He looked up and said as he had been instructed, 'Morning, Mr

23

Ball, you're a bit late,' and Flecker replied, 'Trains from Bromley delayed.'

Without pausing Flecker went to the door by the counter and the man pressed a button out of sight so that the door opened under Flecker's pressure, admitting him to the staircase. The door clicked shut behind him.

The warped tread was uncarpeted and the stair well unventilated under a dirty skylight. The rancid smell from an Italian restaurant kitchen hung in the air.

On the wall by the door at the top was an antiquated metal switch screwed into a worn wooden base. Flecker put his hand over the grooved dome and turned it anti-clockwise until it resisted. Then he swung the board away from the wall on its hinge to show the alarm controls underneath. He disarmed them, closed the board, put his key into the door and went in.

He did not raise the dirty, yellow blind at the window. Instead he switched on the overhead strip lights and put his briefcase on the desk. He took the tape machine from the metal filing cabinet, plugged it in and then he took the tapes from his briefcase.

He ran the number counter to four zeros, fitted the first tape and then sat at the desk. He put on earphones. He opened his notebook and placed his pen beside it. Then he started the tape.

He listened to a conversation which had taken place in Cheltenham on a Sunday afternoon; some of it almost impossible to understand because, although there was very little background noise, they seemed to be at the limit of the range of the microphone. Or perhaps the van was badly placed with obstacles in between. He stopped the tape and ran it back to listen to a blurred section again. It was a special tape, a refinement of the kind first developed in the 1950s to monitor the Russians on manoeuvres in East Germany from listening posts in West Berlin.

Sometimes the Russian tank commanders made a Russian joke and wished their listeners a Happy Christmas. Not in December, but on the date of the festival celebrated by the Russian Orthodox Church in January. Dodgson would have appreciated their sense of humour. His controller did not make jokes. Nor did Flecker, who would have got on with

24

Dodgson's controller, being in the same trade, the same kind of actor. Flecker in a grubby room in Soho playing the part for which he had been cast nearly a quarter of a century before by Lord: listening to an ex-Fleet Air Arm pilot arguing with his son who is a linguist in Signals Intelligence attached to Division J at GCHQ Cheltenham.

4

Everything was unreal, the car, the landscape going by outside, the light. Disconnected thoughts, many of them incoherent as if he were drunk. The shaking inside him went on.

He knew it was shock. He had seen it in the Navy, dealt with it in others. The events of Sunday May 13th, Rose's birthday, kept dissolving into other periods of his life.

When a small boy – he placed it as the time of the book of Newbolt's poems, second-hand, shiny pages with very sharp print smelling a bit mouldy – *The sands of the desert are sodden red, Red with the wreck of a square that broke* – about that time, the last time he said his prayers and meant them, the mind refused to hold, like now; wartime and his Dad-at-sea-time, 'Dear God keep my Dad safe'; terrible guilt, his Dad went down because he, Frank, let his mind wander instead of saying his prayers properly ... but what started this? God and Henry Newbolt? Oh yes, Rose mentioned God in a patronising way which upset Margery almost the moment they arrived.

Margery wanted to argue. Margery was a spiritual person. She knew how to love and wasted no time on false pride. He could see her suppressing her reply rather than rock the precarious boat for three, anxious always to do the best for Bob. She turned the other cheek, which infuriated Frank. He opened his mouth to defend her and then shut it. It was hard for him to say nothing. Always had been.

Suddenly he was nineteen. 'Let's find out about you, Jones,' said the instructor in the Tiger Moth and put her through a series of manoeuvres which made him spew all over the lovely white overalls they issued them. They landed. He could hardly get out of the cockpit for shame. The relief to be down was overwhelming.

'Feel better?' asked the lieutenant.

'Do you?' replied Frank. 'Or shall we go round again – sir?'

He was thirty-one, in civvy street.

'You want to get on in business, my boy,' said the old rogue who employed him green out of the Service, imbued with a sense of duty, ignorant of money and the infinite range of meanness, deception and exploitation that can be safely practised in business. '*First*, what you do is not say too much. You smile and you try not to make people nervous – agree with them, listen to their troubles, don't make remarks behind their backs it comes home in a small town – you got a good face for it, you can look them in the eye. When I first saw you I said, "This is an honest man, you can trust this one" . . . but there is something else, I tell you for your own sake. I see it peeping from your eyes. It's there now!'

The old man had a gap between his front teeth and Frank disliked it when he smiled.

'You know where I come from? My grandfather was selling carpets in the Levant, a world you couldn't dream, my boy, and we know how to look at a man; I said also, "He has not yet learned how to bend, this one," not yet, eh? But you will! I tell you something that will be worth more to you than money: what you do not tell them, what you do not show them – *that* they cannot know.'

Of course – that Sunday they had not come to Cheltenham by car at all. Train. Sunday trains and having to change and the last stretch by coach. Was that the reason for his initial irritation? Or was it later – standing drinking wine which tasted like metallic ink?

He switched on the car radio, pressed the buttons in turn, found every sound unbearable and switched it off. More voices in his head . . .

The taxi – that happened next. To get away from the chat on the roof he used the excuse he must telephone a taxi in good time to take them to the station. It gave him a few minutes in Bob's room on his own. It was an old habit to go quietly away for ten minutes, to take a breath, to control the sharp edge of his mind which tempted him to speak out.

26

He sat at the desk looking for Bob's address book to find the taxi number. The room was its usual shambles. The sound of the voices on the roof came indistinctly through the open window. Near his foot on the floor was a Boots diary. Open. He found the address book. He had given it to Bob some years ago. It was a beautiful job with a green leather cover.

Down the one flight outside the door they were starting to come in. The sun still shone; the light through the window warmed his legs as he sat with them stretched out. He had left the door partly open and the voices were clear.

After the phone call he came into Bob's doorway and stopped. Bob was standing, quite still, on the landing just inside the door to the roof. Frank in the doorway above looked down at him. Other voices came from Mark's part of the house one flight below Bob.

A moment earlier Bob had helped Margery over the sill of the door.

She had said, 'It's getting a little chilly,' which it was not, but someone walked over her grave and she shivered and then suddenly embraced Bob. It was awkward because of his height and he felt uncomfortable. He returned the embrace good-naturedly and said, 'I'm glad you didn't drive this time, Mum.'

'I brought a cake, it's in the kitchen,' said Margery knowing she had said it before two or three times.

'Lovely.'

Then she said, 'Are you happy?' and held him tighter.

' 'Course I am.'

From the floor below Rose called, 'Tea? Coffee?'

'I'll come and help,' said Margery going down, speaking too cheerfully.

Bob stood there. He sighed and no longer smiled. He took off his spectacles and massaged his nose and then stood with them dangling from one hand with that naked, blank look, the world out of focus.

Frank came out at this point. He felt guilty as if spying and shocked because the man on the landing seemed a stranger. It was as if every unquestioned certainty which Frank held about his son was overturned. He knew nothing about this tall, unsmiling young man. He moved deliberately and Bob looked up. He had, the moment before, been holding one hand palm

27

inwards in front of his face close to his short-sighted eyes. Now he flapped the hand, smiled, put back his specs which restored the old Bob, and said, 'Which lifeline is the one that counts, Dad, do you know?'

Frank came down to join him as he went on in his old joking way, 'I wonder. Sinister? Dexter?'

'What?'

'Left, right – comes from a joke about the Roman army on the march – pick 'em up, sinister, dexter, left right – not much of a joke. I don't suppose you marched in the Navy?'

'My boy,' said Frank, in the style of his first employer, 'little do you know! There was a place known as Whale Island where we drilled until we dropped. Do you know I was once daft enough to volunteer for the field gun team. I wanted to stay at Lee-on-Solent, which was our Port Division, they trained there on the far side of the airfield. I wasn't tough enough.'

'I think you're tough enough,' said Bob. 'My goodness, those were the days, I suppose – my country Right or Left.'

'What does that mean?'

'Orwell I think – saying that when it came to it you put your country before political loyalty.'

'Fancy a walk?'

'Yes,' said Bob, 'and then again, no, not really but we'd better get it over – I need to talk to you.' They started down the short flight and Bob tripped on something. 'I'm so clumsy it's bloody ridiculous,' he said. 'I've broken two cups this week already.'

Outside in the street, which was lined with cars parked either side, nothing stirred. The taxi waiting for someone a few doors down was double-parked, its driver reading the *News of the World*. They were well past him when he put the paper down and spoke into his microphone. Perhaps a customer had cancelled or another more urgent job had come up because he drove off.

THREE

1

The liaison man was a plump young American, prematurely bald, who usually wore an English suit – he was Anglophile which was one of the reasons they selected him for the London station – but today wore a hired chauffeur's uniform and a peaked cap. He considered it idiotic but never argued about inessentials.

He stood beyond the customs area at Terminal 3 as the transatlantic passengers came through. He held a card with Mr James P. Shaw on it.

Mr Shaw emerged carrying one small suitcase.

They drove out through the tunnel and on to the last section of the M4 into London. The English car constricted Mr Shaw who unclipped his seat belt and began to fumble under and down the side for a lever to slide the seat back.

'That's against the law here,' said the liaison man.

'Fixing your seat?'

'You don't wear the belt – they fine you.'

'It's my neck.'

'They don't see it that way, Mr Shaw.'

'OK.'

'The British have fixed an apartment,' said the liaison man. 'One of them will give you all they have so far and from that you can structure your questionnaire.'

'How long do I have?'

'You start tomorrow.'

'Where?'

The liaison man indicated a part of London ahead and to the left.

'They have him in prison over there, the district is called Hammersmith.'

'Do I need to remember that?'

'No. I drive you while you're here.'

'How about the black box?' asked Mr Shaw.

'Waiting for you in the apartment, also a typewriter, paper, carbons.'

Immediately before the Cromwell Road they filtered left, turned first right and right again to drive south to the Thames through the early traffic of the morning rush. They crossed the river by Battersea Bridge and the liaison man discarded his cap. He parked short of the block of flats by the park railings. He turned off the ignition and reached behind Mr Shaw's seat for a document case with a combination lock. He fiddled with it, opened the lid and handed over a small ring with two keys and a plastic disc on it. There was a number on the disc.

'Top floor,' he said. 'Don't expect luxury, they don't have our budget. Their man will be waiting. Don't lean on him – I am liaison, I know how they think – if you want something tell me, I'll fix it.'

'You got a number?'

'Use the Embassy, ask for extension 452 – just say your name.'

Mr Shaw started to get out of the car.

'Hold it.'

Mr Shaw sat again with the door partly open. Although a fine morning in late May it felt chilly to him, being used to central heating.

'We have a clear and simple objective: we believe something the Brits do not believe. You are here to make it either affirmative or negative. You are the expert and we go with you. One other thing, there's food up there, you stay in till I call.'

'But this is England for Christ's sake – and I never saw London before.'

'You were never here,' said the liaison man, 'we never had any dealings with the British in this matter except the usual channels. The Dodgson case is closed. Understood?'

'Understood.'

2

Mr Shaw let himself in on the Yale, the Chubb was already unlocked. He put down his case in the dim hall. He heard a stir from behind the door on his left and went through it.

If there are black men built like boxers in Edinburgh the advocate had not met them. Mr Shaw, who suddenly filled the doorway of the sitting room of the flat, could have stepped straight off the gangplank of a slaver were it not for the sharp lightweight coat. He was black, undiluted to milk chocolate or Hollywood tan by white penetration. He seemed, in this light, almost the dark purple of a washed grape.

'Shaw,' he said extending a hand.

'Bruce,' said the surprised advocate.

'You the Interrogator?'

'Er, well er – '

Mr Shaw smiled. He had a wonderful wide smile. He seemed to love life and brim over with confidence.

'Is there coffee?'

He was looking at a tan-coloured Samsonite suitcase with a typewriter case beside it on the floor near the window. He hefted the case in his hand as Mr Bruce, the Interrogator, said, 'I've really no idea,' in the accent of Morningside.

'Oh really! Shall we take a look – you know the cryptonym for what's in this case, Bruce?'

'No.'

'LCFLUTTER. What I do is sometimes known as fluttering. I am,' he said, and Mr Bruce began to realise that there was a little more to him than the all-American first impression, 'Ah am,' he repeated in his cotton-picking voice, 'sometimes referred to, sah, as de Flutter Man, or, if yoh taste is mo' formal, as Mr Flutter – what y'all doin' Mistah Fluttah dey say, an' ah reply – why! ah am pickin' dare brains, Mister Interlockerter, ah am pickin' dem . . . to pieces.'

He flipped the Samsonite case on to the gate-legged table and opened the lid to show the polygraph machine neatly stowed inside.

'Dat ol' black box,' he said, and then in his normal voice, 'have you seen them work, Mr Bruce?'

'No.' A conditioned reply because until they imported six

31

machines into GCHQ it had been Holy Writ that the security services of the United Kingdom had no truck with such things; despite the tame expert and his neat machine tucked away in the Harley Street area for DI5 use years before the recommendations in the Report of the Security Commission, May 1983. In any case Mr Bruce was no career officer. He was one of that army of lawyers, psychiatrists, doctors, economists, bankers who are called on from time to time. Different again from the businessmen who do the one-off mission. His real name was not Mr Bruce. Any more than the Flutter Man was Mr Shaw.

'That coffee,' said the Flutter Man, 'an' then we'll talk about it. There will be ... ' his voice receded, 'a meeting of minds concerning Dodgson.'

The Interrogator cleared his throat but did not reply.

When he first entered the hall, which was one size larger than a cell, the American had noted two doors facing him, and one at either end. The first of the two doors – on his left as he came out of the sitting room – opened into what estate agents call a kitchenette. By holding his stomach in and moving partly sideways he made his way between a greasy wall on one side and a gas stove and refrigerator on the other to the sink under the window. On the draining board was the only clean thing in the kitchen – a cardboard box containing instant coffee, sugar, long-life milk, sliced bread, butter, cooking fat, eggs, bacon, marmalade and something called a television supper which had to be heated in the oven and eaten not later than the day after tomorrow's date.

The top of the electric stove was crusty and spattered like a painter's palette with what had boiled and fried over and become fixed by heat and evaporation. He tried the controls holding his hand over the rings in turn. Two of the four began to warm up. He was examining two dented aluminium saucepans and the frying pan inverted on a rack over the stove when the Interrogator said from the doorway, 'Crockery and cutlery in the sitting room, not too clean, I'm afraid!'

For Mr Bruce, QC of the Faculty of Advocates, to have got out of his chair and looked for a cup and saucer was a remarkable gesture. The last time he had anything to do with a kitchen was in the house of a mistress; a lady in such stark contrast to his wife and way of life in Edinburgh that it added to the sexual *frisson* to do something as unusual as filling kettles and putting spoonfuls of coffee into a non-matching cup. Also he feared she might catch fire while he was there, not from his passion, but from the black, floating, transparent garment she wore as she tripped lightly about the place. It lifted and ballooned round her delicious figure and was, to his practical mind, a terrible hazard in a small kitchen from the gas rings. And think of the subsequent enquiry. In any case he considered men who cooked to be verging on the queer.

Edinburgh society being some twenty years behind the rest of the United Kingdom (if you exclude Ulster) he was used to servants in the house; if, rarely, there was no one available to cook for him he went to his club or to a restaurant. This morning he had, after all, eaten a good breakfast and did not require coffee for another hour and a half.

The black man, whose ancesters had, in all probability, been sold into slavery for the profit of the forbears of the Interrogator, failed to appreciate the gesture.

'You want to wash them?' he said.

'Those!' replied the Interrogator, thinking he meant the cooking utensils.

'The cups,' said the Flutter Man. He had just noticed a fine culture which bloomed in the saucepans; he extended one towards Mr Bruce and said, 'I think maybe we should preserve these, and then if we get sick we have penicillin right here free of charge.'

The Scot failed to understand the joke; but his sense of patriotic pride was lightly awakened. 'I'm sorry about this place,' he said, 'difficult to get cleaners you can trust, if you follow me.'

'Oh sure,' said the Flutter Man, 'we use the blind.'

'The blind?'

'Not so much for clearing the garbage, but we have blind stands where you can grab a cup of coffee and a sandwich – if the guy is blind he can't see what is going on, who comes in and out.'

'I see.'

The Flutter Man shook the kettle. Something in it rattled. He began to fill it. Then he turned and offered the Interrogator a faded plastic container of washing-up liquid. It was unpleasant to the touch.

33

'Use the bathroom,' said the black man, 'there has to be a bathroom – or does there in this place you guys fixed for me?' He smiled his wonderful, broad white smile and the Interrogator responded. When the Interrogator smiled he ceased to be the distant and infuriating figure with whom the official had to deal. He became an instant confessor, a father-figure inviting confidences by the quality of his attention and his honest gaze.

'Don't give all this a thought,' said the Flutter Man. 'A long time ago when I was a kid I lived in Watts, matter of fact I was born there. This apartment is a palace to what I've seen, Mr Bruce – when I was ten, before my uncle got me out of there, I saw the sawn-off head of a baby in the sink, among the dishes, with the flies.'

'Next door, I think,' said the Interrogator referring to the bathroom and hoping to hear no more of Mr Shaw's past which was faintly reminiscent of Mr Bruce's experience of cases from the Gorbals before they pulled it down.

He opened the adjoining door into a bathroom, the bath being the lavatory's width from the wall. At some time a hopeful inmate had painted both the kitchen and bathroom doors a buttercup yellow, and in places the paint had run to coagulate in solid globules like old egg yolk.

The bath was brown stained under each tap; a large spider sat perfectly still by the plug hole. The Interrogator turned on the hot tap and after a moment of gurgling and choking the water came through tepid. The spider moved with extraordinary speed towards the other end of the bath; the Interrogator turned on the cold tap full and its tidal rush caught the creature to carry it back struggling towards the vortex at the plug hole. Just before it got there it died, its legs collapsed inwards, it seemed to shrink, it was sucked down.

As he went for two cups and two saucers and two spoons the Interrogator said, 'I have brought you the transcript.'

'Fine,' replied the voice from the kitchen.

The kettle was on; Mr Flutter came out to pick up his case from the hall floor. He went to the door at the opposite end. The bedroom, like the sitting room, was a dun colour with no paintings on the wall, no old posters, no out-of-date calendars. It contained two single beds with a small table between; a

34

wardrobe with a mirror in its door and a chest of drawers. For a moment Mr Flutter regarded the phone by the bed and then he looked for other fittings where the bugs would be planted. Not that it mattered this trip. This was all between friends. Well almost. He put his bag on one bed and turned back the other. The sheets looked clean.

They took coffee on the gate-legged table in the sitting room. The Crittall windows looked north over Battersea Park. You could not see the river for the trees. Mr Flutter drifted across the room and looked out. Among the empty parked cars was a London cab with its meter off. The driver was reading a newspaper.

'You're looking after me,' he said over his shoulder.

'Oh yes,' said the Interrogator.

In the briefing which he read on the plane it said that distribution included a copy to L Section, so this guy knew the American end, the information supplied by the two defectors and the names of the targets.

'Do you have the photographs?' asked Mr Flutter. The Interrogator took a large manila envelope from his briefcase.

'The names are on the back,' he said, 'with our compliments!'

The black man looked at them.

'Only two?'

'Yes.'

'My information is three. Two with names, one without but I thought your side knew him.'

'Only two at the moment. I realise that in your briefing it says three. We shall do what we can about that.'

'And you have the psychiatric report on Dodgson?'

The Interrogator took it from his case. Mr Flutter flipped it open and read a few lines. Then he said, indicating the polygraph in the Samsonite case, 'Certain kinds of nut can fool the instrument; psychopaths are top of the list.'

'Oh yes,' said the Interrogator politely.

'But Dodgson is not in any of those categories?'

'No,' said the Interrogator.

'How long have you talked to him?'

'So far,' said the Interrogator, 'one hundred and twenty hours.'

He took another file from his case. 'I understand you need a series of facts about Dodgson's life?'

'That's it.'

'These are they,' said the Interrogator and the black man smiled at the phrase.

'They tell me', said the Scot, both to flatter and for the benefit of the listening devices, 'that results depend more on the skill of the operator than on the machine.'

'I have heard that,' said the Flutter Man.

'Which is why they picked you, I imagine.'

'Could be.'

'Oh yes,' said the Interrogator as if he had just remembered it, 'I thought you might care for a little of this.' He took a bottle from his briefcase. 'It's the pure malt.' He held the bottle up to let the light catch its very pale, straw-coloured contents. He smiled. 'I also washed a couple of glasses, because we don't want you down with gastro-enteritis do we?' He took the glasses from the fumed oak sideboard and carefully poured an inch of the whisky into each.

He handed one over. The black man breathed the contents for a moment. Then they raised their glasses and drank. Mr Flutter smiled. 'Man,' he said.

'About Dodgson,' said the Interrogator, as he had been instructed by Lord, 'you know we think he's a loner.'

'They all say that,' said the Flutter Man, 'you must have noticed.'

'Well – ' replied Mr Bruce, becoming distant.

'An' you did miss him for ten years,' said Mr Shaw, 'which is a pity.'

3

The photograph taken by Rose lay on Flecker's desk beside the machine in the office in Soho. The other two from the file were on the gate-legged table in the Battersea flat as the Flutter Man went through the Dodgson briefing.

Flecker liked to fit a face to a voice. In this case the father

36

and son were similar in tone, inflection and accent although the boy was obviously better educated.

A third voice on the tape softly gave the ident: location, date, two names – Frank and Robert Jones, Robert speaking first, picked up in mid sentence.

'... I sort of deluded myself ... you know how you do when it's possibly your first job, you say to yourself well, this is real life, not university any more, and you expect to feel a bit lost, like the first day at school. I ignored the fact that I disliked the place on sight ... they arranged digs for us. It was routine for them and for the landladies, I suppose the eager graduates turned up annually in September. My landlady was the sort who does a big commercial for the food, "I've done you a *lovely* breakfast, dear." There were two days of interviews. It wasn't until afterwards that I realised they arranged the digs by categories so that ...'

Frank's voice broke in to say, 'What categories?'

Flecker noted the place on the tape. Technically, from this point, they could be charged with committing offences under Section 2 of the Official Secrets Act.

In the background on the tape was the faint sound of a silver band.

'In my digs', replied Bob, 'were the linguists of course – in others were the computer people, radio operators, I assume ... and mathematicians ...'

'Like Dodgson,' interrupted Frank.

'That's it.'

'I remembered that from the trial,' said Frank, 'I wondered then if you knew him.'

The sound was breaking up and disappearing. Flecker ran it back and tuned to clarify Bob's reply. He heard the coughing laugh and then, 'That's like asking someone who's just told you he comes from Birmingham if he knows Freddie Green who also comes from Birmingham.'

'I just wondered.'

'Dad,' said Bob, 'do you know what it's like? It's like a factory. It's like rolling up to Fords at Dagenham except for the security and the zones. There are thousands of us. I only know a handful and I don't see many of them outside the job.'

Flecker stopped the tape. The boy sounded relaxed. His

37

delivery was slow and sometimes he paused in odd places and you wondered if it was the tape but then he started again having arranged his thoughts. The father sounded incisive. There was a feeling of something – anxiety? edginess? – in his tone.

The thing that struck Flecker was how English they were. Neither excessive nor over-assertive and up to this point certainly no hint of conspiracy.

He looked at Bob in the centre of the photograph taken nine days earlier, on the afternoon of the conversation he was monitoring. He appeared good-humoured. The father had an expression which reminded Flecker of certain Special Branch men of his acquaintance.

Flecker did not know if the person who took the photograph was also the one who had supplied the print which lay before him. His training automatically precluded curiosity of that sort. All operations worked in separate compartments.

He did not know the source of the information which had made it necessary to put intensive surveillance on the young man in the centre of the photograph. He knew it to be quite separate from the American sources naming the two men in the other photographs. He did not know of the American briefing file (being shared in another part of London by the Interrogator and the Flutter Man) which stated that information supplied by two defectors, one Russian and one East German, with the cryptonyms BEDROCK and ORCHID, plus the confession of an American subject, Luther Berry, indicated that Dodgson had two associates (named) and one other (identified by description only) at GCHQ Cheltenham.

The surveillance teams also worked in separate compartments, reporting independently to Flecker in the Soho office.

What Flecker knew without needing to be told was that the Americans were very angry and it was all stops out to repair the damage caused by Dodgson and his blazingly public trial.

Flecker re-started the machine to hear Frank expressing surprise at the size of the intelligence-gathering operation at GCHQ.

At that moment on the tape Frank had noticed a Post Office detector van cruising slowly past them. His mind wandered for a second trying to remember if his television licence was due for renewal. Bob, half a head taller, strolling beside him had just said something about working at Cheltenham being like Fords at Dagenham. Frank knew Fords at Dagenham on its bleak urban road with the traffic and the dust and he was surprised.

'I never thought of it like that,' he said. 'I always had the idea of a select group actually doing the secret stuff – in a bunker or something. And all the rest making the tea and doing the filing.'

'It's an industry,' said Bob quietly, 'unions or no unions – over seven thousand people, and now lie detectors – and that's just one of the places where it goes on.'

Frank caught something in his tone and said, 'Yes?'

'Yes,' said Bob, 'ordinary, you see? Accepted.'

'Yes?' said Frank again.

The Post Office van parked.

'You intend to chuck it,' said Frank suddenly, 'that's it isn't it?'

'Yes.'

'Why?'

'When you look like that,' said Bob, 'and use that tone it makes it difficult.'

'You must have a reason.'

'Of course. It's just that it's a bit complicated.'

'It would be,' said Frank sharply as all the unease of the day came together round the fact that his son was about to chuck his job. He could not explain to this man beside him – this son who had been a baby, a toddler, a schoolboy, an undergraduate in the shortest time it seemed; five seconds could recall the child sitting in the pram bellowing, the first girlfriend, the changes in hair length, the unfortunate beard, the sound of Russian on tape from the bedroom – he could *not* express the disproportionate anxiety of the moment: an absurd sense in the declining sun of late afternoon that *everything* was not as it should be; he felt fear even, tasted it the way you did when the steam catapult was out of action and they cleared the flight deck and made you take off with rockets to boost the engine power. If the rockets failed – which sometimes they did – you dropped into the sea and the on-rushing carrier ran you under. It came out today as bloody bad temper.

'Don't be so aggressive,' said Bob, 'it doesn't help.'

'It's my nature – you ought to know that by now.'

'Really,' said Bob, 'I never noticed. Shall I start again?'

'Why not!'

They walked from the shadow of the trees into the patches of sun, their own long shadows moved across the grass. It was already too cool to sit on a bench.

'In an odd way', said Bob, 'the Dodgson business focused what I feel. Did you see the photographs of his house at the time of the trial?'

'Don't think so, not in the *Telegraph*.'

'Well,' said Bob, 'there are millions like it, that house, in the Home Counties, on the outskirts of Bath or Brighton – it's a little gem of suburban England – it's the next rung up from Dunroamin and often it has a tennis court, in fact nowadays sometimes it even has a pool. It has canvas awnings in the summer and people go out on to the lawn on Sunday to have drinks and admire the roses. As a matter of fact Dodgson's didn't have a tennis court or a pool and nobody went for drinks on a Sunday but it *felt* like that. He used to teach his son cricket on the lawn, he even collected Wisdens at ten to twenty quid a throw when he could find them – '

'Bob,' said Frank, 'I don't care about this house or what he spent the money on that the Russians gave him, I just want to know – '

'It's the only way I can explain.'

'Sorry.'

'I went to look at the house.'

'Why?'

'A sort of compulsion. There was a copper on the door, of course. I stood there and looked at it. This was about a month ago and the trial had just ended. There had been a hell of a shake-up at our place – '

'GCHQ?'

'Yes. The security people had egg all over their faces – ten years he got away with it, and now all the stable doors were banging shut like a royal salute, they were leaning on the section supervisors to *tell all* about those in their sections – '

'Oh I see,' said Frank suddenly, 'that's what you meant about a "Hammer and Sickle remark" when I put my foot in it this afternoon.'

'Yes,' said Bob. 'You see Rose is a section supervisor and – '

'Yours?'

'No,' said Bob, 'not mine, and she wouldn't dream of reporting anybody on personal grounds, but the business of informing is getting more respectable – they laid on what they call a "programme of security education" and not only supervisors but all of us are now encouraged to report oddities of behaviour, strange events and anything else that strikes us as odd.' He broke off, smiling as usual, then he said quietly, 'Did you ever read the record of the motives which made the French collaborators inform on their colleagues? Millions of them did it – against their own families, their neighbours, the Jews of course, to the Milice and the Gestapo?'

'Oh, come off it, Bob.'

'All right,' said Bob amiably, 'the British are different! And it isn't the main point – but you of all people, Dad, with your "I'll do it my way" attitude should understand what it means to be at the mercy of a secret report by someone you live or work with *just because they think something is odd*; it could easily be someone who dislikes you, or someone who wants the promotion you're going to get, and then you don't, and it isn't explained why. There's no appeal, you know, in the secret world.

'The best you can manage is a tribunal which sits in judgment, and will tell you nothing precise concerning the accusations made against you, but permits you to defend yourself against what you *think* may be the cause of your transfer or dismissal. Consider that! You, being accused by persons unknown, of doing things unspecified, which make you in their view some kind of security risk, then have to try to deduce what it might be and prove that it isn't – now there's the other side of the looking glass for you. Don't you think?'

'Is that what's happening, Bob? Are you accused? Are you being forced to resign?'

41

Bob laughed and put his arm momentarily round his father's shoulders. 'Bloody hell, no,' he said, 'not me – no one's judging me – it's the other way round.' He scratched his untidy hair, pushed his glasses up his nose and tried to recapture the line of thought from which he had been diverted. Then he said, 'Oh yes – house! – I didn't finish about the effect of Dodgson's house. There it was, as I said, a sort of picture of middle-class England, with the spring light on it – but out of sight, in the dark as it were, is what paid for it and kept it going: treachery and porn.'

'Yes, I see that,' said Frank, remembering the recent sensation of Dodgson's trial, 'but what's it got to do with you?'

'Well,' replied Bob, 'I thought "I'm in the same line of business in a way."'

Frank exploded, 'Don't be so bloody wet – of course you're not. The man was a traitor. You're serving your country. I know that sounds a bit old-fashioned but that's what you're doing. It's no different from my time in the Andrew – only you're brighter than me and more use. It's a good job.'

The word 'traitor' was in the air like the long echo of a shot between buildings.

Frank was silent, assessing what Bob had said so far – something clicked and he stopped, taking a grip on Bob's arm. 'Listen, did you say you are being positively vetted at the moment?'

'Yes, it's over five years since the first time.'

'Any rumbles from that? Any awkward bits?'

'None at all, he's rude but so am I when I have to be. He sometimes phones late at night to take up something I said days before. It doesn't bother me.'

'Did you tell him you're going to resign?'

'No. I wanted to talk to you first – and believe me it is *not* the way it was for you in the Navy.'

When Flecker listened to this exchange on the tape he silently congratulated the unknown (to him) informer. Young Mr Jones certainly merited surveillance: those who commit to the secret world do *not* take it upon themselves to judge it and then leave it, their heads stuffed with secret information, free to travel anywhere. (Only in sections like L Section are the passports of those employed kept safely in the Security Directorate at the Ministry.) Young Mr Jones was also being less than frank with his PVIO and that wouldn't do either.

Flecker noted these facts and deplored the policy of giving these upstart linguist graduates more 'job satisfaction' (by letting them ask questions about things that were none of their business) which intensified the risks.

Flecker had seen it all before – discontent leads to disaffection – goodbye loyalty and then anything can happen.

He made this judgment even before he came to the part of the tape which stung him personally. It was not unlike the effect on an actor, slightly insecure in his part, when a cruel and clear-eyed critic takes the knife to him. Long, long after the play is forgotten the wound aches. Long after Bob was dead Flecker heard his scornful voice from a later section of the tape.

5

Frank sat in his parked car in the square where they had talked that Sunday. He wound down the windows to reduce the heat from the afternoon sun. He tried and failed to remember how it had gone after they spoke of vetting and Bob had said it did not bother him. Had he been putting on a brave face? Did it get him down, questions and phone calls? Sometimes he was nervous like Margery, quite small things put him off. What was the man like who asked the questions? They were supposed to be ex-coppers, weren't they? Special Branch. He knew the sort, anyway; in the Service they were called regulating petty officers in his day – RPOs, naval coppers, rough bastards. It was a type.

A similar type had found Bob today, early, after the Welsh woman next door looked out of her kitchen window while making the first cup of tea of the day and then rushed to the telephone.

The 'scene of crime' officer had listened patiently. The Welsh woman stood five foot two, was skinny so that she could hardly have weighed eight stone. Her hair was dyed an unnatural black, her eyes matched it, her beaky nose jabbed towards him, her face was the colour of flour. He wondered what kept her going because she looked at death's door. In fact it was her gasping husband in the corner of the kitchen sitting in a dressing gown who had the 'heart'. She was like a fire-cracker, she kept going off, offering tea, offering the ladder (which they accepted), offering her version as her National Health teeth clicked and her sharp little eyes seldom blinked.

Outside the early light was changed every second by a revolving blue lamp which reflected faintly on the wall near the window.

The body lay on its back. The head was at a slightly odd angle. The cat, Tiger, who had been wailing from before first light, tried to lie close to it and was pushed away by the doctor who had just arrived.

The Welsh neighbour was saying, ' . . . I heard the cat, you see – it's their cat next door, he comes in here sometimes because he can get down all right but not get back so one of them 'as to rescue him. I was filling the kettle and I happened to look out, it was terrible I couldn't believe it at first.'

Outside there were bright flashes as the police photographer took photographs of the body and of its relationship to the wall of the building from which it fell and the garden wall which it may have struck. The cat butted its head against his legs and he swept it away.

'Oh no,' said the Welsh neighbour, 'we never 'eard anything in the night did we, Glyn? There's three of them next door, you know, but two was away for the weekend I believe.'

The 'scene of crime' officer recognised one of nature's concierges.

When the photographs were over they began to mark the position of the body with thick white chalk.

The Welsh neighbour said, 'We was up watching telly until midnight and never 'eard a sound, the walls of these 'ouses are thick, mind you. He must have slipped, we've 'ad some rain lately and it's dangerous on these roofs, I only use ours for the washing.'

After the chalk marks came the men with the stretcher to lift him and cover him and take him away. Leaving the cat.

'No we didn't know him,' she said, 'he worked at that government place didn't he. Knew them by sight of course to say "good morning" – or out on the roof when it was fine.'

Her cawing voice filled the kitchen. She was elated and felt better than she had for days.

7

Some of what she said had been conveyed to Frank by a police inspector when Frank telephoned before leaving his home. All he could remember now, sitting in the car dreading what was to come, were the directions to the mortuary in the grounds behind the hospital. He thought of having a drink first then realised the pubs were closed. He started the car. It was six hours since a policeman had rung his doorbell to tell him his son was dead.

PART TWO

FOUR

1

Mr Bruce the Interrogator and Mr Shaw the Flutter Man waited in the disused storeroom. Two strip lights overhead had been installed to supplement the poor light from a single barred window.

Mr Shaw put the finishing touches to the furniture and properties for the impending drama. He had placed the wooden table end-on against a wall. On the table he set up the polygraph with its dials, graph paper and narrow pens. Beside the table and close to the instrument stood a wooden chair facing the wall. Anyone sitting in this chair would be unable to see either the dials or the graphs made by the pens as the graph paper moved through the machine. In the centre of the room he placed a second wooden chair – isolated, facing the window.

There was a knock on the door. The Interrogator said, 'Come.' A warder urged Dodgson into the room and then closed the door, leaving him. Dodgson looked at the black man then at the polygraph. The Flutter Man registered Dodgson's pudgy features, the quick eyes behind the glasses, the sweaty dome of a head with its fringe of fair hair. The Flutter Man sniffed the hatred in Dodgson. He expected it. He had spent half the night framing and re-framing the questions after absorbing the material on Dodgson given to him by the

49

Interrogator. The Flutter Man's game was like stud poker – over half the cards are dealt face up.

'Good morning, Dodgson,' said the Interrogator, as he had every day for three weeks in this room.

'Change of furniture,' said Dodgson, 'what a good idea. I was getting bored with the old arrangement.'

The Interrogator smiled his transforming smile. 'Do sit down.'

He indicated the chair by itself in the centre of the room. Dodgson sat, folded his hands carefully in his lap as he had trained himself to do, and relaxed, half closing his eyes. So that was what it looked like – the famous lie detector. Less cumbersome than an electric chair and only fifty per cent as effective. Excellent odds.

The Flutter Man picked up a folder and took some pages stapled together to Dodgson. His large black hands, with an impressive ring on the third finger of the right, wafted a pleasant scent from the soap he used. Dodgson let him stand there for a moment before accepting the offered papers.

'These are the questions,' said the Flutter Man, and noted Dodgson's slight movement of aversion at the sound of his American voice.

Dodgson immediately began to read the questions. The Flutter Man handed a duplicate set to the Interrogator and held the top copy for himself. In a leisurely way he took a pen from his pocket and placed it ready to mark the graph paper when necessary. Then, as if he had just noticed Dodgson's concentration, he said 'When you've read them we'll go through them.'

Dodgson continued to read.

'After that I'll give you half an hour to think about them on your own.'

The Interrogator looked surprised. Dodgson continued to read.

'All you have to do is answer either "Yes" or "No" to each question.'

Dodgson stopped reading and looked up. The black man stood over him looking down as if he were looking into him.

'If there's any problem we fix the questions so you can give one of those answers.'

'The truth can't be reduced to "Yes" and "No".'
'I'll worry about that, Mr Dodgson.'

2

When Dodgson had gone the Interrogator said, 'Why give him time on his own with the questions?'

'Because I'm like the ju-ju man, when you know I've put my spell on you ... dare ain' nutting' yawl can do 'bout it, boy.'

'And how long will it take do you think?'

The Flutter Man chuckled. 'Less than one hundred and twenty hours, Mr Bruce — did I get that right? You've been talking to him for a hundred and twenty hours?'

'So far.'

'You realise that we have a unique situation here?'

'In what way?'

'This', indicating the polygraph, 'is no magic box and ninety-nine per cent of the time it has only two purposes — counter-intelligence questioning and full life-style questioning. Now, what we have here is a self-confessed spy and sexual pervert. So what is there left for him to hide?'

'His associates as I understand it, which you people seem convinced about and which we ... '

The Interrogator let it hang. His brief was to maintain the lie that the British believed Dodgson to be a loner.

'Right,' said the Flutter Man and took the two photographs from the folder, 'these guys if we're right.'

'It will be clear to him what you're after from the questions.'

'Oh sure.'

For a moment the Interrogator glanced at a long disused fitting high on the wall of the room in the corner. It had once been a gas pipe but was cut off and its end sealed. Installed in it at present was a microphone. This led to an adjacent area which had once been a boiler room. In there a balding, moustached man with headphones sat uncomfortably with the recorder. A complete record of the Flutter Man's technique and Dodgson's response would be recorded and transcribed daily and sent to Lord.

'How do you rate your chances with him?'

'A hundred per cent.'

'It's fair to say from my experience that Dodgson is not the impulsive creature he likes to appear.'

The man with the headphones in the boiler room chuckled and said aloud, 'You can say that again.'

In the whitewashed room the Flutter Man said, 'I have a degree in psychology, for eight years I was an investigator – you know why they recruited me in the first place? – the boy who came out of Watts and was illiterate until his uncle saved him? They recruited me because I'm *really* black. I look like every nigger that ever caused trouble. I look like the kind of nigger they used to lynch every once in a while. You must have noticed, Mr Bruce, that I am in the Paul Robeson mould an' so when I join this or that organisation an' tell them how I hate the white man an' how I admire the Soviet Union or Castro or whatever the hell – those subversives find it easy to believe me. An' when I tell them how it was in Watts when I was a boy, an' what happened to my mother they take me to their hearts.'

Mr Shaw caught the slight change of expression on the Interrogator's face and said at once, 'They told me you people don't like to talk about these things, and I guess you never did that line of work yourself – what you might call the Judas business?'

'No.'

'It is amazing how close you get to the ones you're going to betray and wipe out. An' you develop a kind of instinct. Dodgson now, he's full of hatred – for the system, for you an' most of all for me – not me personally, but the sound of my mouth, the sound of America. Also he despises us. I really took to the polygraph business when I got into it. So tell me, Mr Bruce, what are you so delicately hinting? What is Dodgson going to do to get by me, an' that machine?'

'I think', said the Interrogator carefully, 'he will create a diversion of some sort to confuse the results.'

'Ah! but how? He's human isn't he? I mean he breathes, he sweats, his heart pumps, his blood has pressure – that's what I need from him.'

When Lord briefed the Interrogator he said, 'Give them a

chance. They're cocksure about their sources, they're cocksure they've got the right names. We are *almost* certain they are wrong on both counts. If they are it was set up with Dodgson a long time ago for just this contingency, that he would be caught and his real associates would be in peril. We think Dodgson's neck depends on misleading our good friends. If he pulls it off they'll do everything short of World War Three to get him out. I suspect that's the arrangement.'

The Interrogator had replied, 'Then there *are* two more like Dodgson, but not the two in the photographs?'

'That's our view – but our good friends want immediate action on what they believe they know. They shall have it. Promises have been made! But give them the chance to change their minds would you? It might be healthier in the end.'

Having fulfilled Lord's wish the Interrogator dropped the subject of Dodgson's ability to dissemble and addressed himself to the Flutter Man's methods.

'I take it', he said, 'that you talk to the back of his head and he talks to the wall.'

'Right.'

'So you don't watch his face?'

'I watch the dials. I watch the graph as it feeds through.'

'Do you explain how it works to him?'

'Sure.'

'You don't mind if I stand so that I can watch his face in profile?'

'Be my guest, just don't speak while the instrument is running and stay out of the corner of his eye.'

'Of course. I shall be very interested to see how it works.'

'The way they define this', said the Flutter Man, 'is that the pens record on the graph, a quadruple graph, the blood pressure, pulse rate, galvanic skin response, thoracic and abdominal respiration of the subject. Every subject is different from every other subject. So we run, and re-run, and run again, and re-run and the ol' ju-ju-man reads dem entrails – in other words, my dear sir, I specialise in interpreting the physiological pointers to the psychological stress of the subject . . . in particular when he is telling goddam lies or when his guts is all churned up over some apparently innocent and simple matter.

'One of the things that troubles the smart ones is there is

53

nothing to hide. Not only does he have all the questions in advance, he has the purpose of the questions. There is, if I may say so, a very unpleasing feeling in the guts of the less than innocent that *inevitably* their breathing and blood pressure and sweat is going to betray them. They are their own accusers because, like the man said, you got no worries if you got nothing to hide, baby.'

'Quite,' said the Interrogator, deciding that there was no useful purpose in attempting to warn the American further about the possible resources of Dodgson in a tight corner.

'Shall we have him in?' he asked.

'Why not?'

3

Dodgson was surprised how much he disliked being attached to the instrument. He faced the rough, whitewashed wall which had the smell of a cricket pavilion where he used to play wicket keeper. He concentrated on that – playing wicket keeper with his contact lenses in and his large bottom bulging his cricket trousers which had once split up the seam to the hilarity of both teams and the onlookers. He concentrated on remembering the name of the place; the pitch had not been flat; it was in a park and the actual ground was at the bottom of a large bowl of grass between trees with a circular boundary in white: a very shallow, white-edged saucer of green with the whitewash-smelling pavilion up on one rim backed by the dark green of hedge and shrubs; the scoreboard by hand; dogs running, bored girlfriends putting up with it not having a better place to go.

Round his chest the pneumograph tube made him think of a harness like those nineteenth-century harnesses on women and children pulling tubs of coal down there in the stench and filth, working naked often. The black man was saying, 'This takes care of the rate of breathing, OK?' The blood pressure cuff on his left bicep brought back a muddled recollection of many medical inspections – that moment of concentration as it pumped up until it was uncomfortable. The black man said,

54

'I expect you'll know that this measures pulse and blood pressure, Mr Dodgson. I have your medical report with me and I see you're normally a little high. Also you have a fast pulse rate – that would be the smoking, I expect you know that, too?'

Dodgson did not reply.

'Smokers beat out that rhythm of life a few thousand times a day more than the rest of us – would you just hold out your right hand? That's the way.'

The device was a hand-held electrode secured across the palm by springs over the back of the hand.

'Sometimes', said the Flutter Man cheerfully, 'we just use an index and ring finger attachment instead of the full palm but we don't want to make any mistakes, I'm sure you'll agree, so with you, Mr Dodgson, it's the full palm electrode to measure how much you ... ' he let it hang for a few moments and then said with emphasis, 'sweat.'

Dodgson automatically closing his hand on the electrode and feeling the springs pull at hairs on the back of his hand thought of knuckle dusters.

'Statistically', he said, 'this machine is useless.'

'I have heard that.'

'There is no scientific criterion by which you can decide whether its results are accurate or false.'

'I want you to be comfortable,' said the Flutter Man, 'and I am grateful for your co-operation.'

'I have nothing more to hide.'

'More?'

'More.'

'Great. You probably observed there is a pattern to the questions – many of them are about things we already know for certain, like your name, your age. That way we are sure the answers you give to them are truthful, and from there we can see how you react, on the graphs, when giving a truthful answer.'

Dodgson started to speak but the American went straight on, 'Of course there is the stress factor of being attached to the instrument. Everyone experiences it. We allow for that. We shall go through the questions maybe four, five, six times until there is a pattern. Even though we have already checked the

55

questions, if we have any difficulties we stop and we fix them again, OK?'

'This whole rigmarole has about as much validity as fortune telling.'

The Flutter Man smiled showing his wonderful teeth.

'Face the wall,' he said. Dodgson faced the wall. Instead of switching on the instrument the Flutter Man leaned close to the back of Dodgson's head and said, 'How do you think they rate it at the Lubianka? Did they mention that to you? Do they have a training method to stop yourself sweating? Or to control the valves of the heart?'

He did not start the instrument. He waited. Dodgson shifted in his chair. The Interrogator, who seemed to have melted into a corner, said quietly, 'Just think of your wife – and relax.'

It was a subtle threat.

The Flutter Man switched on. The blood pressure cuff inflated, the corrugated tube round Dodgson's chest seemed more restrictive. He knew he was already sweating against the electrode across his palm.

The Flutter Man glanced at his sheet of questions; in the corner the Interrogator looked over the top of his duplicate sheets at Dodgson's profile. The man seemed composed, slightly scornful, as usual. Who would win? Well, thought the Interrogator, not the truth, certainly not the truth. Had all of them been in complete accord, even then not the truth because between them they knew possibly half or less than half of the truth in this matter. The one who knew most was Lord. With Lord the buck stopped. Lord kept an objective distance from plump, sweating traitors attached to suspect machines, a necessary distance from large black men who came from places and conditions unimaginable in well-trimmed England.

As for such misty figures as the two defectors known as BEDROCK and ORCHID kept jealously from the British by the good friends – who at this end could begin to untangle their layers of cover? Or assess the competence of those de-briefing them first in Germany then in America? – lovingly cocooning them while they recovered from the shock of plastic surgery and became used or resigned to their new faces: BEDROCK and ORCHID, at some point after weeks or months, letting drop a hint about GCHQ at Cheltenham, England, possibly a description, a name even, leading eventually to the two photographs in the folder in the black man's hand.

And Berry? Luther Berry, American citizen and traitor, whose activities had complemented those of Dodgson? The Russians believed for months that both men were a plant, feeding disinformation on a grand scale. But it was *real*. A security catastrophe for the West.

No wonder Luther Berry never surfaced in the American press or anywhere else after they caught him.

The Interrogator hid his sense of distaste for the present exercise. It was too reminiscent of those real-life American courtroom documentaries shown on television: the embarrassing histrionics, loose reasoning and suspect informality . . . the vulgarity.

He regretted the break in his interrogation of Dodgson. And this charade. It would not get them nearer to 'One' and 'Two'. The Interrogator thought of Dodgson's uncaught associates as 'One' and 'Two'; and of the two men in the photographs – whom the Americans believed to be the associates – as the 'Stooges'.

Lord had shown him the results of Flecker's teams who had investigated the 'Stooges' back almost to the womb. They had been cleverly chosen by the opposition. Each had something to hide. Each had misled his PVIO in the slack, old days before Prime. Each inevitably had been connected to Dodgson.

No move had been made against the 'Stooges', but that would end if Dodgson persuaded the black man and deceived the overrated (in the Interrogator's view) polygraph.

That 'One' and 'Two' existed was certain. Otherwise the whole elaborate exercise mounted by the opposition using BEDROCK, ORCHID and Luther Berry would be pointless. To salvage something, and at Lord's insistence, the British line both publicly (at the Dodgson trial) and privately (at the highest levels in Washington) was that Dodgson had done it alone. The myth of Dodgson the loner would permit, if it came to it, the 'Stooges' being mopped up and 'One' and 'Two' remaining confidently in place.

This confidence might undo them. Particularly if there was no possibility of a leak that they had ever been suspected of existing.

The only hope of getting at them was to come back to brother Dodgson and stay close; never give him the comfort of an audience like this conceited black to raise his morale and stimulate him to win; never reveal by an eyelash what you know of 'One' and 'Two' and BEDROCK and the rest – never specify the aim, the area, the intention in the manner of this absurd machine: after one hundred and twenty hours Dodgson had already become an altered man, this Dodgson who sweated so profusely and looked from side to side behind his glasses and believed himself a master chess player. It now oozed from every pore the damage done by giving him a new face, a living symbol of the thing he loathed, the thing that made him tick, to compete against, to deceive.

More than that: if Lord had it right the price of Dodgson's 'freedom', of an opposition attempt to get him out, was to beat this American by confirming that the 'Stooges' – whom the research teams had shown to be innocent of treachery – were the real thing.

We were, after all, for ever in the hands of, at the beck and call of, the good friends.

They had us in a vice because out there was the coming wrath.

Long gone was the belief at the highest levels that nuclear stalemate meant no nuclear war. Now nuclear war was expected and planned for – only the extent of it was blurred in the official mind. The bunkers were ready for the surviving bureaucracy, and the death of the rest was expected and accepted. Survivors would be a bonus.

And how was it that they and the good friends could know when and at what targets the button would be pressed? By electronic espionage. By GCHQ at Cheltenham and its linked stations at home and abroad.

What could not be permitted at any cost was a major malfunction in that giant spy machine. So Dodgson must not be let out of his sights. The Interrogator must attack again and again and no Queensberry rules. The wife had been a windfall and the son more than that. Dodgson's Achilles' heel.

There was an irritating loose end. Not strictly the Interrogator's business. Lord's business but it irked the

Interrogator. The supposed number three. The unnamed third spy insisted on by the good friends.

'A bureaucratic cock-up,' said Lord. 'Our good friends are often very Teutonic have you noticed; it shows in their education – and in their driving laws, those boring convoys at fifty miles an hour or whatever it is. They are absolute. Not flexible. No wonder they're forehead to forehead with the opposition. However – the third man, if I dare utter that dreadful phrase, it's rather like the man at a Jewish party who inadvertently refers to a final solution to his host's problems – in my view there is *no* third man – or rather the third man was Dodgson himself. Without going into detail we have reason to believe the opposition "burned" Dodgson. They tried to get him to defect and he wouldn't leave his wife and that son.

'The good friends got this slightly cocked up somewhere in the dark reaches of the National Security Agency and it came out as three. I think you can depend on that.'

'I am to ignore it?'

'I should.'

But it would not quite go away.

Just as Flecker did not know of the American briefing and Flecker's surveillance teams knew nothing of each other, the Interrogator did not know that someone living under the same roof as a GCHQ linguist named Robert Arthur Jones had, in the time of near hysteria among security personnel at GCHQ following the arrest of Dodgson, felt it a duty to report that Bob Jones sometimes said – and wrote – odd things.

The informer had been apologetic and shame-faced. The Higher Executive Officer had been reassuring. A quick check showed Robert Arthur Jones to be undergoing his quinquennial review. The PV Investigating Officer was called in. He had nothing to report against Jones so far, except that he found him unhelpful and offhand. Bloody stroppy in fact.

There was a tenuous connection with Dodgson. Jones played chess with a mathematician who worked in Dodgson's section. This mathematician turned out to be one of the 'Stooges' already under surveillance. Immediate surveillance of Jones was begun.

As the Flutter Man started to question Dodgson in prison Flecker, on the other side of London in the Soho 'office', was listening to more of the conversation between Bob and his father. This part of the tape, recorded under difficult conditions, was sufficiently clear to show that Bob, like the Interrogator, was also concerned with the truth. Or rather its opposite – with the effect of lies.

Flecker almost said aloud, 'You silly young bastard – don't you know there isn't room for that sort of scruple any more? Don't you know *yet* that there's a war on?'

Lord read the transcript with growing distaste. Surely people of this sort had a larger idea of the country's institutions – parliament, the civil service, the judiciary – than this exchange implied? Of course the words on the page lacked the humanity of the voices: that urgency of debate as father and son clashed. But had Lord listened to the tape, the underlying affection, the seeming excess would merely have embarrassed him, not affected his judgment that Bob's opinions were insolent, intemperate and incipiently treacherous.

Even their accents and use of the language – indicating that they did not belong to the world which had formed Lord and which he now devoted his life to perpetuating – would have counted subtly against them. Lord's education, grounded in the classics, removed from the vulgarities of common life, persuaded him of the completeness, the civilised detachment, of his judgment. Reduced to a single sentence – Lord stood for the life of a gentleman. It was this, ultimately, which Bob threatened.

Lord's revulsion, masked as pragmatism, focused itself particularly upon those who, having taken service and signed the Act, then dared to set their own moral standards against those which he defended. He would never have conceded that the matter was in any way personal, or that this voice from the intellectual picket line in any way threatened him. He simply wanted it stilled.

4

'Dad, when you first apply you haven't the faintest what it's about. Then you get short-listed and come here and they fix the digs and you go out to the place and they put a security tag on you. Then you go to a sort of classroom and they get you to sign the Official Secrets Act and then the man starts to talk to you. Only then. He appears to answer your questions – '

'But, Bob, this is nearly six years ago.'

'Tell you what – ask a priest if time diminishes the evil of sins committed – no, ask the Jews.'

The sound of footsteps. Cars in the distance.

'But you told me the job was interesting and worthwhile – I remember, because it was a relief to hear you say it, your mother said that I'd influenced you and – '

'You did.'

'I didn't mean to.'

'Yes, you did.'

'Well . . . I could see the 1930s coming again, Bob.'

'I know. Anyway the buck stops with me, as little Harry Truman remarked when he pressed the button – '

'Pressed the button! Oh Christ! You haven't gone pacifist have you? I can't wear that.'

'No. No. Nothing at all to do with any of that. Forget all that. It's the lies.'

'What?'

'The lies. It starts the first day. The man I mentioned is not what he seems. You never realise until later, years later in my case. If he's talking to the linguists he's a mathematician, but with the mathematicians he's a linguist – '

'Sounds daft.'

On the tape the coughing laugh; in the distance a motor scooter buzzing over it.

'No, not daft – it's basic once you think about it. He can't say what he really is; after all, many of those being interviewed will be rejected, and even though they've signed the Official Secrets Act – and there have already been enquiries into their backgrounds or they wouldn't have been short-listed – it is still the best policy to say as little as possible (from the point of view of the authorities) at this stage.

'If the man, who in my case was pleasant and tweed-jacketed and mid-thirties, told the linguists that he was one of them, which is what you'd expect, then some bright lad might try his Russian on him – or if he told the computer boys he was one of them, when the guided tour (which happened next) gets to the computer complex they might ask him technical questions he can't answer.

'So you see from the first day the truth recedes; a man who is not a mathematician says he is, or a linguist as the case may be, and then purports to answer your general questions, which he deflects in a casual British sort of way making jokes about how German tourists in a Merc have been found driving round inside the place having got straight past Security – all that sort of thing, but the truth recedes and something else takes its place.'

A throat being cleared on the tape, they must be very close to the microphone at this point. The feet stop on the tape.

'Look, Bob – if you're fed up with it here get a transfer. Go to Hong Kong, go foreign and enjoy yourself. It's wonderful out east. You'd be surprised what a bit of sunshine and footy footy can do for you, my boy!'

The coughing laugh again like a kick start.

'I don't think I'll ask what footy footy is.'

'Ah! Got you! To the pure all is pure. Footy footy, my lad, is small oriental feet doing sentry-go up and down your spine. A real tone-up. In fact I could do with it now.'

Feet again on the pavement, not on spines.

'You know that Signals Intelligence is heavily funded and partly run by the American National Security Agency, don't you?'

'No I don't. And you shouldn't tell me.'

'It's no longer a secret, Dad, believe me.'

'What about it?'

'Did you ever happen to read any of the stuff that came out after Watergate? About the way the CIA and NSA function?'

'No ... there was a film wasn't there, not that I've been to the pictures for years. Bob, as for the lies and all that – whatever we have to do in that department – it's necessary.'

'That's a fatal argument, Dad.'

'It's common sense. And what you need is a posting or a holiday – do one or the other but for God's sake don't chuck away six years' seniority. No! listen, don't interrupt, bloody well listen – when I came out after my twelve it was no joke earning a living. It's taken me over twenty years since then to find my way and even now it's dodgy, very dodgy; cleverer blokes than me are going bankrupt all the time, and don't tell me I shouldn't vote Tory because the other lot would wipe me out in a year – I've had all that. I never told you what it was like getting through the 1970s – it was bloody murder after '74 ... and don't forget *young as I was* I remember the feel of the back end of the 1930s. What do you think it was like when we got the telegram that my Dad had gone down and all my Mum could do was put me in the Service as a boy at that bloody nautical school? I was a shit-scared little jack-me-hearty climbing the mast at thirteen. I wasn't having anything like that for my kids if I could help it, I tell you. You've done wonders, so has your sister, out there in Los Angeles this minute doing her Ph.D. – Dr Jones, do you mind, in my family – and don't give me any of that rubbish that it's for my satisfaction or I'm living by proxy – I'm not. I'm doing what a man should. I'm head of the family and it's my business to face the responsibility.

'These are bad times and getting worse. You have no idea, and I don't want you to find out, what it means to face the bills with the certainty that there is no money in the bank or the drawer at home. Another thing – who wants to kotow, yes sir, no sir, three bags full, here I am would you please be so kind as to take me on? Eh? Who wants to get in the long, long queue – and I do mean the queue of graduates, not your yobs but the ones with degrees – for work? Do you? Let's face it – you're not an engineer or computer man or doctor – you're a linguist. Who wants them?'

'Are we going to have a row?'

'Shouldn't be surprised.'

'I'm all for a quiet life, you know that.'

'That's true – you never rub people up the wrong way like I do. You're like your Mum.'

'Then you can see that this is important to me.'

'No. I can't see that. I *mean* – I can't see why.'

'It's very hard to explain. I knew it would be. It's a bit like pebbles starting to roll and you hardly notice – that's how it was at the beginning – then suddenly you end up with an avalanche. That's what it's like now.'

The father's voice rises. His control has snapped.

'You end up making a fool of yourself and going on the dole. You don't know you're born. You went to university until you were over twenty, you got the second job you applied for, you live in a decent place in decent conditions with decent people and you're not exactly worked to death – so what the hell is up with you?'

The voice of the son is quiet on the tape so that Flecker has to run back and adjust in order to hear his reply.

'Is it time for your taxi to the station? Should we get back now?'

After that the sound was too bad for the voices to be understood.

5

'Is your name Ramsay Charles Dodgson?'
'Yes.'
'Were you born December 23rd 1940?'
'Yes.'
'Were you illegitimate?'
'Yes.'
'Did your mother marry?'
'Yes.'
'Was the man she married your real father?'
'No.'
'Did your mother marry in 1944?'
'Yes.'
'Was your stepfather American?'
'Yes.'
'Did you hate him?'
A slight hesitation.
'No.'
The Flutter Man marked a circle on the graph paper with his felt pen.
'Did you spy for the Russians?'
'Yes.'
'For ten years?'
'Yes.'

64

'Do you regret that?'

'Yes.'

The Flutter Man marked the graph paper flowing out under the pens.

'Was the name of your real father, or your stepfather, or your mother's maiden name – Dodgson?'

'No.'

'Is Dodgson the real name of the author known as Lewis Carroll?'

'Yes.'

'Did anyone else – British, American, Australian or Canadian – help you to spy for the Soviet Union?'

'No.'

The Flutter Man made another circle on the graph.

'Did Lewis Carroll write *Alice in Wonderland* and *Alice Through the Looking Glass*?'

'Yes.'

'Was Lewis Carroll a mathematician?'

'No.'

The Flutter Man stopped the instrument and the cuff on Dodgson's arm deflated.

'No,' said the Flutter Man, 'what do you mean "no"?'

Dodgson without smiling said, 'Dodgson was the mathematician, Charles Dodgson; Lewis Carroll was the author.'

'Why thank you,' said the Flutter Man and started the instrument. The blood pressure cuff inflated. The Flutter Man began spacing the questions.

'Did you change your name to Dodgson?'

'Yes.'

'Did Lewis Carroll like little girls?'

'Yes.'

The black man ringed the graph paper.

'Do you know Stephen Kedge?'

'Yes.'

'Did you watch videos with Stephen Kedge?'

'Yes.'

The Flutter Man opened the folder and took out the first of the two photographs. It was glossy, blown up. It showed a scraggy man of about thirty-five who stooped. The man stood close to the railings of a primary school looking through them.

On the other side in the playground were lively little girls playing what looked like Salt, Mustard, Vinegar, Pepper. Some of their skirts were blown upwards with this activity. Stephen Kedge had both his hands bunched in his trouser pockets. He was attempting to hide an erection.

The Flutter Man, standing behind Dodgson, lowered the photograph in front of his face and said, 'Is this Stephen Kedge?'

Dodgson immediately shouted, 'You didn't warn me about photographs.'

The Flutter Man stopped the instrument and the cuff deflated.

'That's an extra question.'

'An' that troubles you, Mr Dodgson?'

'It's a trick.'

The Interrogator made a brief note in the margin of his question sheet but said nothing.

'But Mr Dodgson,' said the Flutter Man, and to the Interrogator's ear he was deliberately exaggerating his American accent which Dodgson detested, 'you already told me this "machine" is no better than fortune telling at the fair. To you this is junk. So what is your problem?'

'I've already made a full confession.'

'Oh really – now that is very helpful. But take it easy, Ramsay, every once in a while I may throw in a lil' ole supplementary just to stop it being boring. For me I mean. You know how long I've been doing this? Three years. Three long years, Ramsay, of standing behind guys who don't like it and asking questions that as an ordinary citizen I would definitely say invaded my privacy. I am, you might say, like a doctor. Sometimes it is necessary for health reasons to look right up the arse of even the most modest citizen. Someone has to do it. Three years! – and they only give you four before they transfer you – due, Ramsay, to the strain!

'I have really lost count of the number of good people who have sat where you are sitting . . . so give me a break, Ramsay, let me show you a picture from time to time will you? Eh? I never read it myself but they tell me Alice said, "What good is a book without pictures?" Right? Shall we take another crack at

66

it? You just stick to "Yes" and "No" because you're doing fine.'

The Interrogator looked out of the window and sighed. The instrument was running and the cuff had inflated.

'Did Lewis Carroll take a lot of pictures of little girls?'

'Yes.'

'And did you watch a lot of videos with little girls in them?'

'Yes.'

'Did you blackmail Stephen Kedge to help you spy.'

'No.'

The Flutter Man ringed the graph paper.

'Did your American stepfather run out on your mother when his unit went Stateside in 1946?'

'Yes.'

The Flutter Man paused slightly longer than usual before asking:

'Did your mother die from overwork?'

'Yes.'

'Because she had to work when she was sick?'

'Yes.'

'Do you hate your stepfather?'

'Yes.'

As the Flutter Man started to ring the graph paper Dodgson half turned in his chair –

'That appears to – '

The Flutter Man turned off the instrument. As the cuff deflated Dodgson repeated, ' – appears to contradict my previous reply to a similar question – but you will note that the earlier question was in the past tense, meaning did I hate him when I was a child. I did not. He gave me new clothes, he got us extra food that other people did not get because of rationing. He gave me toys and sweets. He made my mother laugh. She was never a strong woman and it was her happiest time. I loved him then.'

'And then he betrayed you.'

'You can', said Dodgson, 'spare me the psychology for infants – it makes the gorge rise.'

Without comment the Flutter Man re-started the polygraph. When the cuff was fully inflated and Dodgson was once again looking at the whitewashed wall he read the next question.

'Your sentence is for twenty-eight years?'

'Yes.'

'Are you still anti-American?'

'Yes.'

'Is Stephen Kedge anti-American?'

'No.'

The Flutter Man marked the graph.

'Did you have trouble with the last question?'

'No.'

The Flutter Man marked the graph and then switched off. 'I think we have a problem with that question.'

'A lot of people', said Dodgson, raising his voice again, 'are anti-American. In fact the world is full of people who detest America and all it stands for, but in this country that is not a crime.'

From the corner the Interrogator said, 'Now that depends where you work.' He moved to stand across the table from Dodgson. 'While we're having a break,' he said, 'this might be the moment to tell you that your wife has taken a second opinion – he thinks she'd benefit from a course of treatment.'

Dodgson tried to ease his chair round to face the Interrogator. The Flutter Man put his large hands on Dodgson's shoulders and held him in place.

'Take it easy,' he said, 'we don't want any damage to my li'l black box.'

'Get these things off me. I will not co-operate any more. Get them off.'

'Of course,' said the Interrogator, 'if that's what you want.'

The Flutter Man stepped back. Dodgson slumped in the chair. The almost hysterical attitude was replaced by apparent despair. It seemed he might weep. He said, 'She did everything you wanted, she told the press and the court what you told her to say. I know that. You've done something to turn her against me. Or you're blackmailing her. I don't blame her, I blame you. She won't come to see me. She won't bring the boy. You told me if I co-operated I could see the boy. Well, if I can't then to hell with you – and this black American pig.'

The Interrogator said in his prim voice, 'I'm sure your wife told the truth both in and out of court, she's a brave woman and she deserved rather better than you.'

'I've co-operated,' said Dodgson, 'but I won't if you hurt them.'

'The trouble is,' said the Interrogator, bringing the other chair to sit close to Dodgson, 'that knowing you was like being in contact with a carrier of the Black Death, you can never tell where else it will crop up.'

'What treatment?' asked Dodgson, averting his face from the Interrogator. 'I know she must be terribly upset, but what treatment.'

'Psychiatric,' said the Interrogator.

'Oh I see,' flared Dodgson, 'it's a crime in the Soviet Union to use psychiatry as a state weapon but all right when people like you fix it up here.'

'All we want,' said the Interrogator, 'as you fully understand from going through the questions, is your honest opinion of two gentlemen whom you knew – Kedge and – '

He made a gesture and the Flutter Man passed him the second photograph. He extended it towards Dodgson who ignored it.

' – and Goodburn,' he said.

Dodgson was silent.

'Psychiatry,' said the Interrogator, 'as no doubt you know, is a very loose discipline. Sometimes people do get shut up in those places by mistake and after a few years you can't distinguish the mistakes from the real cases – now there is Lewis Carroll for you, wouldn't you say?'

Dodgson remained silent.

'Coffee?' said the black man. 'Do they make coffee around here?'

'Oh by the way – don't worry about your son,' said the Interrogator, 'he'll be taken into care by the local authority. Yes, by all means coffee.'

'I want to go back to my cell,' said Dodgson.

'I expect you need time to think,' said the Interrogator.

When he had gone and they were drinking coffee the Flutter Man said, 'He's bluffing.'

'Hmm!' said the Interrogator. He had made more notes in his minute handwriting on the margin of the questionnaire at the point where Dodgson appeared to have lost control completely; in brackets at the end of these notes he had written:

(Dodgson's first diversionary tactic extremely well timed and executed, the black man has totally misread it).

Mr Shaw, the Flutter Man, was expansive and affable. 'Not bad,' he said. 'You notice how he's trying to get away from our friend Stephen Kedge? You notice how that really troubles him. Not even your stuff about his wife and kid could get him back on the machine and he sure as hell loves that kid of his if your report is right.'

'Hmmm!' said the Interrogator.

The Flutter Man took another sip of his coffee, made a face and said, 'Do they really give this stuff to the prisoners in here?'

'Good lord, no,' said the Interrogator, 'this is staff coffee.'

'I think', said Mr Shaw, 'you may be putting me on, Mr Bruce.'

Mr Bruce smiled. 'Only in respect of this disgusting beverage,' he said. 'I suggest we now pack up for the day. Dodgson will probably cheer up in an hour or two but I shall tell my associate to leave him to stew.'

'Your associate?' said the Flutter Man.

'Hmm! We don't leave him solely to the prison staff as you may imagine.'

In the adjoining space the balding, moustached man felt very cheerful as he spoke softly on to the tape giving the date, time, names of those involved. He would be home before the rush-hour. Tomorrow was another day – another day, another tape and that crafty Scot running rings round everybody. He switched off and left.

FIVE

1

On the way back from the square they were silent. Frank occasionally caught Bob's eye and they smiled as if to say, 'That was a bit overheated and unnecessary.' When they got back to the house they made fresh tea in the kitchen. Margery came in. 'Is everything all right? You were away ages.'

'Fine, fine.'

'I thought we might catch a later train, Frank, so I changed the taxi.'

'Good idea.'

'Your room's a terrible mess, Bob, I thought I might – '

'No, no, no,' said Bob. 'If you did I'd never find anything. I mean it may look a bit – '

'It does,' said Frank.

'But basically it is very *clean*.'

'Of course it is, dear, I didn't mean – '

'I know you didn't, Mamushka, as we Russian speakers say – and in any case Dad and I are going up there so there wouldn't be time.'

Margery hesitated in the doorway of the kitchen; from Mark's sitting room came the sound of his voice and Rose's and another which was the television they were talking across.

'Shall I?' asked Margery indicating the sounds. 'Will I be in the way?'

'Of course,' said Bob, 'they'll probably throw you out.'

Reluctantly she left them. In the train later she wanted to know what they had said. Frank seldom lied to her but he did

71

on that occasion. After Bob's death she remembered and accused Frank of hiding things from her. He kept on lying.

After Margery left the kitchen they cut fat slices of the birthday cake she had brought for Rose and took the tea up on a tray to Bob's room. The low late sun shone across his ceiling reflecting down on them. Bob cleared a space on the floor to sit with his legs stuck out and his back against the divan bed. Frank, who hated eating on his knee, sat at the desk and moved the telephone to make a place for his plate and cup. He carefully avoided putting his saucer on the leather cover of the address book.

When Flecker heard this conversation Frank was loud in the foreground and Bob slightly muffled but completely clear in the background because it was only a small room, low-ceilinged. The informer in the house had let in a selected member of the staff of British Telecom when no one else was there; the device had been fitted in under five minutes. Even the beady-eyed Welsh neighbour, who seemed to monitor the street continuously when not eating or watching television, missed the yellow van outside the door. The bug functioned with the phone both on and off the hook. To activate it they dialled the number and on the last digit added ultrasonic sound which stopped the phone ringing at that time but made its line 'live' to transmit from the room. A similar ultrasonic device is sold commercially to activate telephone answering machines at any distance after dialling.

It was peaceful after the walk in the square. It was this moment of the day with the warm, late light and Bob smiling and dropping crumbs on the carpet and the taste of strong sweet tea on the tongue that was in Frank's mind as he stood looking down at the face of his dead son on a trolley in the mortuary.

The spirit had gone from the body. The face was pale and unmarked, even the unruly hair had been combed; without the big glasses slipping down the nose it could almost have been the face of a stranger. It was not believable, not credible, not possible. My beloved son. Anguish seized him – it was for ever, his son was dead for ever, nothing could be done, nothing put right, they could not go back.

Someone was speaking to him, asking a question. He did not

want to listen, he did not want to move, he gazed down and it seemed like the end of the world. He understood not just how much he loved his son but how much his son had loved him. He knew also what the events of the day had kept from him, the anaesthetic of action had worn off, the raw mind knew that Margery's love for Bob was greater than her love for him, Frank; when she had screamed and seemed to go from him it was as final as Bob's death.

Why not me, he thought, why couldn't it have been me? It's all wrong, it's not natural, I should have gone first – it's not as if there's a war on when the young ones –

'Are you all right, sir?'

'Yes.'

'Is he your son, sir?'

'Yes.'

'You formally identify him as Robert Arthur Jones?'

'Yes.'

'Thank you.'

He did not move. The coroner's officer, a police constable in plain clothes, touched Frank's arm.

Frank jerked away and turned to look at a face with a moustache like thousands of other faces: nondescript, brown hair, pale eyes, squarish. It had a practised expression, combining firmness and sympathy, for dealing with the bereaved.

The policeman instinctively moved back a pace. Frank turned to look at his son for the last time. He bent and kissed his forehead. They left the small brick building. Afterwards he could not remember going back into the main building until he found himself near the canteen with the smell and sounds of the hospital all round him. He did not know which way to go. He stopped and the coroner's officer caught up.

'Will you be at your home the next few days?'

'I don't know.'

'We shall want to get in touch with you.'

'Why?'

'The pathologist's report – after that, Mr Jones – '

'Pathologist?'

'There will be a post mortem.'

Frank stopped. 'Why?'

'That's the law, every death that is accidental or – '

'You said his neck was broken.'

'No,' replied the policeman, 'what I said, sir, is that according to the doctor who attended the scene of the accident there appeared to be fractured vertebrae.'

They were walking again. The place was full of busy people. Strangers.

'How could it have happened?'

'It appears to have been an accident.'

'I know that for God's sake – I mean *how*? Did anyone see it?'

'Not that we've found. It was dark.'

'Did anyone hear anything?'

'No, sir.'

'A neighbour found him?'

'Yes.'

'She didn't hear or see anything?'

'No.'

Frank said without meaning to say it, 'Heights never bothered him – they did me, but not Bob.'

The coroner's officer did not respond.

'So what happens now?'

'I confirm your son's identity to the pathologist, the day after tomorrow there'll be the inquest – if it's all straightforward there'll be a certificate to hand the body over to you for burial – I think you'll be able to make your arrangements for the funeral by the end of the week, Mr Jones.'

They came to a door. The policeman unlocked it and went in. Frank followed into the small office. On a desk was a grey plastic sack of the kind used to line dustbins. It was about half full with a string and label closing its top. The policeman did not immediately pick it up. He seemed to consider the label. Then he said, 'This is all your son's gear in here.'

He offered it and Frank found himself taking it. It was light. He held it and looked at it.

'That's all he had on him when we found him. It's been examined.'

Frank continued to look at the sack. For the rest of his life he would remember that sack.

'He was dressed.'

Frank was silent.

'The bed wasn't slept in.'

Frank did not look up or appear to hear him.

'Did you see him often?'

Silence.

'Sir?'

No response.

'Your son, did you use to see him often?'

The policeman had raised his voice slightly.

'What?'

'I asked you if you saw your son very often.'

'Why?'

Frank now looked from the sack to the pale eyes. He said, reverting all the way back to those Navy days when they beat the shit out of him until he learned to beat the shit out of them – long before the flying days, 'Spit it out, sonny – why do you want to know how often I saw my son?'

'I wondered if anything was bothering him – sir?'

'Did you? And why was that?'

'Because the coroner will want as much information as possible in order to establish the cause of death.'

'Well, he didn't kill himself if that's what you think.'

'I don't think anything, sir – I'm asking.'

Frank said, raising the sack, 'I expect these are cheaper than say a cardboard box or something decent.'

The coroner's officer said, 'A lot of young people get worried and depressed.'

There was something in the way he said it. Frank caught the faintest underlining. A faculty long buried by the drudgery of getting and spending, the tedium of years of marriage, the anaesthetic of the daily round unrelieved by surprise or challenge suddenly functioned: the shock, the despair, the anger – the pressure on his senses of the hospital and the presence of this policeman in his drab suit and tie had stripped the dull certitudes of thirty years leaving him as if flayed; the long-buried Frank who once flew listening to the note of the engine and to his own instinct and intuition came painfully to life with a single certainty.

They had it in mind to say it was suicide.

He shook his head. He put down the rage. He stopped looking at the policeman and looked past him. This man would shortly record their conversation when he was alone.

'He wasn't,' he said carefully. 'He was neither worried nor depressed. I would have known.'

'So you did see something of him.'

'Yes, of course, as often as we could, my wife and I. It's over a two-hour drive and I am self-employed which means not a lot of free time, but at least every month or so.'

As he spoke, moderating his tone, part of his mind considered how much they could check. Instinctively he began to think in that way. He had years of training, in one sense, by dealing with the Inland Revenue, and fly salesmen and credit agencies and over the last decade the Customs and Excise VAT man. You cross-checked, you looked at it from their point of view. You never, in the words of W.C. Fields, gave a sucker an even break.

If this lad was going to form the coroner's opinion then let us sort him out, mealy-mouthed if necessary, because whatever else was going to happen no one was going to destroy his wife by bringing in a verdict of suicide on her beloved son. And then a small Judas voice whispered, 'Are you sure he didn't? He got just as het up as Margie over things; that last day, although he was very steady, when we talked in his room and he put it to me I could see (although I wouldn't own up to it) just what he meant ... I never knew, I never even guessed, that things went on like that in our world; on the other side of the Iron Curtain – yes. But in America? And here? England?'

'What was that?' he said. 'Sorry, I was thinking about my wife at home and I missed what you said; she's in a bad way.'

'I was asking if your son had money troubles, Mr Jones.'

'No, none at all.'

'And sex?'

'What do you mean?'

'Well, girls – did he have girl trouble?'

'No.'

Frank caught another nuance and knowing he would explode if the man dared put the question to him he said, 'And he was normal – you can confirm that with the security man that was vetting him if you like – they don't encourage queers in those establishments.'

'I wouldn't know anything about that.'

'What else?' said Frank.

'The post mortem will show if he had been drinking or taking drugs.'

Frank said deliberately, 'His bed was unslept in you said?'

'Yes.'

'How do you know?'

'The "scene of crime" officer went through – '

'Did he?'

'Yes.'

'Who let him in? First thing I was told by your Inspector Brown – '

'Bourne.'

' – Inspector Bourne on the phone this morning is that Bob had been alone in the house over the weekend – the other two were away.'

And click, as he said it, the voice in his head said, 'That was convenient, alone in the house.'

'My colleagues', said the coroner's officer, 'borrowed a ladder and went up on to the roof and into the house that way.'

'Did they,' said Frank, 'and I expect someone waited for the others to come home to talk to them about Bob?'

'I don't know about that, sir.'

Frank looked at the label on the sack with Bob's name on it.

'It's all there,' said the coroner's officer, 'if you'll just sign for it.'

Frank signed. The plastic sack had a faint, detestable smell.

2

The section of the conversation in Bob's room which got Flecker on the raw concerned Bob's assessment of security services as a whole. He said, his mouth half full of cake, 'Do you know what was the most surprising thing? About the CIA revelations? Their paranoia. It had never occurred to me, but people who spend their lives spying and telling lies are like mental patients. It is a form of flight from reality. One of the reasons I'm talking to you, Dad, is I want to be challenged. I may have got it wrong so I must face criticism. I don't like it much, who does? But if the idea of an open society means anything you have to face conflicting and hostile opinions, don't you? The raincoat men, like the guy who is vetting me at the moment, who seem to live in the same world as us – don't. They are not answerable. And they know they are not. In a small way I'm one of them, do you see? And it won't do. This situation – which is getting worse because of the enormous increase in the use and flexibility of computers – has dire results.

'For one thing these people are absolutely incapable of distinguishing dissent from treason. As far as they're concerned *anyone* who rocks the boat is a threat. To what? To *their* idea of good order.'

Frank said, 'All right, I don't know what you know. I don't read what you read. But I do know that in security – secret means secret. You have to have it to protect us.'

'Against whom, Dad?'

'Don't be wet.'

'I'm not.'

'It's obvious.'

'That's what I used to think, but you don't have to look very far, Dad, to find out it isn't like that at all. For example, when the Dodgson case came to trial one paper published a chronological list of every known traitor since Nunn May in 1944. Forty glorious years of spilling the beans to the Russians – Vassal and Winifred Gee and Pontecorvo and Blunt and Uncle Kim Philby and all. Not to mention those English gentlemen who still enjoy their honours and draw their pensions and go to royal garden parties because various Attorney-Generals did a deal with them rather than bring them to trial ... it must have struck you that the Russians obviously know the unnamed traitors but we – the betrayed you might say – don't. And I suppose it is too obvious even to remark that those jovial old Soviets also know all the secrets that all the traitors have spilled – but we don't. So secret is secret from whom?

'And if forty years of spilled secrets were so vital to our safety – why are we still here? Why not Soviet Britain already, my boy, I ask you? I can't help being facetious, it is like an enormous and deadly farce. Why, for example, are the authorities more anxious to hide the fact that Top Secret documents are *missing* than to hide Top Secret documents? I can show you chapter and verse if you like?'

Frank sat up sharply. 'You haven't brought stuff out? Surely you haven't – '

''Course not. It happened, to give just one example, at the Little Sai Wan GCHQ base in Hong Kong. *World In Action* got hold of the story and made a documentary, so the IBA banned it as possibly prejudicial to national security. It's wonderful when you think about it – over two hundred classified documents are missing, whoever has them knows that and knows what is in them – but it is prejudicial to national security if you, Frank Jones, turn on your telly and are told about it. So nobody got the sack and the register of documents was amended.'

'It sounds to me', said Frank, 'the way students get hot under the collar and want to reform the world, they're like that until they get out into it. Even *I* – your grim old Pa – used to go on about it when I was on leave with my mates; not about the same things, but it was real enough, the Korean War was on and I was in it with United Nations markings on the main-planes . . . and I read George Orwell too, you know – matter of fact I first picked him up in a *Reader's Digest* in a Fleet Air Arm base called Golden Hind in Australia in 1951.'

He chuckled and flicked with his shoe the open copy of the large Boots diary which still lay on the floor. He had noticed it earlier when telephoning for a taxi. The neat entries were both in English and in Russian. 'We're there,' he said, 'and you don't look much like Winston Smith to me, chum – own up! You look like someone whose boss has got up his nose, someone who needs a change . . . someone who should not, in his present state of mind, make any important decisions. Isn't that reasonable?'

'Yes it is if we were talking about the same thing.'

'I'm talking about the slump,' said Frank, 'that's what we've all got to bother about. Because none of them, Right, Left or Centre can handle it. I'm talking about mugs like you and me surviving. I'm talking about money and unemployment.'

'I know, and I appreciate it – but I'm talking about personal freedom, and not conniving in something now that I've got some idea of what it actually involves.'

'And lies, you said.'

'That most of all.'

Frank sighed. He felt old. He was conscious of the wrinkles round his eyes, the slack on his belly and thighs. He was tempted to put on his reading specs, which he detested at the best of times, because the light in the room was going and Bob's face down there near the carpet was shadowed.

'Oh shit,' he said, 'don't you know that everybody tells lies? Life runs on it. Take money which I have to deal with all the time because I both buy and sell – which I detest – '

'Do you?' said Bob surprised. 'You never said that.'

'No, I never said it; anyway everybody, including me, lies about money. They lie to each other, to the tax man and the VAT man and to their bank managers and in most cases even to themselves. What do you think you're going to do, Bob? Get a job where they don't have some nasty boardroom secrets? Where they don't launder the cash? Where nobody fiddles?'

Bob heaved himself up into a more comfortable position and said, 'I never knew you felt like that.'

'No. Well I do.'

'And you don't much enjoy life. I thought that you and Mum ... '

'We're fine.'

'I understand very well what you're saying but ... it's not what I'm on about.'

'It should be, that's what you have to deal with – not all this theory.'

'I was afraid you'd say that – I know you like to tackle matters in a practical way.'

'Not always. I would have voted for the first Labour government after the war if I'd been old enough.'

'Good God – would you!'

'Yes. And now you can reply that I'm the usual middle-aged man who's gone steadily Right due to self-interest.'

'Well did you?'

'No. Gaitskell died.'

'Ah!'

'And smarmy little Wilson looked at me out of the box ... I remembered Attlee and Bevin, even Bevan, and all the ones with guts who understood that an English socialist is nothing to do with anything across the Channel but is to do with us, here. So I turned, you might say – at least the Tories won't bankrupt the whole country – just a few thousand firms!'

Bob was astonished. 'You never said anything like that before.'

'No point – I can't alter it.'

'You let Helen and me think you were Colonel Blimp.'

'Admiral Blimp, if you don't mind – the Senior Service.'

'I think you actually know what I mean about the lies but you won't say so because you're afraid it will encourage me and I'll be in trouble.'

'I mean every word I've said – and yes, I am worried you'll get into a mess.'

Bob smiled. 'You'd do it in my place – I bet you would.'

Frank shook his head.

Bob stretched out a large foot to tap his father's shoe. 'Listen, I know I may sound a bit like Antigone – '

'Who?'

'A Greek lady in a play by Sophocles, but I'm thinking of a later version by Anouilh – she insisted on martyrdom by giving her brother a proper burial when he had been left outside the city to be eaten by carrion. He stood for subversion and King Creon wasn't having any. She did not have to do it. She was due to marry the king's son and live happily ever after. Her action could not affect the tyranny under which the city of Thebes now lived. You can imagine the pressure put on her. She did not have to ... but she did it and died for it. In the Anouilh piece it was a parable about the Vichy government, the occupying Nazis and the question of resistance.'

'I see. Yes, I do see – and it doesn't make me feel any better.'

'Well, that's not me. I'm not made of stuff like that. You won't find me chained to any railings or inviting prosecution.'

Frank considered this. 'All right, but what's the real point of resigning, Bob – ?'

'It seems to me that underneath ordinary life, I mean underneath the commonplace things – buses in the streets, and newspapers and radio and television and different political parties and paying the mortgage and heatwaves and arranging a holiday and making a fuss about the run-down of the National Health Service and ... it is so hard to put it clearly

– underneath all that, there is another and entirely secret world in the dark.

'The people who run it, thousands of them, appear to live in the light but they don't. I don't. Me. Your son. Bob Jones of no particular distinction. Bad eyesight, awkward, lover of classical music, not very brave. Every day, or nearly every day I go to a place where I translate surprising, boring, sometimes terrifying and sometimes appalling things, all of them secret. Me. One small cog.

'I don't know if I ever told you but I love the Russian language and their literature. Take dissolute young Pushkin, for example, who ended up being shot in the stomach in a duel provoked by his unfaithful and capricious wife – it still upsets me; and Tolstoy stinking and with all that guilt and Dostoevsky missing the firing squad and gambling like a maniac – Lermontov and Gogol ... I love the plays of Chekhov and the way Stanislavsky ran the Moscow Arts Theatre ... and the operas, *Boris*, and ... you see I have a world in my head, and obviously, as the politicians insist on saying, I have a perspective of Russian life to set against long, long telephone conversations between party officials – '

'Russian telephone conversations?'

'Oh yes, out of the Kremlin even, I learn at first hand what can become of a great language and a great literature in the mouths and minds of bigots and tyrants. I don't care if this argument is considered naive. I don't care at all when the professional sceptics, the hard-boiled boys who run the world, talk casually of, for example, the Bolshoi being merely a cultural weapon – which it is – *and feel nothing* as they say it. I feel something. I know it isn't news to anyone what has become of that culture, that language, that art, that music, that spirit in the name of ... the future. But it hurts me personally if the Bolshoi comes, if I watch and listen to *Romeo and Juliet*, the joy of that is poisoned by the certainty of the KGB man in the prompt corner.

'Their secret world has put out the light of the ordinary world.' He paused and shifted, he licked some icing from his fingers then he went on, 'And all I can tell you is that I believe with all my heart that our secret world and the American secret world is on *exactly* the same tack as theirs – supposedly in

82

defence of the light. To understand the scale of what I'm saying you need to read what the American secret world has done so far in the way of secret wars, secret coups using secret fleets of aircraft and secret armies – also murder, bribery, blackmail, burglary, drug trafficking across the world – in particular, before Watergate blew it up in their faces, *the extent to which they worked against their own people.* All that is what I mean by lies.'

'But it's over in America. Finished, isn't it?'

'No, it has merely been stemmed,' said Bob, 'and here we have had no Watergate. Here it would always be covered up. Have you ever known a judicial enquiry under one of our impeccable judges bring in a result contrary to the wishes of the government in power? The Official Secrets Act does the rest. Our secret world is beyond the law. In any case the judiciary is already half nobbled by its taste for power, its vanity, its private interaction with the political world where the rewards are dished out.' He finished his tea and put the cup on the carpet ignoring the saucer. 'Which brings us back to what I said at the beginning, Dad – this place, GCHQ Cheltenham, is hugely funded by and totally integrated with the Americans. Can you believe that what they do – we do not? Do you want me to go on being part of it?'

Five weeks and one day later, sitting in his car in the hospital car-park with the grey sack beside him and the driving door open to ease the heat, Frank remembered the moment. He had got out of the chair and gone to the window. He looked down on the roof where Tiger lay in the last small area of sun by the bamboo table with the empty bottles and glasses on it; the sense of foreboding which he had felt in the square earlier lay heavily on him. Without turning he said, 'I could have had a commission once, and against all reason I blew it. You have the right. But for God's sake leave it at that. Resign and walk away.'

Bob did not reply. Frank turned to see him looking down at the carpet.

'Well?'

There was a sound outside the door and Margery was saying, 'Can I come in, we've only got about a quarter of an hour, Frank?'

Bob said quietly, 'Sorry Dad, I won't look for trouble,' and then he opened the door to his mother, smiling and saying, 'We've been putting the world right, it happens all over England on Sundays – all those newspapers.'

'I do hate politics,' said Margery, 'honestly who cares,' and then as if it were part of the same sentence, 'did you know that Mark's mother's first husband was sent to Australia in the hold of a ship like a transportee at the beginning of the war? Something to do with enemy aliens or something, we were talking to Rose about Australia and her parents and the fact that you were there at one time, Frank, he never knew him of course because they divorced and his mother married his father just *after* the war.'

'Oh yes,' said Frank hardly listening.

Frank lacked the will to start and drive the car. His head ached. Margery's remarks about Mark's mother's first husband being an enemy alien and something about Australia came senselessly into his head.

The coroner's officer and another man watched him from a first-floor window in the hospital. After about five minutes he closed the door and the car drove away.

3

'What's keeping him this time?' asked the Flutter Man. He looked at his watch. He was hungry.

'Prostate,' said the Interrogator.

'Oh really?'

'He plays it up to give himself time to think. He did it under interrogation to break my concentration.' The Interrogator glanced at the point on the questionnaire where the session had broken and tapped the page. 'Of course he's much too clever to do it every time things get a little sticky for him, he does it at the most misleading places as well,' he indicated the polygraph, 'all the same he prefers this to facing me.'

'You could have fooled me.'

'It got him off the hook,' said the Interrogator. 'Dodgson

was barely a half-peeled onion when we were ordered to pass him to you.'

'It's been hurry, hurry, hurry, since they connected him with our little problem.'

It was the first time they had spoken of the contents of the briefing concerning BEDROCK, ORCHID and Luther Berry. There were one or two things the Interrogator wanted to know that the Flutter Man might tell him. At the gossip level more than anything else.

'Luther Berry?' he said.

'The very same.'

'Wasn't Berry fluttered on your ju-ju machine?'

'Oh sure. Fluttered – yes; by me – no.'

'Ah,' said the Interrogator sounding sympathetic.

'Or he wouldn't have got away with it for five years.'

'Five!'

'But you knew that?'

'Certainly, and probably you know that when we put the dates together we worked out that our friends on the other side had Dodgson and Berry *at the same time* in – '

'Vienna.'

'No, only Dodgson there – both of them in East Berlin. For four days in 1981. It wasn't friendly. Meetings in the open. No vodka and backslapping. They kept them apart, of course – the two controllers were cross-checking because what Dodgson provided fitted so well into Berry's information they thought it was a plant. They even considered eliminating our two friends but then, when it became obvious what they'd got, they couldn't believe their luck.'

The Interrogator did not say that Lord believed it was at this time that Dodgson worked out with his controller the way to incriminate the 'Stooges' in order to cover 'One' and 'Two' if the worst came to the worst and he, Dodgson, was caught. That was after Dodgson refused to defect leaving his wife and slightly sub-normal son.

It was also at this time that they let Berry know about the three at GCHQ: one, apparently incautious, sentence on the third day in East Berlin, hastily retracted. Berry was selling for money not conviction. They knew that when the Americans inevitably caught him he would tell everything including that

85

sentence. BEDROCK had already 'defected'. ORCHID, a personable woman, 'defected' that year.

The Flutter Man said, 'Luther ain't gonna travel like that no mo', no mo'.'

When you cross-examine there is a time to be silent. The Interrogator glanced at his copy of the questions with his notes in the tiny, neat writing in the margin and waited. Mr Shaw crossed the whitewashed room and took the bars on the window in his large black hands.

'Oh Lord, let my people go,' he parodied and then, 'since your Mr Dodgson spoke those unkind words this morning about me being a Judas to my black brothers groaning under American imperialism I have had friend Luther in my mind – now there *was* a black gentleman who wanted to give the American people a hard time. And for money! Which is good old capitalism in action you have to admit.'

'I admire the way he never came to trial and you kept him out of the news. That was clever.'

'Have you any idea how long he could have kept the thing going under our legal system? Years!' said the Flutter Man dusting his hands and pacing back across the room. 'We did a deal an' then he just talked, and talked and then again – he talked. We gave him a little break for being so helpful. After that, according to what I read in his home-town newspaper Luther took a fishing trip with an old buddy – did you ever visit New England?'

'No.'

'There's a pretty li'l town called Concord and not half an hour away a small place called Hillsboro, out of there you take a dirt road and you're in among the pines on the shores of Loon Pond. No swimming because it's a reservoir – but fishing is no problem. There was this real pretty cabin – did you ever see the movie *On Golden Pond*?'

'I'm afraid not.'

'That kind of lake, beautiful sunsets, rocking-chair out on the porch, screens to keep the bugs out, a few bottles of whisky and a few crates of beer from the liquor store in Hillsboro – that's where Luther's ol' buddy took him to relax after all that talking. I imagine you've heard of Louisa M. Alcott?'

'Er ... possibly?'

'Wrote a fine book called *Little Women*.'

'Yes. I don't think I ever – '

'Well it was Louisa M. Alcott country, I mean she may even have written that book somewhere near where poor Luther drowned.'

'Ah!'

'Fell in and panicked. Nearly drowned his old buddy who was trying to save him – it said in his home-town newspaper.'

'Hmmm.'

'The only person that didn't buy it was Luther's pappy. Said Luther had always been a fine swimmer. So ... they put Pa Berry in touch with Parent Bereavement Outreach of Santa Monica, California.'

The Interrogator was faintly incredulous, not about the end of Luther Berry but about the organisation which dealt with Luther's unhappy father.

'Parent Bereavement what?'

'Outreach.'

'Outreach!'

'That's it.'

'And they're genuine?' It was the Interrogator's none too subtle way of asking if the organisation was a CIA front.

'Oh sure!' The Flutter Man managed to sound faintly indignant. 'They are really good people, every one a bereaved parent – those excellent people told ol' Berry in a really caring way that all bereaved parents are positively plagued with doubts.'

'Yes I see.'

'Also that bereaved parents suffer terrible guilt and many have strange ideas.'

'Hmmm.'

'Matter of fact,' said Mr Shaw, his hands in a praying position in front of him, 'an' sad to say – sometimes their minds just go altogether.'

4

'Did you like your Russian controller?'

'Yes.'

'Did you enjoy doing what they taught you?'
'Yes.'
'Because it was secret?'
'Yes.'
'Because it made you feel important?'
'Yes.'
'Because you got paid?'
'No.'
'Did you enter the Civil Service with the intention of betraying your country?'
'No.'
The Flutter Man marked the graph paper.
'Did you resent criticism of your skill as a mathematician?'
'Yes.'
'Did you resent others being promoted?'
'Yes.'
'Do you enjoy kiddy porn?'
'I can't help it.'
'Yes or no, Mr Dodgson.'
'Yes.'
The Flutter Man opened the folder and took out the second photograph. Dodgson sensed the movement and began to turn. The Flutter Man said in a soothing voice, 'No need to strain, Ramsay, I'm coming right beside you with one of these ol' photographs that relieves my boredom, you'll have seen it once before – here we have your old friend Allen Goodburn and his wife Cynthia, or so they tell me – would you say that was a good likeness?'

He switched off the polygraph. The cuff deflated. The photograph taken by flash was blown up to the same size as the photograph of Stephen Kedge. Allen Goodburn was older than Kedge, he had receding dark hair and a dark beard. His smile was forced, perhaps that was the effect of the flash. He was sitting at a table with a drink in his hand. His wife Cynthia, about ten years his junior, was holding his arm and leaning to him in an attitude of affection. She wore a paper hat and was slightly drunk. Discernible behind them was another face – cheerful, hair untidy, specs slipping a little on the nose, a glass raised towards the photographer. Bob Jones recorded for as long as the negative would last as enjoying himself –

possibly in the company of Goodburn and his wife – at Christmas.

Dodgson looked at the photograph and said nothing. From the corner the Interrogator watched him intently.

'With your permission,' said Mr Shaw, 'we'll just start up the black box and proceed.'

Dodgson sat still, holding the photograph. The cuff inflated unpleasantly on his upper arm and he became aware again of his own heartbeat somewhere near the elbow. It seemed more difficult for him to breathe, as if he had become conscious of an automatic function and inhibited it by noticing it.

The Flutter Man made no move to take the photograph from his hand, nor did he hurry to ask the next question. Dodgson touched the rim of his spectacles with his free hand, dipping his head because the cuff connection tightened on that side as he bent his arm. The hand with the photograph had the palm electrode and the springs to keep it in place; this restriction made him appear to hold the print delicately between finger and thumb as if it were either precious or liable to bite him.

The Flutter Man leaned over his shoulder and took it. He laid it by the photograph of Kedge eternally watching the little girls while hiding his eternal erection. The haggard face and the uneasily-smiling bearded face of the two known to the Interrogator as the 'Stooges' rested face up on the table beside the so-called lie detector; the man attached to the polygraph looked hard at the whitewashed wall two feet in front of his nose.

The Flutter Man could see the sweat forming on Dodgson's bald dome: white, partly wrinkled skin with a slight greasy sheen over bone, hiding the unfeeling brain working at maximum capacity.

The Interrogator could smell Dodgson who had only one bath a week in prison. Despite the Flutter Man's fastidious use of soap and aftershave the smell of Dodgson dominated the room. The Interrogator was familiar with the smell which came off those under pressure.

Dodgson was deliberately concentrating on his wife and son. He imagined her being given electroconvulsive therapy without anaesthetic; then he imagined a Victorian workhouse

89

(he tensed against the corrugated pneumograph tube round his chest to revive the images of squalor and torment for the poor children in Victorian mines) in which a man resembling the Interrogator shouted and bullied his son, and then beat him because the child was slow and could not understand. The self-generation of fear and hatred induced an added feeling of claustrophobia. Dodgson was gearing for the climax. This was the afternoon of the third day. In the adjoining room the man with the recording machine, a Welshman this time with thinning sandy hair, sat yawning with one earphone off wishing he had the will to stop smoking.

'Is this a photograph of Allen Goodburn?'

'Yes.'

'Was Allen Goodburn in your section?'

'Yes.'

'Did you sometimes meet Allen Goodburn socially?'

'Yes.'

In the margin of his list of the questions the Interrogator wrote, '*After* the meeting in East Berlin in 1981 – Dodgson cultivated Goodburn.'

'Did you play chess with Allen Goodburn?'

'Yes.'

'Did you recruit Allen Goodburn?'

'No.'

The Flutter Man ringed the graph paper.

'Was that because Allen Goodburn already worked for the Russians?'

'No.'

The Flutter Man made another mark.

'You knew Goodburn was a spy?'

'No.'

'Goodburn like Kedge was anti-American?'

'No.'

The Flutter Man stopped the instrument. The cuff deflated.

'You're still having a little trouble, Ramsay.'

'No.'

'Let's just relax and then try it again.'

Dodgson suddenly shouted, 'We've done it five times. I've said the same thing five times.'

'So what is your problem?'

'I have mixed feelings,' said Dodgson, waving his arms as far as he could and seeming to writhe in the embrace of the three connections, 'you must have met it before? Half "Yes", half "No". Yes, yes, yes I liked my Russian controller and – *no* I did not. I resented him because when I was away from him it was horribly lonely and it was his fault.'

'Hearts and flowers,' noted the Interrogator, 'not up to his previous standard.'

'Yes, I am abnormal,' shouted Dodgson, seeming on the verge of tearing himself away from the polygraph and out of the chair, 'and to get an erection I use kiddy porn; and *no*, I detest it and I'm ashamed, masturbating in a dark room with the video running. Yes – I shared it with Stephen Kedge and sold it to one or two others on the side – that's why I was arrested you *know* that. It was nothing to do with spying. So, yes I feel *guilty* when you mention Kedge, and no, I never recruited him into helping me to spy. Yes, Allen Goodburn was in my section and no I did not – '

The Interrogator took the spare chair to sit very close to Dodgson invading his private space. The smell of Dodgson at such close quarters was rank. His whole face ran with sweat. Behind the glasses his eyes, which were a curious opaque green, looked rapidly from side to side but not at the Interrogator.

'There now,' said Mr Bruce, 'I understand. You're a poor fellow who somehow blundered along stealing and photographing Top Secret documents, hundreds of them, taking them to Vienna and East Berlin on a series of impulses. You managed it by sheer chance for ten years.' He paused, he almost smiled. Dodgson had become very still. This, thought the Interrogator, is your last chance to catch on, Mr Flutter Man from Watts – if things turn over later and your people tackle us we can say, hand on heart, we tried to tell you but you wouldn't listen – it's all going on tape in the next room.

To Dodgson he said, 'I understand. You're not faking your responses. You're not dedicated or well trained. You don't have a small support team you're covering. You're just an emotional pervert as capricious as the Red Queen – isn't that it? What's more you were never rehearsed to resist interrogation and keep on lying and dissembling because somehow or other they'll get you out the way they got Blake and Abel out.'

The Flutter Man was examining the graph paper.

The Interrogator leaned closer. Dodgson averted his face.

'They won't, Dodgson. Those days are over. We've all stopped being soft and even if they frame twenty Western businessmen and try an exchange we shall let the poor fellows freeze their balls off in the Gulag and hang on to you.'

Dodgson made as if to stand up and pull the connections from the instrument. The Flutter Man without seeming to notice immediately pinned him into the chair.

'Your trial was painful to us,' said the Interrogator. 'We do not forgive you, Ramsay, for making us look foolish and for putting another wedge between us and our good friends. You are here to help make amends. You are here to answer "Yes" or "No" to the agreed questions.'

He got up to reach for the two photographs. The Flutter Man still restrained Dodgson by the shoulders. The Interrogator held the photographs in front of Dodgson's face.

'"Yes" or "No",' he said, 'get on with it.'

The only thing the three men had in common was a complete lack of interest in the cheerful young man in the background of the Goodburn photograph at the Christmas party.

SIX

The Interrogator, a frugal man, took the tube to Marble Arch. He emerged to a babel of tourists on the pavement, many of them Arab. Veiled women went past him with bold, not downcast eyes. A German had an altercation with the only Englishman in sight who was selling papers.

He turned right breathing exhaust fumes and when he passed McDonald's Hamburgers he thought of Mr Shaw flying back to somewhere in America after being de-briefed at the American Embassy in Berkeley Square only ten minutes from here on foot. Not that Americans ever went on foot. The liaison man had been an unobtrusive chauffeur for the five days of the Flutter Man's stay.

Walking up the Edgware Road the Interrogator, who did not have the professional inhibitions of Flecker, considered whether Mr Shaw was more than a mere polygraph operator. He had seemed rather too familiar with Hillsboro; and the late Luther Berry would have had, most probably, a black companion not a white on his well-earned fishing trip to Loon Pond.

At another expansive moment Mr Shaw had spoken of his uncle who saved him from Watts and took him north one blazing summer to Cleveland. This same uncle subsequently paid for Mr Shaw to go through Hiram College, Ohio, with all the farm-fed kids from the Midwest, the boys sweating, at that time, over Vietnam, and marrying, and having kids they did not want in order to avoid the draft, the compulsory ride to the killing ground in Indo-China.

Mr Shaw had mentioned ketchup. His uncle used a lot of

ketchup; Mr Shaw had caught the habit and regretted the lack of ketchup in the dingy flat in Battersea where they had the conversation.

Young Shaw, aged fourteen, and his taciturn uncle took two weeks driving north. At each motel his uncle made him shower and scrub himself. He made him eat sitting at the table cutting up the food with a knife, using the fork. Until then the boy had mostly eaten standing holding whatever it was – sandwich or hamburger – in his dirty hands. On the second day they stopped in a small town and bought him new jeans, two shirts, a zipper jacket, socks and shoes. His uncle threw away the old gear. He had already taken the gun and got rid of it.

At night they shared a motel room and his uncle prayed before going to sleep. When they reached the frame-house in a suburb of Cleveland his aunt said, 'God be praised,' and embraced him. They had no children.

On the trip his uncle had said nothing except things like, 'You want to eat now?'

The first night he was in his room his uncle came in and sat on the bed.

'You like the house?'

'Sure.'

'You like the food?'

'Yeah.'

A silence and then he said, 'You want this or you want the penitentiary?'

The boy was taken aback, what was this shit?

'What did I do?'

'Nothin'. I'm giving you a choice.'

'I don't get it.'

'I'm giving it you. I've talked to your aunt.'

'You mean I work for you?'

'I mean you get educated.'

The hardened fourteen-year-old laughed in his uncle's face. His uncle, who was not a big man, smacked him hard across both cheeks and then pinned him to the bed and leaned over him.

'You can laugh when you know something. You know nothing. You're like an animal, boy, because that's what your

94

life has been; your mother was wild and never would listen – you want to go back to all that? Do you?'

From another room the newscaster on CBS was talking about Vietnam.

'What else would I do?'

'Go to school, get the grades, go to college.'

'With what?'

'You make the grades, I'll lend you the money.'

'You mean I can live here – with you?'

'Where else?'

At breakfast the next morning his uncle put a lot of ketchup on his eggs.

: They recruited him the second year at college when he was nineteen, the year Simon and Garfunkel did a gig at the college and sang the way it was in the mid-1960s before the National Guard shot the guys at Kent State.

These were the last days of something and despite the green grass and the elegant houses of the Greek Revival and the rich patrons of music, despite the fact that it was not oven-hot, not seething tenements, the young black smelled the coming violence and the end of an old sort of authority.

Simon and Garfunkel sang of graffiti, old age, death, rootlessness and looking for America and Mr Shaw wanted it to stay like that because he knew, as he had told the Interrogator, what the severed head of a baby looked like covered with blowflies in a filthy sink among unwashed dishes; he knew how easy it was to go from *this*, with a girl beside him for whom he lusted, to *that* which was lower than any lower depths that anyone ever wrote about. He did not intend to lose the America he had found.

The girl's father recruited him. The girl's father gave him beer and talked to him about the time he had commanded a rifle company in Korea. Perhaps the girl's father had looked up from a foxhole and seen an out-of-date piston-engined fighter bomber come in from the sea to give support. With Frank Jones in the cockpit hoping the North Korean MiGs would not jump him before he had found his target.

The Interrogator missed the company of the Flutter Man – and went as far as to wonder if it had not all been a triple bluff. Perhaps Mr Shaw did not really believe in the 'Stooges'. Or

95

worse – perhaps there was a whole piece of the picture missing and the 'Stooges' were actually 'One' and 'Two' despite Lord's apparently irrefutable evidence to the contrary.

The Interrogator found the doorway and pressed the bell. When the voice answered he identified himself. The door buzzed and he went in, making sure it closed behind him. He avoided the lift and took the stairs. On the top floor he pressed the bell of the flat and knew himself observed through the spyhole before the door opened.

'Come in,' said Lord, 'sticky sort of a day, do go through would you?'

The Interrogator had visited the flat twice in the previous fifteen years. The painting of the Delhi Durbar, based on a contemporary photograph, was still on the wall. There were no books, newspapers or periodicals to indicate the taste of the occupant.

Lord limped into the room after him. Lord obviously had a magnificent tailor to cut a suit to accommodate that slight twist in the body and the leg which looked as if it might snap off below the knee, the distortion being so great.

'Do sit down.'

'Thank you.'

'Which would you prefer, tea or a drink?'

'A drink would be pleasant.'

Lord used his hands with an elegance which suggested vanity to the Interrogator.

'You like this I believe?'

The Interrogator looked at the bottle being held up and smiled, 'Quite right.'

While pouring Lord said, 'We're in for a heatwave I think, you don't take ice?'

'No, thank you.'

The voice was precise and well produced as if it had been trained. Its tone, even when he was being pleasant, was chilling as the sea sometimes is under a warm layer on the surface.

When he sat he twisted the thin leg tightly round the other spoiling the cut of the trousers and giving the impression the leg functioned like a creeper.

Although betrayed neither by voice nor expression the Interrogator sensed an extraordinary tension in Lord, as if a war raged in him. It had been his first impression fifteen years earlier and it remained. He had wondered then if Lord, who had about him the quality of a black Merlin, had ever been destined for the stage – that sanctuary where the unbalanced, amateur and professional, can express the passions, terrors and violence lurking in them and be applauded for it: a profession sufficiently close in spirit to the law – with its rituals, its enormous vanities, its public triumphs and disasters and its dispensation (while performing) from the shackles of what is expected as normal behaviour – for the Interrogator to feel both sympathetic and superior to it.

There was the faint pleasant smell of polish. The Interrogator wondered if this was one of the many WD or FO or HO properties in London.

They drank.

'So the American has gone and you can now get on with Mr Dodgson.'

'Yes.'

'They seem pleased.'

'Good.'

'I have read the transcript – perhaps you would interpret it for me?'

'I would say that Dodgson's confirmation that Kedge and Goodburn were involved was convincing.'

'To you?'

'Not at all, to the American.'

'Despite the machine? – I'm no good at machines, I'm good at men. I gather you did your homework on the machine?'

'Yes, despite the machine. Dodgson's main problem was to convey the guilt of Kedge and Goodburn while actually telling the truth about them – which is that they're innocent. He had obviously been briefed by our friends on the other side about the dangers of the polygraph because they instruct their people to avoid it – it is one of the few areas where the good friends feel confident they have an edge on the KGB.

'To pull it off he had to establish misleading results to the questions which were *not* in doubt because these are, as it were, the norms from which variations are noted and lying or evasion inferred. If you can blur the norm you're halfway home. The questions about which answers are not in doubt are

97

of two sorts – the emotionally neutral such as, "Is your name John Bull?" and the emotionally loaded, as in his case, "Do you really enjoy watching kiddy porn in which fully-grown men penetrate young girls?"'

'Hmmm.'

'What he did was to stoke up the emotions, heart rate, breathing over the former and, as far as I could make out, practise a sort of "concentrate on the blank wall and empty the mind" over the latter. Then, whenever it came to Kedge and Goodburn, he jibbed. He argued, he made the American stop the machine, he seemed outraged. Finally when the machine was *off* after a major tantrum he suddenly staged a breakdown – criminals, incidentally, quite often do this genuinely and he probably knew it, they suddenly break down and confess. The machine is designed only to deal with "Yes" and "No" so the confession automatically happens when it is off and no dials are monitoring.

'So Dodgson, as I say, appeared to break down as if he had to get it off his chest at last. He then made a moving plea to spare his wife and son.'

'Where is she, by the way?'

'On holiday in Spain with friends.'

'My dear fellow – I hope she doesn't catch something nasty from that filthy Mediterranean or their cooking. We might be blamed!'

'Yes! So, our good friends have what they want.'

'Not quite.'

'Oh yes of course. Number three. I can't be of much help there, I'm afraid.'

'You're doing very well,' said Lord, 'and I think we might put their hearts at rest about that.'

Lord untwisted his leg and stood up. The Interrogator stirred but Lord's hand indicated he should stay.

'Just to tie up some loose ends for you,' he said, 'it may be of some use, both the mother and father of Goodburn's first wife were card-carrying members. He knew but failed to reveal it. Obviously the other side knew. BEDROCK brought it to the attention of the Americans who told us. Goodburn's first wife was also inclined that way, which we missed.'

Lord was looking out of the window at the grey building

opposite. He did not appear to be angry. Against the light he looked much younger than his age, like some women who, seen from the back, appear twenty and when they turn ... Lord turned, 'It used to be said, and I was inclined to agree, that such mistakes are forgivable because, unlike the enemy, we err on the side of decency and trust. When we pry we do it blunderingly, and even the most hardened of our snoopers is given to thoughts of fair play. Or should I put it that we tend to distinguish between our own, the professionals, and the rest, the civil servants and such who come under the Act. With the latter we were inclined to give them the benefit of the doubt.'

The Interrogator noted the past tense.

'As for Kedge,' said Lord, 'he'd twice sought psychiatric treatment for his perversion, he even asked for some form of aversion therapy. Of course he shut up about it – and again we failed to find out. As for Dodgson's arrest – we had, as you know, no idea either of his perversions or his spying activity. The police got on to him after receiving an anonymous letter. It was timed so that they caught him selling some of the stuff.'

The Interrogator listened carefully to detect Lord's real theme. These facts were not new to him.

'When he had been charged the police received an anonymous phone call telling them that they were looking in quite the wrong direction and they should look in certain specified places. They did. They found the spy paraphernalia. How we dealt with that and Mrs Dodgson you know already.

'The Russians certainly "burned" him. They had sucked him dry. Sooner or later he was going to trip up over the porn business and they failed to persuade him to defect. They knew Berry's days were numbered in America. We are certain that neither Kedge nor Goodburn were involved in the anonymous calls, and equally certain it was someone locally placed at GCHQ and not done from outside.

'Now that our good friends are convinced about Kedge and Goodburn there can be no question of another trial, you can see that?'

'Given the evidence,' said the Interrogator, 'the inadmissibility of defector testimony leaves only Dodgson, and a good counsel would demolish him. The best you can do is sack them. I take it Kedge will remain immune from prosecution over the porn business to avoid another field-day in the press?'

'Exactly,' said Lord, 'it is a problem. We can hardly depend on an act of God to solve it.'

The Interrogator thought for a moment that Lord was referring to 'One' and 'Two' still safely in place.

'I by no means despair of getting more out of Dodgson,' he said.

'Yes,' said Lord, as if it were the first time he had considered the matter, 'yes, from your point of view – but perhaps what I am referring to is our first priority – the protection of Anglo-American co-operation in electronic intelligence.'

The Interrogator at once understood.

'Our good friends', said Lord, 'accept the result of what they call "the technical interview" with Dodgson which you so brilliantly analysed for me a few minutes ago. Had they been here and listened they would have dismissed your interpretation. They believe in the authenticity of BEDROCK and ORCHID. They would not accept our surveillance conclusions on Kedge and Goodburn were I unwise enough to show them. Even the word of the late Mr Berry carries more weight with them than anything I may have to say at the moment ... they now wish to act.'

'I see.'

'From your tone I take it you have qualms.'

'Reservations.'

'Ah.'

'It is my experience', said the Interrogator carefully, 'that our good friends are not always as efficient as they boast of being. I imagine they intend a clean sweep.'

'Hmmm!'

'They are in a strong position?'

'Overwhelming – they reached the end of their patience when Dodgson was flushed, certain promises had to be made in order that they did not deny us further access to their ... machines, and that they did not cut off the budget ... '

'Understood.'

'Had they done so we would, in terms of the enemy, have been like a blind beggar at a bad street crossing.'

'Extreme,' said the Interrogator, 'and given their dependence

n us as an aircraft and missile carrier and reinforcement
rea – unlikely.'

'So you say, so you say – but in the circumstances the PM
ad to make a special journey to Washington. And I', said
ord, 'was nearly choked by humble pie at that time. You
eferred to efficiency?'

'To give them a free hand *in this country* seems an unneces-
ary risk – although I imagine it has been done before.'

The Interrogator had fixed his position. Without con-
ciously summoning the arguments he had considered his
uture, part of which he intended to spend in parliament and
art on the bench. A man has only one life. Lord could blight
t if he chose.

At this time Bob Jones was also considering his future in
he face of an ethical problem. Earlier in the week he had
one to see an old school friend in Manchester. Bob had
lways admired Matty's judgment.

Curiously, between Matty and Lord there was the faintest
onnection: one of Lord's recruiters, a partially disgraced
areer officer working out his last years in the security
ervice, had tried to hook Matty at university and failed.

Lord did not, of course, know about the routine attempt
y one of the foot soldiers in his section years before – but
e did know about the journey of Bob Jones. Flecker's
ndefatigable team reported it. The name Matthew Snelgrove
nd other names were being investigated.

A rush job had been done to tap Snelgrove's telephone at
he exchange; his mail began to arrive one post late having
een put on the interception list which exists at many post
ffices to be separately sorted and taken by special messenger
o another place: there opened, read, photocopied as neces-
ary, re-sealed and returned for delivery.

These precautions were a day too late to discover whom
Matty contacted on Bob's behalf.

Lord, accepting that the Interrogator had chosen, poured a
econd drink, sat again twisting the one leg round the other.
He said, 'I very much take your point; things can be botched,
he police are not the fools and thugs some people like to
make out and the press, although much of it is trash, can be
damned awkward at times. However the risk has always been

101

accepted in the extreme case.'

The Interrogator wondered how often.

'Let me give you an example – you remember that – ' h
hesitated slightly and then said, 'entertainer person in the war
American? Nearly as famous as Churchill himself, they still tal
about him. Well, he got himself involved with ... something o
other in Paris after we liberated it, and someone put a knife int
him in an hotel room. One of our chaps to be precise. RAF.

'The effect of that on American public opinion, if it had com
out, would have been similar to the effect on British publi
opinion if a GI had raped Vera Lynn.

'It would have been disastrous for the Alliance. It wa
necessary to invent a tragic accident. We had the precedent, i
the public mind, of the Leslie Howard plane crash. The thing
had to be done in a hurry and wasn't quite foolproof so we als
leaked medical reports to the effect that the poor fellow ha
been mortally ill and bravely carrying on until the pain mad
him ... ' Lord took a gunmetal cigarette case from his pocket
To the Interrogator it seemed an extraordinary anachronism i
an age when those who smoked always did so from the packet
It was almost as if Lord were taking snuff. He lit the cigarett
and considered it.

'At the same time, as you can see, it was necessary to dea
with certain others involved. As it is in this case. Of course w
got the co-operation of the good friends. The problem then, a
now, is the *public* effect of such revelations and the subsequen
pressure of American public opinion on the president and th
politicians.'

'Yes,' said the Interrogator, 'yes, of course.'

'Our business', said Lord, 'is to see to it that we and the goo
friends always hang together – not separately.'

It was quiet for a few moments in the room. The Interrogato
disliked the smell of the cigarette. Had there not been enough
publicity about death from heart disease and lung cancer to
convince any intelligent man?

He began to consider how to deal with Dodgson the next
day. As he thought of Dodgson into his mind came the jingle
from *Alice*: 'I'll be judge, I'll be jury,' said the cunning old fury.
'I'll try the whole cause and condemn you to death.'

He caught Lord looking at him.

PART THREE

SEVEN

1

Frank drove carefully between the cars parked either side, his windows down to ease the heat. Nothing moved – no car, cat, bird, citizen or twist of foil in the gutter. Bob had said that his first, and abiding, impression of the place – not just this street but the whole town – was of emptiness.

Nothing was real since this morning. The unreal was all around him in the sunlight; the *real* was an invisible dimension in which he moved, from which he looked out, driving down the street, breathing, hearing Bob's voice speak of Antigone – who must have been a pain in the arse to have about the house ... even though what she did survived the centuries to disturb an ordinary man now pressing a doorbell.

He rang a second time. The car was double-parked, with its driving door open. The grey sack hung from his left hand. Creon lost that round; Antigone covered her brother with earth and died for it; even if the dust of Thebes was long blown to the upper atmosphere her action was more real at this moment of thumb on bell-push than the dead town at his back.

Antigone's brother was put out naked for the carrion; Bob lay naked on a metal table over holes in regular rows so that when they opened him what ran out would go down the centre column to the gutter underneath ...

Something moved, was walking towards his back away from the sound of a car door clacking shut. Before he had fully turned a voice said, 'Mr Jones?'

They say you're past it when the coppers seem young.

Young or not they all have a certain expression. This one was the exception. Long hair, not quite the Jesus Christ cut of previous decades but long and fair and round the ears. Easy he stood in the jeans and the collarless shirt his granddad might have worn. Big spectacles and a face like an overgrown choirboy ready to pipe up 'Oh for the wings of a dove' still favourite on request programmes for neo-geriatrics.

Frank was silent. What you don't tell them ... unless, said another voice in his head sharply, they're listening when you don't know. He had read about it a hundred times in newspapers, thrillers (seen it on the telly) – the James Bond stuff. Nothing to do with him. The secret listeners were the good guys; those listened to were criminals, Reds, moles, terrorists – the enemies of law and ordinary self-employed businessmen like him.

The thought jolted him. He might be counted among the bad guys simply by being Bob's father. The idea was part of the new reality. He *felt* it. It made the things Bob said also become real. Until now, or until the knock on the door this morning, all that had concerned him were the possible consequences to Bob if he resigned. Hearing about the secret world had been similar to hearing a news item about Ulster. So there was bombing and murder? So what? He wasn't there to see blood, hear shouting voices and gunfire, smell the air after an explosion. It wasn't his business.

Now, facing the young man, his heart banging in his chest he knew that being Frank Jones, ordinary tax payer, Tory voter, did not exempt him. Despite its problems his life until yesterday had been lived in a state of innocence.

The jolt was the greater for the speed with which it hit him: a feeling of dread as if he were about to be sent into action unprepared; a series of thoughts that were neither words nor images but something else; the sort of response an ape or a lion might have when the fight or flight mechanism is triggered.

The young man said, 'Mr Jones.'

'Yes?'

'Bill Pickett – ' He hesitated deliberately to see if Frank reacted. Frank was silent.

'I knew your son.'

No response.

'I'm very sorry to hear what happened, Mr Jones.'

Frank turned his back to ring the bell again. The previous feeling had gone as fast as it came, swamped by a need to be alone, preferably in a shaded room; to have a drink and then to sleep for a long time.

'Could you spare a minute?'

'What for?'

'I'd be grateful to talk to you.'

Coppers don't talk like that. Coppers don't say words like 'grateful'.

'How did you know me?'

'I guessed.'

'No you didn't,' said Frank, 'you were waiting. I don't even live in this town. Who are you?'

'A journalist.'

Frank detected, as he had with the coroner's officer, an assumption of authority and the anger started to rise again.

'I don't want to talk.'

'I wouldn't bother you but – '

'Which paper?'

The words 'paper' came out like a threat. Pickett paused to look properly at Frank. He took in the stance, the Marks and Spencer suit, the hard face and the short hair brushed straight back making the man look continental, the way some Poles look; a round head emphasised the impression; a head that was used to going down and butting its way through. It was slightly down now and the eyes were looking up under the brow. They were an indeterminate colour between blue and green, they looked at him without blinking.

'Which paper?' It was louder this time. Pickett revised his assumption of a nondescript or stricken parent.

'You're not local,' said Frank. Pickett had a voice that came from somewhere in the South-East, slightly nasal.

'No, I work for a weekly, the *Senator*.'

No response.

'Bob may have mentioned me?'

'No.'

'I was at university with a mate of his – '

'Which mate?'

'Matty Snelgrove.'

'Which university?'

'Kent.'

'Snelgrove?'

'Yes, he read economics.'

'And then?'

'What do you mean?' said Pickett.

'What did he do then? If he's a chum of yours?'

'Oh. Computers. He audits computer accounts.'

'Where?'

'Now look, Mr Jones, all I want – '

'I know what you want.'

'Manchester,' said Pickett.

Snelgrove had been home with Bob. Snelgrove was a little dynamo. Not much to Frank's taste. But he was in computers in Manchester.

Frank considered Pickett, noting the shift of expression, a shading of the baby-blue eyes behind the spectacles expressing slight displeasure that this particular member of the public was not co-operating as members of the public were expected to when the word 'journalist' or 'interviewer' was uttered.

'Matty put Bob on to me.'

When Frank wrote it down later he wrote it in capitals – *Snelgrove put Bob on to the journalist* – and underlined it.

'Who did you say you are?' said Frank, and the journalist wondered if he was a nutcase.

'Pickett, Bill Pickett.'

'The *Senator*,' said Frank politely.

'That's it.'

'Prove it.'

Pickett shrugged and took his wallet from his back pocket. He showed a card with his signature.

'NUJ,' he said, 'oh sorry, National Union of Journalists.'

'Why did Matty Snelgrove put Bob on to you?'

'I'm not sure, Mr Jones, I thought you might help.'

'Well, what did he talk to you about?'

'Bob?'

Frank took a breath and then said quietly, 'Yes – Bob.'

'Nothing really.'

Without warning or premeditation Frank seized him by his shirt front and swung him round at arm's length to bang him against the front door of the house. Pickett made a gasping sound as the breath went out of him. For a second Frank moved closer and the journalist put his hands up in front of his face.

'Don't fuck about with me – he's dead.'

Frank let him go, turned abruptly to his car as if to get in, slammed the door shut and walked away up the road twenty fast paces raving under his breath wanting to kill someone. He turned and came back to the car, opened the door and then shut it again.

By this time Pickett had moved along the short path on to the pavement tucking his shirt in, smoothing his hair back and trying to control his feelings. He lit a cigarette and stood a car's width from Frank's double-parked car looking at him over a luggage rack.

'Right then,' said Frank, 'why are you here? Eh? Why here on Bob's doorstep when I come back from identifying the body?'

'Because', said Pickett, 'I was supposed to meet him this afternoon when he came home from work.'

'You're a Leftie, aren't you?'

'What else?'

'You want to stir up the Dodgson business – it's that isn't it? Now Bob's dead you'll use him!'

'I don't need to use him to do that I assure you.'

'You say he came to you.'

'No – he *telephoned* me. I checked with Matty afterwards to make sure it wasn't something else.'

'What?'

'Well,' said Pickett, and he no longer looked like a choirboy, 'you don't exactly take it on trust when someone you've never heard of phones you and says they work at GCHQ and they want to talk – I mean there are laws, and things are very jumpy since brother Dodgson.'

'Ten days ago he phoned, did he?'

'That's it.'

'All right – why the delay? I mean in getting together?'

Pickett now seemed to think it safe to move to a normal talking distance from Frank. Also he was aware of the level of their voices.

He came round the kerbside car to lean on Frank's car roof.

'Bob said that what he wanted to discuss involved someone else. The other person didn't want him to talk to me about it. He hoped to persuade him. That's the lot.'

'No it isn't – why the appointment today?'

'Bob told me he'd be in touch with the other person this weekend.'

'In touch?'

'Yes.'

'Telephone or meeting?'

'I've no idea.'

'That's not "nothing" is it? That's something if it's true.'

'It's true all right. I brought this to discuss with him today.'

He held out a sealed envelope. He put it on the bonnet of the car, produced a biro and began to write on it.

'Look – I'll give you my name and phone number. You might want to call me.'

'Don't you believe it.'

The journalist held out the envelope. After a moment Frank took it and put it in his inside pocket. The obvious questions came into his mind.

'Who told you he was dead? No one knows except his family and the police.'

'The press know by now – but in fact ... '

Pickett indicated a small, black-haired woman hovering in the partly open front door next to Bob's house.

'That one,' he said, and walked away to a car parked on the opposite side of the road.

Frank went back to the front door. A low wall divided him from the Welsh neighbour. He vaguely remembered having seen her before. It was impossible to avoid her. She began at once poking her sharp white beak towards him and snapping her eyes; she seemed full of unnatural energy in contrast to her skinny little form.

'Are you another reporter? I told him I don't think anyone's in ... oh I believe I've seen you haven't I? On the roof out there, I am sorry, I expect you're related?'

'Yes.'

'Aaawww,' said the Welsh woman, cawing with sympathy, watching him closely for some sign of suffering to which she could respond, 'so sorry, woulden' you like to come in for a nice cup of tea, I'm just going to make one and – '

'No.'

'Oh.'

For a moment she was silent. Frank, hating to have to do it with her watching, was carefully opening the grey sack.

'I was the one dialled 999,' she said.

'You mean you saw my son?'

'Yes I did, from the kitchen window, you see, I was filling the kettle and I could hear Tiger, that's the cat, you know, he comes in to us sometimes and – '

'The police told me there were no witnesses.'

'Aaawww, I never saw it happen, mind, I tol' them that, they borrowed our ladder to get on the roof, they even took the cat up after they finished.'

'Finished?'

'Looking. They went in by the door from the roof, two of them, very nice men they were, very patient, listening, and then they took Tiger up the ladder before they gave it back, you see.'

Frank had found a paper bag within the sack. This contained the contents of Bob's pockets. He took out the keys.

'Oh you got some keys then?'

Touching the keys, the cheque book, the bank card, the used handkerchief made him want to weep.

He put the key in the door and the Welsh crow said, 'If you change your mind about the tea – '

He went into the hall without reply and closed the door. He stood in the small lobby and listened. The house was still. There was a faint smell of gas from somewhere on the ground floor, Rose's section. Her part of the house was a separate flat partitioned off and locked. On the lobby table was some mail. Nothing for Bob.

He went up the long flight of stairs to the first floor and stopped again; he put down the sack and went into the kitchen. They kept the drinks in a wall cupboard. There were dirty cups and plates on the wooden table, chairs pulled out and left blocking the way round.

He moved two chairs, opened the cupboard and found the Scotch. He washed a glass, aware of the overflowing waste bin and the smell of stale food mixed with garlic. Flies cruised an eccentric circuit under the ceiling.

He poured two inches of Scotch and drank an inch. He sat at the table clearing a space with his arms. A cup went over and dregs of tea spilled to drip on the floor on the far side. Theatre posters and smart postcards from friends, slightly dulled by grease, hung or were stuck on the wall nearest to him. The silence hummed in his ears. Something moved and he turned, half rising. Tiger stood inside the door watching. The cat made its odd seagull-like squawk and then lay on its side inviting attention.

'You were bloody down there,' said Frank, 'but were you out there when it happened?'

He went to the window with the glass in his hand. The cat jumped on the ledge beside him. It was from here that the animal got out through a cat 'door' in the window. Frank looked down into the garden with its enclosing wall. From where he stood he could not see the narrow path that ran beside Rose's part of the house between the building and the garden wall. The trees in all the gardens seemed thicker than five weeks earlier, making solid shadows across the houses.

He finished his drink and left the kitchen, picking up the sack from outside the door. Deliberately he opened the doors in turn – bathroom, lavatory, Mark's bedroom. He stopped there, in the doorway, and looked round. He listened for the sound of anyone entering the front door below. He did not know what he was looking for; yes, the bed was made. On the chest of drawers a brush, comb, scissors, a pot with pens; in the bookshelves the books neatly, tightly placed. Shoes in trees in the corner; a notice board attached to the wall with letters, reminders, cards, tacked to it; a portable television, black and white, its screen the size of a postcard. A wall cupboard which would not close properly because of the clothes hung in it. A photograph in a frame on the small table used as a desk. Frank went in to look at it. A strong-faced woman with a small boy. Unmistakably the 1950s with that tucked-in waist, calf-length skirt. Mark and his Mum.

An air of impermanence, which Frank associated with student houses from visiting his children through their university years, faintly reminded him of the days when all his and

112

Margie's gear went into one suitcase and one tea chest. The days when a reading lamp and a portable radio were luxuries, as were pieces of material with patterns chosen and treasured by Margery to cover the ugly surfaces in bedsitters and squalid flats when he worked for other people in places he did not want to be: sometimes they cooked, ate, washed, washed-up, read a book in the one other room; and at night listened to the portable radio with the soft light of the bedside lamp on a square of William Morris design covering a chair used as a bedside table. When she was pregnant with Bob, twenty-eight years ago – no, more recently, his brain ticked off the years – it was when she was pregnant with Helen, a mistake not too gladly accepted at first, and Bob was in the cot only a couple of feet away from the bed that they lay close, loving, he and Margie with her swelling belly and her calm; and in the mornings Bob waking, talking to himself, smiling. Bob always smiled.

He now stood in the middle of the sitting room. In Edwardian days it would have been floridly papered; now it was painted, do-it-yourself by Mark, a pale green with the woodwork and the door white. This emphasised the shabbiness of the brown fitted carpet and the furniture – armchairs and sofa which sagged where you sat.

There were cushions almost under his feet and a glass. He bent to pick it up and smell it. Beer. Half under a cushion was a book on its face, open. Pushkin's poems. He turned it over. The poems were in Russian with a literal translation.

Bob had been lying here, reading. A place was marked. Frank looked at the translation.

He read: 'A deaf man summoned a deaf man to be judged by a deaf judge. The deaf man shouted, "He's taken my cow." "For goodness' sake," the deaf man cried out in reply, "my late grandfather already owned that plot of waste ground." The judge decided: "So that there should be no depravity the young man must marry – although it's the girl who's guilty." '

He went up the short flight with the book in his hand. On the landing he tried the door to the roof. Locked. He left it and went up to Bob's room. He hesitated outside the door and then entered.

He was astonished. Not only was the bed made but the

whole room had been cleared. Everything was in order. Nothing on the floor, books not falling against each other in the bookcases, the desk top clear but for the telephone and local directory.

He dropped the sack on the bed. He put the book of poems on the desk and sat. He looked at the room from that angle, the position he had occupied when he telephoned the taxi five weeks earlier.

Bob's voice had shouted up, 'Did you find it, Dad? It's by the phone, if not try the desk drawers and there should be a taxi card stuck on the wall somewhere with Blu-Tack – or on the floor if it's dropped off!'

Frank had picked things up and put them down. Most of the desk drawers were partly open and stuffed full.

Now they were all shut.

On that Sunday when looking for the taxi phone number he had come across the previous year's Boots diary in the second drawer down on the right. He looked there first. No diary. And no current diary with its entries in Russian and English which last time had lain open on the floor by his feet. He found only empty cheque books, unused envelopes, writing paper, typing paper, carbons, staples, plastic rulers and all the usual clutter.

There was not a single letter to Bob in any drawer. There were no bank statements and no paying-in books. There was no sign of the green leather-covered address book he had given Bob.

Frank closed the drawers one by one. He put the phone on the carpet before moving the desk from the wall. This revealed blanket fluff, paper clips and a card for the taxi firm with a small blob of Blu-Tack still on it. He pushed the desk back, replaced the telephone and crossed the small room to pull the bed its own width from the wall. Under it was blanket fluff and a dirty handkerchief. He pushed the bed back.

He could not think coherently. His heart pounded. The heat at the top of the house made him sweat heavily; he could feel it trickling down under his arms and from his forehead.

He took off his jacket and tie.

Very carefully he moved the hi-fi equipment and then each speaker to look behind them. Fluff, dust and what looked like

114

a few mouse dirts despite Tiger in the house. He put the equipment back.

He took a row of books at a time. He removed them on to the carpet, held each book by its covers and shook it to see what would fall out and then replaced the row. After half an hour he had collected three bookmarks, an envelope with a second-class stamp two price rises out of date, and some pieces of string.

The telephone rang. He jumped and gasped with the sound. He picked it up.

'Bob?'

'No, this is his father.'

'Oh yes, Mr Jones, we met, Matty Snelgrove here – is Bob there?'

'No.'

'Oh, well, I'll phone later, when do you think he'll – '

'He's dead.'

'Oh God.'

'It was an accident,' said Frank, looking round the neat room which no longer contained his son's diaries, address book, letters.

'Oh God, how awful – I am sorry.'

'Yes ... well.'

'Is there anything I can do?'

'Perhaps', said Frank slowly, 'you would come to the funeral, we would want his friends, you see.'

'Yes, of course, of course. When is that?'

'I don't know, I think in about a week, there has to be a post mortem.'

For the first time Frank detected something from the other end as if the man had collected himself.

'Yes, I see,' said Matty Snelgrove, 'a post mortem. And it was an accident?'

Frank said, 'I've just met a journalist – Bill Pickett.'

Snelgrove replied at once, 'Don't tell me now! Tell me when we meet, Mr Jones.'

The old Frank would have been puzzled. The Frank holding the phone took it from his ear, looked at it and then put it back saying, 'Yes, of course – I'll need your address.'

Matty Snelgrove gave him an address and telephone number

in Manchester. Frank hung up. He put the piece of paper with the address in his inside pocket. His hand touched the envelope given to him by the journalist but his mind ignored it concentrating on the room and Matty's voice saying sharply, 'Don't tell me now!'

'Oh Jesus,' he said aloud, 'I'm slow. I used to be fast up here,' he banged his aching head with the flat of one hand, 'but I'm slow, I can't put it together.'

This remark out loud, like the phone call, went down the line and found its way to Flecker.

The front door opened and closed downstairs. He moved into the doorway of Bob's room. Feet sounded on the first flight. He came out on to the top landing and called, 'Hello.' The feet stopped. He said, 'This is Bob's father up here.' The feet started and he went down to meet them.

Rose was nearly his height. She was panting slightly and she avoided his eye.

'Mr Jones,' she said sounding put out, 'can I get you a cup of tea? I can certainly do with one after – '

She tailed off. She was already clearing the kitchen with too much energy.

'I'm sorry about this mess. There really wasn't time – don't come in.'

It was an order and Frank turned away.

'I'll bring it up in a minute – all right?'

He returned to Bob's room and its neatness was still a slap in the face. That, and Pickett, and bouncy little Snelgrove. He could not leave it there. He phoned his sister-in-law who was looking after Margery. He said that he had to stay overnight, giving no reason. She replied that she would have to leave by early evening the next day.

He sat for a moment after putting down the phone. Something was different, not just the order of the room. When they came back from the square and he sat where he was now with Bob sprawling on the floor opposite eating cake he had been alerted to something that previously he had never noticed ... something in the eye-line connected with what Bob was saying ... a colour ... red. Then he remembered.

He got out of the chair, crouched to examine the bookshelves. They were gone. The books on the police, the security services, the CIA. The red covers had been a pair, volumes one and two, on that shelf.

He relaxed on to the carpet. He could even remember some of the titles because he disapproved of them. Leftie stuff, no good Bob denying it.

Then Margie had come in talking about ? . . . Australia, and Mark's mother's first husband being some kind of enemy alien or something.

For a moment his mind's eye rested on the strong-faced woman in the photograph in Mark's room holding the hand of the timid boy.

Then he thought: 'Why the books? Perhaps he made notes in them.'

He said softly to himself, 'Don't go round the bend; if it was you and you wanted to make sure no nosy press people got their hands on anything you'd take the stuff wouldn't you? If the bloke's dead it can't do him any harm.'

He said to himself, 'At least look at the roof.' Both these remarks were too soft to be picked up by the device in the telephone.

He found the key to the roof door on Bob's ring and let himself out. Tiger must have heard because he came from somewhere and went past Frank at a rush. Then he circled, making his odd croak, confident of affection.

'Was it you,' said Frank, 'or did you see it?' He looked round the roof. Like the room it was neater than he remembered. And smaller. Reluctantly he walked to the unwalled edge to look over. Down there were the chalk marks. He moved to where Bob must have gone over. He looked at the surface. It had been wet, the sun had dried it. There were no marks that he could see.

The cat butted against his leg. From the kitchen came the sound of the kettle whistling. In the kitchen window next door the curtain seemed to stir.

2

He held open Bob's door for Rose to bring in a tray. On it was a teapot, milk, sugar – and a single cup and saucer. She put it on the nearest surface, the divan bed, and turned briskly to go.

Frank stood in the doorway as if he was not conscious of stopping her and said, 'I shall want to settle up.'

'Oh.'

As with Pickett, the journalist, he watched her without appearing to.

'Any bills,' he said, 'electricity and so on?'

'Those we split three ways, and Bob's telephone is separate.'

'Yes.'

'We buy our own food. I can show you Bob's cupboard.'

She moved as if to pass. He did not appear to notice and said, 'I'd like to thank you, Rose.'

She was surprised, 'Why? I er?'

'This,' he said, indicating the room.

'I don't understand.'

He continued to appear vague.

'I really don't understand,' she said. 'I never came up here, except at odd times when invited – you mean letting Bob have the room?'

'Clearing it up like this.'

'I didn't, what makes you think – ' Then she stopped.

'And thank you for the tea,' said Frank, 'very good of you, I hope you used Bob's.'

She began to go red. It moved up to the roots of her hair.

'I expect the police talked to you,' he said smiling as if to imply that they had both been through it today.

'Yes.'

'When you went through the house with them.'

'No, I didn't.'

'Someone did.'

'Mark.'

'Ah, Mark. He was the first home off weekend was he?'

She turned away from him and sat on the divan beside the tea-tray. Some of the tea slopped from the spout as it tilted.

'Mr Jones – '

'I wanted to phone a friend of Bob's – couldn't find his address book, perhaps it's downstairs?'

'Mr Jones, there's – '

'I'll have a look when I've had a cup of tea, and when Mark comes in – '

'Mr Jones,' she said sharply, 'you were in the Navy.'

'Yes.'

'So you'll understand about orders. I have to say this now and then we all know where we stand.'

'Oh?'

'You must be very shocked,' she said, 'and believe me it has not been easy at my end either.'

'In what way?'

'I can't discuss it, but I've had a difficult day. I *am* a section leader, I *do* live under the same roof and – ' She stopped as she had earlier. Frank carefully put the tray on the desk. There was no longer any need to block the door. He began to pour with his back to her. Spacing the words he said, 'I am sorry you've had a difficult day.'

She seemed mollified by his tone.

'I knew you would understand, Bob always spoke of the way you were like the old sort of Englishman – I mean a kind of 1940s man.'

He concentrated on putting in milk and sugar. A small aberration of the mind suddenly threw up Margery making a joke about how the upper classes put the milk in last.

'Did he? I was ten in 1940, perhaps he meant a 1940s boy?'

'Yes, so what I have to say is this – we have orders, Mark and I, *not* to discuss Bob's . . . what happened.'

'Orders?'

'Yes. Particularly with relation to the press.'

'And?'

'Everyone else really. So if we can just observe that, Mr Jones.'

'Even the relatives? You can't speak to Bob's father and mother about their dead son.'

The red which had receded to her cheeks rose again.

'You can't say anything even if it might be comforting?'

He drank a whole cup of tea and began to pour another.

'What I find a bit difficult, Rose, is why it is not in the national interest if the press print a story saying that you, or Mark, or even both, liked having him about the place and that although he tended to have two left feet and fall over the cat he was a decent hand with a good heart.'

'That's absolutely not fair – you're perfectly aware of the

way the press twist things and make things up. We have our jobs and our futures, you know.'

'Oh yes, yes I do know.'

Frank finished the second cup of tea. His mouth and throat burned. As she got up to go he stopped her again by putting the tray in her hand and said, 'I can see you're really going to miss him.'

'How dare you?' she said and actually began to cry. 'How dare you?'

'I'm staying the night,' he said, 'it being Bob's room. You can put a notice on his food cupboard and a label on his towel in the bathroom.'

She went with the tray.

He closed the door, removed the plastic sack from the divan bed and lay down.

3

When he woke it was dark. He groped in the wrong direction for a light switch and took half a minute to realise. He lay still and listened. There was very little light through the uncurtained window; few sounds, and those distant. Nothing stirred in the house.

He sat up and rested his head in his hands. He was very thirsty and his stomach had a hunger ache. The word 'orders' was in his head. Obeying orders. That went out with Nuremberg didn't it? That and an Englishman's word being his bond. Hoist the ladder, Jack, I'm inboard.

His eyes got partially used to the gloom as the shape of things registered. He put on his shoes and went out on to the landing. He listened. No sound.

He went down the short flight and opened the roof door. It creaked. He stepped out and stood again to listen. A motorbike a long way off. The wall on his left with the chimneys shut out any view of the adjoining roof. This was the opposite side from the Welsh woman's house and he wondered what had been said to the police by the people that side. He edged across the roof diagonally in the direction of the place from which

Bob fell, sensing the cane table and the chairs on his left. He could just make out the low bulk of the wall at the end. He could not see the edge of the roof to his right, not even the shape of the old sinks and pots against the trees and the gound below. He stepped carefully, feeling with his toe. He hit a sink and almost jumped back

He crouched and felt for the sink with his hands and found it. He eased forward, still squatting, going round the sink to find the edge of the roof. He could smell the earth in the sink and whatever was growing in it. Something butted him and he nearly screamed and went over. Tiger began to purr in the dark.

'You dozy bugger,' he said, 'you could have had me over – is that what happened? Did you get under his feet? No. You were down there.'

Tiger rubbed against his hip. Frank eased forward to sit with his legs over the edge of the roof and the cat continued to butt against him. When he put a hand on it, it nipped him and he swore, pushing it away. He was glad he could not see the drop.

He looked up. There was either haze or cloud cover. No stars and no moon. He had not checked the phase of the moon. What time was it? He could not see the face of his watch.

No one could have seen Bob, or anybody else, crossing the roof if last night was like tonight, or rather this morning. To be fair – if you were a bit awkward you could go over in the dark.

He went back into the house and down to the kitchen. He switched the light on and closed the door. He was eating bread and butter and cheese and drinking lager when Rose came in.

He had heard her coming up the stairs. The light caught her fair hair which was down making her seem more feminine than on previous occasions. Her big breasts were not restrained by her dressing gown. He wondered why, with that equipment and long legs, there was nothing sexually attractive about her. She wasn't a dyke because homosexuality still topped the list for unacceptability when they PVed those who had access to SIGINT material.

Frank had not wasted the time since he talked to Bob. He had read the 1983 Report of the Security Commission and the subsequent partial report on positive vetting procedures. It amused him to discover that the major obstacle to clearance in

121

his old service was excessive drunkenness, while with the RAF
– the crabfats – it was excessive sexual activity. It came out at
three to one : three randy crabfats to one pissed matelot. Good
old-fashioned vices.

He held up the lager can. 'Not yours I hope, I was thinking
of having another.'

'You woke me.'

'Sorry about that.'

Perhaps, he thought, as she sat opposite him, she's not sexy
because she's an imitation man and the imitation doesn't work
– or it does and I'm not inclined to be queer.

His mind had been closed to such thoughts for many years.
Now he could even imagine screwing her to find out how she
would respond. And that made him think about the white
gloves joke, although she wasn't upper class, of course – just a
sharp suburban girl with a doctor Daddy who emigrated to
Australia. He looked away.

'Do you really think', she said, 'that if there was something I
felt you ought to know we would not tell you?'

'Yes.'

'Well you're wrong, Mr Jones.'

'Who gives you the right to decide, Rose?'

'You must realise that after Dodgson we all have to be very
careful.'

'We?'

'It's secret work, what do you expect?'

'Well,' said Frank, 'I expect to find out from his friends, I
mean you were his friends? ... what had gone on in the last
week or so, that's all. I can't understand what happened.'

'Nothing,' she said, 'nothing here and nothing at work ... so
far as I know. I haven't of course spoken to anyone in his
section. It was just a tragic accident.'

'You mean nothing out of the ordinary.'

'Nothing.'

'Well, what was ordinary?'

'We went our own ways. That's why we got on, because we
are different from each other and in the communal parts of the
house – here and the bathroom – we didn't get in each other's
way. Bob listened to music a lot in his room and read. He used
to go away for weekends, but you know that – he came to you,

122

let me see my birthday was five weeks ago and he was — we all were — here the following weekend so it was the one after that. Right?'

Without hesitation Frank said, 'Right,' and noted that it was three weekends ago.

'Didn't he see you the weekend after that as usual? — I thought he mentioned it — I know he was away the two consecutive weekends because I did some shopping for him the second time.'

'Ah yes,' lied Frank, 'I'd forgotten.'

'So you must have talked to him,' she said, 'you must have noticed if there was anything unusual. Didn't you? You *are* his father.'

He finished the bread and cheese. He was grateful that each time he talked to this bossy cow he had something to do with his hands. Who did Bob see besides Snelgrove? Where? Not Pickett. Pickett said that Bob phoned him.

When Frank wrote it down next day it read:

Bob away two weekends
Bob saw Snelgrove
Bob saw someone else (Mr X)

Those entries were above —

Snelgrove put Bob on to journalist

'I didn't', he said, 'notice anything. Bob was his normal cheerful self.'

A door opened outside and Mark in a dressing gown came towards the kitchen. As he blinked in the light he saw Rose first and said, 'Can't you sleep either?' Then he saw Frank and was taken aback.

'Er ... I'm terribly sorry,' he said with his head hanging, 'about Bob, terribly sorry.'

'Thank you.'

'I'm just ...' He went out. A few minutes later there was the sound of the flush.

'I think I'll make a cup of tea and then go back to bed,' said Rose. She indicated a cupboard. 'That's Bob's and please use

123

the eggs and bacon in the fridge when you have breakfast in the morning. Mark and I will be clear by eight thirty. If I don't see you, please give my condolences to Mrs Jones.'

'Thank you,' said Frank, 'and for talking.'

'Well, good heavens,' she said. 'This isn't the Soviet Union. I sometimes had to tell Bob that.'

He was dismissed.

'Good night,' he said, and went back to Bob's room. He put the light on.

He sat on the bed with his back against the pillows. He looked at his watch. Two thirty-five. His jacket hung on the back of the desk chair. What else? ... The envelope!

He opened it carefully in order to preserve Pickett's telephone number written on the outside.

Inside were two press cuttings with the name of the newspaper and the date written in biro at the top.

He put on his spectacles. Newsprint was hell in artificial light.

He read, under a sub-heading 'No Spy Link in Suicide': 'A civil servant who worked in the same section as the convicted spy Charles Dodgson took his life because he was depressed – and not because of anything more sinister, an inquest heard yesterday.

'Allen Michael Goodburn, aged thirty-eight, was found dead in his car in the closed garage at his home last Tuesday; the engine was still running. This was only a week after the first birthday of his daughter, Penny.

'His widow, Mrs Cynthia Goodburn, said ...'

He put it down and picked up the other. This time the sub-heading said 'Dodgson Friend Dies in Accident', and underneath: 'An inquest heard yesterday that the civil servant who fell in front of an underground train and was killed last Thursday had been one of the very few friends of the convicted spy Ramsay Charles Dodgson.

'Stephen Barry Kedge, aged thirty-three and single, appeared suddenly to faint and fall before anyone could prevent it according to ...'

Frank stopped reading. In his head Bob said, 'After a bit you can detect what the papers and telly are not saying from what they do say.'

124

Frank could see him, walking slightly ahead and then stopping to make a point. 'You can even spot the stories inspired by the raincoat men – they are reported by compliant or deceived journalists. The latter are known as Willies by the way.'

Frank had said, 'Are they!'

'Hmmm. That's the disinformation department.'

'How do you know, Bob?'

'Oh you read, you listen. You begin *never* to accept face value. That's the important thing, Dad.'

Further down the inquest report on Kedge was a sentence about Goodburn whose inquest had been the week before. It went on to say, 'A government spokesman said there had been no MI5 or Special Branch enquiry into either death – both men were ordinary civil servants who had died in unexceptional circumstances which would normally have attracted no attention but for the recent notoriety of the Dodgson case.'

Frank read the government spokesman's statement twice.

They were sufficiently bothered to put out a statement, further drawing attention to themselves.

He re-read each cutting. Goodburn, Kedge and now Bob. He got off the divan bed and began to look through the local telephone directory. He could not find a Kedge with the right initials but he found Goodburn. He wrote the address and telephone number on the envelope with Pickett's number. He put the cuttings back.

It made no sense, except in sensation terms for a journalist. How many of them were out there, Bob said? Thousands. So obviously, every now and again, one of them fell under a bus or took an overdose. But . . . these two had been connected with Dodgson. Not like Bob. Bob just wanted to resign. Didn't he? But why did he contact a journalist? And who was this other person whose permission he needed before he could talk to the journalist?

For a long time Frank sat with the light on. Then he switched it off and lay down. He had made up his mind. He slept.

4

Frank bought the hard-cover notebook as soon as the shop opened. Then he scoured the bookshops to find a textbook on forensic medicine and another on methods the police use for investigating violence. He still had time before the appointment to check the index in the library. An assistant librarian, inevitably with large spectacles, was helpful, suggesting that Frank detour to Bristol on his way home and go through the bookshops in Park Street. The man was obviously puzzled by the discrepancy between Frank's appearance and the titles he was after. Frank told him that he was researching for part of his sociology degree in the Open University.

Frank had a similar problem the following day, Wednesday, in London – at a bookshop recommended to him in Bristol. The two assistants looked at him: the word 'Fuzz' seemed to rise from their heads in balloons; he was obviously Special Branch; a routine check on recent anti-police, anti-state publications to be analysed for names and put in the DI5 computer.

The two had the kind of relationship with Special Branch that DI5 tails have with their Soviet, and other diplomatic, targets – a mildly jolly, enforced collaboration to make everybody's life easier. Until somebody slips the tail.

To Frank's surprise – when he found the book and paid – the one who was dressed in tight jeans, women's high heels, a nylon blouse and had eye make-up said, 'You're going to enjoy that, ducky – *Police Gazette* give it full marks for detail, they don't *like* it but they can't fault it, read the jacket.' Despite the eye make-up the chin was unshaven making a grotesque contrast.

Frank turned to go. The other, a girl, said, 'Don' you wan' the bill then?'

He took it.

'I mean I know, don' we all, it comes out of that dirty great secret fund – but the feller before you said they was dead mean unless you give 'em a chitty.'

Frank took a little time to realise who he was supposed to be. He sat in a sandwich bar drinking tea and checking the indexes for other titles covering the secret world and returned to buy them. This time they ignored him so he deliberately said, 'Gissa receipt, then.' As the girl gave it to him she said, 'You Irish?' and Frank replied, 'Dat's right – an' I'm not tellin' you which bog I come from, darlin'.'

The appointment on Tuesday, before the detour to Bristol, was at the County Police HQ. It was difficult to park. To the waiting coroner's officer Frank seemed calm and resigned.

'The inspector won't be long, Mr Jones.'

'Thank you.'

'If you won't mind just waiting?'

'Of course not. It's very good of him to see me.'

'Not at all, sir – it's our business to do all we can.'

'Yes.'

'I'm sorry I can't help . . . so if you'll excuse me I've got to – '

'Yes,' said Frank, sitting on the bench, 'of course, you must be busy, by the way – did you deal with Allen Goodburn?'

The coroner's officer said at once, 'Did you know him?'

'No,' said Frank, 'neither him nor Kedge.'

'Kedge?'

'Went under a train.'

'Not here, sir.'

'No,' said Frank, 'London. The Underground. Worked here though, like Goodburn.'

'Friends of your son, sir?'

'No,' said Frank, 'not that I know of.'

The coroner's officer left. People passed Frank as they went in and out. Telephones and talk-back sounded through the partition. As Frank read posters about rabies and little girls found in woods and 'Have you seen anyone wearing boots like these?' and tips on not having your bike stolen, and compensation for victims of violence, he reflected that when he was a boy sailor and the seniors wanted to soften you up they left you to sweat.

The attitude and methods of the hard men who dished it out were familiar and international. He had once seen a Japanese film about the training of their wartime pilots. The attitude of the trainers was so similar to those in his early naval days it was quite like home.

What he remembered most clearly was a scene in which the recruits had to take the NCO his evening meal, a bowl of rice; they had to take it fast, keep it hot, bring it before him with

127

humility. They stopped very briefly en route behind a hut; they bent their heads in turn over the bowl – and with vigour they rubbed the dandruff from their round cropped skulls on to the rice.

Even if you have no power at all there is always a way. It was while sitting and waiting that he made his notes in the hard-cover notebook, one fact to a line.

They now read:

> *Bob told me he intended to resign*
> *Bob away two weekends*
> *Bob saw Snelgrove. Manchester?*
> *Bob saw someone else. Mr. X?*
> *Snelgrove put Bob on to journalist*
> *Bob wanted Mr X ? or someone else's agreement to talk to journalist*

On the facing page he began another list:

> *Bob's room cleared. Diaries, letters, address book and books abt. police, CIA, MI5 etc. missing.*
> *Goodburn and Kedge dead. Govt. statement.*
> *Rose and Mark forbidden to talk to me abt. Bob.*

He looked at the list. He decided what he wanted to know. He put the notebook in his pocket with the envelope. 'You'll be lucky,' he thought.

On the telephone making the appointment he had been very polite.

A police officer gave him a visitor's badge, took him to an interview room and closed the door on him. Bare walls, small table, two straight-back chairs with plastic seats; smell of stale smoke. He sat to face the wall with the door. A man came through in a grey suit and before Frank could react an Inspector in uniform followed him. If Frank had looked back at the hospital from the car-park yesterday afternoon he could have seen the man in the suit at the shoulder of the coroner's officer.

Of course, thought Frank, two to one.

The man stood against the wall behind his left shoulder. The inspector, a big man, eased himself into the chair opposite. He had the regulation police expression. It was a face known, just across the border from here, as Welsh Indian, probably come down from Armada survivors mixing with Celts. A flat face with a very dark moustache that he touched sometimes with the back of his left hand. The voice was not Welsh, it was West Country. Frank recognised it from the phone call yesterday morning giving him directions to the hospital.

'Mr Jones,' it said. The inspector never looked directly at him after that.

'Very good of you to see me.'

'What's the trouble that the coroner's officer couldn't deal with?'

'Well ... there's something that bothers me since I went to my son's room after identifying him, Inspector.'

The inspector continued to look at the wall behind Frank's right shoulder. The one on the other side behind him stirred slightly.

'Just to clear my mind,' said Frank, 'I'd be very grateful if you would tell me if your "scene of crime" officer took anything away as evidence?'

'As evidence of what, sir?'

'I don't know.'

'Is something missing then, is that what you're saying?'

'Yes – I think so.'

The inspector shifted. His feet were too close to Frank's under the table.

'You ... think so?'

'Yes,' said Frank, 'I think that my son's diaries for last year and this, his address book, letters to him and a number of books are missing.'

'You think?'

'Yes.'

'Presumably because you know they were in the room on Sunday last. You could be definite about that, Mr Jones?'

'No.'

'I see. When were they there to your certain knowledge?'

'Five weeks ago.'

The inspector smiled. Frank made sure that from the beginning his hands were under the table flat on each thigh and that

129

he sat with his back upright not quite touching the chair. He waited.

'Is that all, sir?'

'No, Inspector. But was anything taken away?'

'Nothing was removed from the premises, to my knowledge.'

Frank noted the last phrase.

'It would help to set some other things straight in my head,' said Frank. 'It's been a bit difficult to understand – your men went through the house?'

The inspector said, 'Yes?' and the other man stirred again.

'None of the beds had been slept in, and there was no sign of anyone having broken in?'

'Correct.'

'Which leaves', said Frank, 'the security people.'

'What "security people"?'

'Oh,' said Frank as if surprised, 'GCHQ of course, you must have been in contact with them.'

'What we do is our business, Mr Jones.'

'Yes, of course,' said Frank bending over the rice bowl, 'I'll remember that for the interview.'

'What interview?'

'BBC,' said Frank at once, 'they phoned.'

The inspector said, 'Right!' and then, 'We informed your son's place of work. A sergeant interviewed some of his colleagues. We received full co-operation. There is nothing unusual to report. I hope that sets your mind at rest.'

'How did he die?'

'The coroner will decide.'

Frank leaned forward. 'But how do *you* think he died from the reports you received; I have to go home and tell his mother. We both have to live with it.'

Frank regretted having to crawl but who doesn't want to be appealed to? Frank's tone to the inspector throughout had been muted, slightly uncertain. It was not difficult to dissimulate, the Service was a university for it if you were both bloody-minded and ambitious.

'It was almost certainly an accident,' said the inspector and that seemed one hurdle over until he added, 'but it could have been suicide. There's no evidence either way, no witnesses.'

'There's me,' said Frank, 'and the two he lived with and others to say that Bob was cheerful, had no problems and was the last bloke in the world to kill himself. He would never have done that.'

'People do it every day – off bridges, high-rise buildings, off cliffs. It's very common, sir.'

'As your men took nothing away there was no note or letter. If my son had killed himself he would have said why.'

The inspector did not reply.

'And then', said Frank, 'there was the state of his room.'

'What do you mean?'

'Tidy. Really squared off. Someone did that. He never did. Never in his life.'

The inspector permitted himself to glance at the other man.

'So?'

'Well,' said Frank, 'having taken the things I mentioned earlier the ones who did it might think – looking at the usual state of the room, which was chaos – they'd better square it off because when your people arrived it might look to them as if it had been turned over – which would indicate an intruder, wouldn't it?'

'With respect, sir, you've been seeing too much television. A friendly word – our experience is that when this happens to people they often get very funny ideas from the shock – why don't you have a chat with your doctor?'

Frank lowered his head to hide his expression. The inspector said in a friendly tone, 'Whenever there's an incident like this, sir, the first thought in the mind of the "scene of crime" officers is the possibility of murder. Let me put that to you straight. They look very hard and if there's a sniff of doubt they follow up. There is no possibility that your son was murdered, which is what you've been hinting at. None.'

For the first time Frank felt he was talking to a fellow human being. He lifted his head.

'Right,' he said, 'I believe you.'

He meant that he believed the man's sincerity and that the ordinary police were not involved.

On the way out when he signed his name and put his address someone told him about the Compassionate Friends.

131

About six weeks earlier in California they had told Luther Berry's doubting old Pa about Parent Bereavement Outreach of Santa Monica.

The one in the suit never spoke.

EIGHT

1

The weather broke that day with tremendous thunderstorms. Driving from Bristol after buying the books Frank watched clouds come up to fill the sky, ten-tenths, dropping veils of rain on to the edges of the horizon. The lightning was both sheet and forked; the colours ranged from flickering green to pale rose in the receding folds of thick grey and dark bruise. When the rain hit the car the wipers could not clear it fast enough and he pulled off.

It changed to hail and hammered over his head. He put his lights on to reduce the risk of being hit. He knew that lightning ran all round a car body without hurting the one inside. He wondered if it would happen as zigzags of it sprang out of the ground like something from a Dracula film.

He went to sleep.

He dreamed. It was the old terror, the naval dream; he could not find his uniform, he did not know where they were going; he knew he was too old, fifty-four was too old, and he could not remember the cockpit drill; he knew he was both no longer in the Service and trapped in it – this happened in an atmosphere, a mental ambience, of terrible foreboding; his heart ached and felt as if it would crack with the effort of trying to catch up; also he was half naked and could not hide it.

He woke. It felt as if someone had taken out his guts. He

could hardly move. He switched off the car lights. The rain was steady but the real storm had gone ahead of him to London and out to the Thames Estuary.

He said aloud, 'Did you really just slip, old Bob? Am I going round the bend? Those were just ordinary coppers doing their job.'

2

Anne had closed the shop and gone. He looked through the plate glass window from habit checking that the display stands, typewriters, calculators were well placed to catch the eye. They were doing an offer on duplicating paper suitable for typing, neatly stacked up to head-height in green packets, with the cut price red on white card. He could see the IBM on the counter had its cover on and the door to his back office was closed.

He let himself into the hall, more like a passage, by the house door. He stood listening with one hand on the wood panelling which divided him from the shop. When these houses were built wood had been cheap and men, also cheap, had cut and fitted it with care. Years ago to please Margie he had stripped and polished it. He liked the feel and the smell.

The inner tremor which started yesterday in the car as he approached Cheltenham and disappeared overnight began again as he stood there: it felt, through his hand, as if not he but the house itself were trembling. Also it was difficult to breathe, as if by shutting the door behind him he had shut out the air.

Heart attack? Let's find out. Test to destruction. He ran the hall in three strides. He carried the books in a plastic shopping bag and they banged against his thigh as he took the first two flights as fast as he could. He stopped on the landing. Now he could breathe. He glanced into the kitchen. A new pin. That would be sister-in-law Eileen, with a fag in her mouth, doing it under protest and letting poor Margie *know*. It was not by chance that Bob had always been shambolic – he got it from Margie.

Frank detested disorder and usually shut his trap. Where was she? He looked into the sitting room.

Windows open for fresh air on a fine day, pity Eileen had gone before the storm; water glistened on the sills and darkened the carpet. The chairs were geometrically arranged, fresh flowers in the vase on the coffee table and the clock actually set at the right time. How unreasonable to knock Eileen, good old Eileen doing what Frank would have liked done every day – but by doing it she was knocking her sister and he wasn't having that ... Where was Margie?

He ran the next two flights noting the window open on the landing, the slight overflow of water not from the storm on this side but from the freshly watered plant pots; an unusual clear run, nothing left on the stairs to be taken either up or down.

He stopped appalled at his thoughts. They came fast like pop-up targets on a range. Bang! Bang! Bang! But they kept rising: he hated being home; it was all junk – the business, the customers, the deadly, familiar rooms with their deadly, familiar contents, smells and shapes and the deadly, familiar views from their windows; this was what he'd put the good years of his life into – this! Strip it, sell the contents (other than the stock in the shop) and you wouldn't get enough to pay next year's rates.

What did he get out of it? This, with its insurances, telephone, electricity, gas bills, car tax, car insurance, telly licence, AA relay, BUPA ... what a load of junk. What did he need? Any bed would do, any caff serve a meal, any water closet deal with the result. The rest was getting a living – a what? This? Living? This was living? Selling office junk and before that – life insurance.

Life insurance! Bang!

He stood outside their bedroom door. No sound from inside, only an evening level of traffic noise through the window on the landing. He eased the door gently open. The bed was made. Nobody there. The bathroom door was ajar. He pushed it wide. Empty.

That left Bob's old room. The door was closed. He opened it and went in. Twilight, the curtains were drawn. It was a shock to make her out, still, on the floor propped with her back against Bob's bed which sagged like a hammock. She showed

135

no sign of hearing him enter. Instinctively he put on the light. She turned her head. She looked very bad from crying.

'You've been hours, I was worried, Jay.'

From long ago, because she disliked the name Frank, she called him 'J for Jones'. 'Hello J for Jones, darling, how's the fleet today – under control?' By habit he became Jay.

'I'm sorry, Margie, bit of a storm, I drove carefully.'

'You'd like a cup of tea?'

Round her on the carpet were model ships made by Bob when he was ten or eleven. Not from kits but from wood and tins; crude models which either capsized or went straight down when launched making them all laugh out of proportion to the event. Bob's race-track stuck out of the garish box, its two cars had spilled on to the carpet.

When he opened the curtain he noticed the Beatles poster for *Sergeant Pepper's Lonely Hearts Club Band* on the bed, curled at the edges.

She was holding a pillow in her lap. As he helped her up she gripped it tightly to her stomach.

'It's all right,' he said, 'I'll put the kettle on.'

'I'm a bit dopey, Jay.'

''Course you are.'

'Those pills the doctor . . . '

She stood, her head drooping, in profile to him. Before he could stop himself he looked at her clinically, made no allowance and said in his head, 'She's an old woman, looks like her mother.'

When it was J for Jones they used to cling together. Now it was as if they had never pined when separated, never been intimate or suffered jealousy, never shared dreams or comforted one another after failures. Like Bob's boats they had been uneasily glued together – by habit, by love for and from the children. The residue was a knowledge of varicose veins, irritating habits, the repetitious tedium of attitudes once found mysterious or delightful: a state as common and unremarkable as death until it happens to you, personally; until, suffering, you hold your wife, suffering, and she says, 'Why did it happen, Jay?' and you take it to mean everything which has died and you shut your trap; and then she says, 'Oh God! Oh God!' to the mystery in which she has always believed, to

136

which she has prayed, from which she has received comfort . . .
but there is no reply today – only the prospect of filling and
putting on the kettle.

Later she said, 'Why did you encourage him – you did – to
work there? I know he wasn't happy. He didn't tell me, he told
you, but I know.'

'No,' said Frank.

They sat in the neat kitchen and as she tried not to cry again
she pressed the palm of her left hand with her right forefinger
in a sweeping motion as if she were trying to clear it to read her
fate, then she held her wedding ring and rotated it on the finger
and said, 'You've gone away from me, Jay – why have you? I
can feel it.'

'No,' he said, 'no, Margie, of course I haven't.'

'How could he have fallen? He was right on the edge the
other day when we were there. I know he was awkward but
height never bothered him. Do you remember how he used to
jump off things when he was a little boy?'

'Yes,' said Frank, 'but it was so dark, you see.'

'No I don't,' she said, 'it wasn't deliberate was it?'

'Of course not, put that right out of your head – I'm certain,
Margie. It was an accident.'

She got up so that he could not see her face. Then she said,
'Did it hurt him, please tell me the truth, did it?'

'No,' said Frank, 'no, girl. It was immediate.'

'I can't bear it,' she said, 'I can't bear it.'

She went to bed in Bob's room. With great reluctance Frank
made telephone calls until he found someone who was a
member of the Compassionate Friends. She promised to come
tomorrow. He liked the sound of her.

3

He intended to read and understand the book on forensic
medicine and the book on police methods of investigating
violence before the inquest. He decided on a routine of three or
four hours' sleep to allow him to make the necessary journeys
and keep the business going in the day, leaving the nights to

137

read and make notes on the relevant parts of the other books when the inquest was over.

The thought which dominated his mind was to reach a definite conclusion about Bob. The thoughts of the day, after the storm, moving among normal people in normal traffic were in such contrast to the thoughts of the night and the subsequent police interview that he wondered how he could possibly trust his judgment. He must only deal in facts, note the facts in the notebook which he now thought of as the Bob notebook. He must also hold himself together with a strict routine: set the alarm for six daily and neglect nothing. He must read what he thought Bob had read and see if it supported what Bob had said.

He lay on the marital bed propped with two pillows against the headboard with both lamps on. He was still in trousers, shirt and socks. The night was cooler after the storm and he had the window wide open. He was trying to hoist in the medical names for the parts of the skull in case the pathologist used them, when he sensed rather than heard a faint vibration which said 'shop phone'. He had not put it through in case someone woke Margie. He got off the bed and went fast down the four flights thinking 'Helen' and wondering what time it was in America. One of the worst things about yesterday was when he phoned Helen. He looked at his watch. Two thirty BST. Helen was eight hours behind GMT so one thirty less eight equals five thirty in the afternoon, perhaps she had already fixed the flight home. It would be – he unlocked the hall door into the shop – wonderful to see her, she took it like a heroine on the phone yesterday, poor girl.

There was enough light from the street through the plate glass window. He picked up the phone.

'Hello.'

Automatically he picked up a pencil as he put the phone to his ear. The first sound was heavy breathing – that's all he needed.

'Yes?' he said sharply. 'Yes?'

'Mr Jones?'

'Yes – what do you want at this time of night?'

'I'm sorry, couldn't make up my mind, it's about Bob.'

Frank pressed the telephone to his ear. His whole being

138

concentrated on that sound. He stopped seeing anything around him. It was as if he was moving down the dark line to the place where the voice came from. Instantaneous impressions: a man in middle-age, a man who smoked, a man drunk, slurring very slightly — could be the voice of anyone from a loft insulation salesman to —

'I was a friend ... he was a good feller, Bob ... bit of a Charlie, but he'd got bottle an' I feel bad about it ... I was really pissed-off, I mean that feller ...'

The voice tailed away. The breathing went on and a scratching sound. A match?

Frank said in a friendly voice, 'Good of you to ring, Mr ... ?'

'Never mind that,' said the voice, 'I'm jus' bloody sorry that's all, an' did you find the notebooks?'

'What notebooks?'

'I think my name's in, so if you've gottem jus' tell me, I wanna know ...'

'Where should I look?' asked Frank as if the caller were his closest friend. 'I'll tell you all right, just tell *me* where — '

'The bloody bank!'

'The bank?'

Frank had called at the bank, before going to the police station, to tell the manager Bob was dead. The manager had expressed his condolences and asked for Frank's bank in order to check his identity. Frank gave him the name and told him also to confirm with the police. They agreed to talk later in the week.

'Bob tol' me his ol' man — thas you ennit, right? — tol' *him* there was a grass in the house.'

Frank bit on it as the breathing set in again, then the man said, 'He would never have thought of that himself, Bob — a grass gettin' details for a Hammer an' Sickle file, that right? You said that?'

'Right,' said Frank, 'I did say that.'

''Course there was,' said the voice and its accent improved slightly, 'what do you expect? He was like a child.'

'So the notebooks you're talking about', said Frank, 'were put in the bank for safety by Bob after I said that — '

'Lissen,' said the voice, 'I'm so pissed I can hardly stand up; I'm an idiot to phone you; he would of bin tapped but they woulden' worry you. I'm bloody sorry about Bob but I don' want my name attached, all right?'

'All right.'

'He trusted you. He said you went on like them but inside you was like him – so jus' burn the notebooks – '

'Diaries,' said Frank sharply, 'you haven't got it quite right.' A pause.

'You have them, then,' said the good accent.

Frank was silent.

'Lissen, now he's dead no one's going to do it, an' put a bomb up their arses.'

'Let's meet and talk about *it*, whatever it is, Mr – '

'Can't do that, squire.'

'Just tell me your bit of it,' said Frank, 'just your end. Bob trusted me and so can you. What was he going to do?'

He willed the man not to ring off. There were odd scuffling sounds from the other end and muttering, then the voice said, 'Used to play chess wiv him.'

'You did?' said Frank incredulously.

'Not me, you berk, that feller . . . he was really choked about that, I mean wiv a kid an' all.'

'About what?'

'So I tol' him the feller hadden' done it himself.'

It went click and Frank said, 'Which one – Kedge or Goodburn?'

The man at the other end started to laugh; it was a smoker's laugh, 'Oh Christ, which one!'

'Yes, which one did he play chess with?'

'So I tol' Bob, which I shoulden' have done but I did, I tol' what happened to someone I knew . . . an' his wife, not in this country, mind you, not in Merry England, squire, but . . . abroad, an' that upset him more.'

'Upset Bob?'

'I said so. After he seen the wife – '

'Ah,' said Frank involuntarily. Kedge had no wife, it must be Goodburn – who had a wife named Cynthia and a daughter aged one according to the press cutting.

'Can't prove it, tol' Bob that – you'll never prove it. 'Course that wassen' what he intended, it jus' got him going.'

'Did you see Bob on Sunday?' said Frank. 'Did you talk to

him? Did you give him permission to talk to the journalist? To Pickett?'

There was a disgusting noise at the other end, then gasping, then the voice said, 'I jus' bin sick.'

'Could we meet?'

'No.'

'Don't ring off, please. Bob's dead. You were his friend.'

'No I wassen'. I jus' knew him.'

'Did you work with him?'

'Me! No.'

'If you don't want to talk you could write to me – '

The man started to laugh again; Frank raised his voice, – anonymously, just tell me – '

'Oh dear,' said the voice, 'oh dearie me, you're another – put it in writing! Ditch my pension! They have a little list at sorting offices diden' you know, squire? I'm on that, could be, till the stink dies down. Letters delivered intact one day late – an' why do you think I'm out in a call-box this time of night when I could be snug in my kip using my own phone eh? Just in case. I haven' had the phone call yet but that dossen' mean they missed him coming here does it?'

Frank wrote on the pad on the counter – *One of them* – under the word *Bank*.

The voice seemed to have run out of steam, it mumbled something that sounded like, 'Sea air dowry.'

Frank said carefully, 'Can't quite hear that.'

'It give him the idea, sea air dowry.'

'What?'

'You read it?'

Frank said, 'I haven't read it so I don't understand.'

The pips started to go.

Frank said, 'Give me your number.'

'Better ask the journalist, Bob wanted to find out – '

The voice cut off. Frank sat with the phone in his hand; his heart banged in his chest as if he had been running. He wrote *journalist* and then put the phone down. Then he wrote *Mr X phoned (?).*

He went slowly upstairs with the sheet from the pad. No sound from Bob's room. He sat back on the bed and opened the Bob notebook at the other end. For twenty minutes he wrote down what he could remember of the conversation. He underlined certain words and phrases. The key word was *Bank*.

He got off the bed and went to the open window and breathed slowly to calm himself. Then he set the alarm for six, put it under his pillow and before undressing he wrote under the telephone conversation notes – *A drunk. Anonymous. All a bit pat. You don't trust that.*

4

He got the name of the Tottenham Court Road shop from a rep who sold him calculators. From it he bought a small tape recorder with a built-in microphone. That was Wednesday – the day they mistook him for Special Branch in the bookshop. He ate at a sandwich bar just off Leicester Square, then he telephoned the Goodburn number from a call-box with tourists drifting by and the big cinemas all round him. He had never really noticed them before. Now he noticed everything and everything seemed to refer to Bob's death. Spy movies, men with guns, men being hunted. He had telephoned the Goodburn number four times already. He waited as it rang.

Every time he was near a telephone he was tempted to ring Pickett. But not yet, not yet.

A woman answered. Knowing how she must feel Frank said clearly and calmly, 'Mrs Goodburn, this is Bob Jones's father,' so she would know it was not the press and not an official.

'Oh.'

'Is this an inconvenient moment?'

'No ... no.'

He heard the child in the background.

'Mrs Goodburn, I have to be in Cheltenham tomorrow for Bob's inquest.'

'I'm terribly sorry.'

'Yes. Thank you. And *I'm* very sorry about your husband. I wonder if I could just drop in to see you for a few moments tomorrow.'

'Er ... well ... um.'

Normally he would never have pushed it.

'Just a few moments, if you could possibly ... '

'Yes, all right – when?'

'I'll have to phone you ... no! The inquest is in the afternoon at two thirty, if I could come about midday? I have to drive, you see?'

There was a silence in which the child made demanding noises and she said 'Sh! Sh!' Then she said, 'I don't want any more trouble, Mr Jones.'

'Why do you say that?'

'The baby,' she said, 'I have to bring her up now, I have to protect her, there's just her and me, I ... '

Frank said, 'You can trust me.'

Then he telephoned Bob's bank manager to make an appointment. The man was friendly, having checked Frank's identity the day before.

He came out of the box. Once during the war when his Dad was on leave he had brought him here – he was standing looking at it now, the cinema – to see *Gone with the Wind*. It had been winter. A day of tremendous excitement. There was even a raid on the way back. Was it possible?

Yes. Him. Aged about eleven. Before his Dad went down. Most of the people round him weren't born then. Most of them spoke a different slang, saw a different world; Jesus, he thought, who's left? Where are they, off the squadron? Do they feel like me? Do they have the naval dream? Why is it so empty I don't exist except I can look down, see my legs, front of the jacket, the hands.

Would it have been better to be like Bob, read a lot of books? Have the life of theory in the head. I did read a bit – Jeffrey Farnol and Maurice Walsh and Sapper. I never knew what I wanted, I only knew what I didn't want. I didn't want anyone bossing me after the Service ... or in it, but there were ways round that. But then again, I didn't want to be a bloody shopkeeper, either. I don't care enough about money. You can keep the Masons and the Round Table and the Rotary and the little badges.

How long has the bell been tolling for me and I shut my ears? If it was the old days I'd find a woman. They didn't much any more, him and Margie – and after this perhaps not at all.

143

Better get out of this place then, where it gets at you in the atmosphere, off the bookstands and from Soho just round the corner.

His car was in a park just north of Cambridge Circus. Striding up Shaftesbury Avenue past the Queens Theatre he bumped into a man who was turning from looking at the photographs of actors.

'Look where you're going,' said Flecker.

Frank stopped and said, 'You look, Charlie!' And then went on. Flecker dismissed the idea that it was the one in the photograph. There were so many mistaken identity cases an old hand knew better.

NINE

1

The small tape recorder was in his inside pocket. He had tested it. The microphone was very sensitive.

The bank manager's office was pleasant; cool with a bare desk and two tasteful paintings. The man himself younger than Frank had imagined, recognisable: the young businessman; there were many like him in the 'new' Reading of the past ten years. Instead of 'Hello' they often said 'Hello there' and when they left they said 'Goodbye now'; when something was agreed or achieved they said 'There you go' and sometimes Frank replied 'Where?'

This one had an expression to match his tone of condolence. He regretted not to have known Bob. But he, himself, had been manager here only six months or so; as there was no will and, he understood from Frank, Bob had few assets there was no question of probate. The account had been frozen, of course, since Frank telephoned, and any cheques which came in would be returned marked 'DD'. He hesitated, not wishing to say 'Drawer Dead'. Frank said nothing. The account was in credit to the sum of, he looked at a note, fifty pounds and thirty-four pence; if Frank would care to sign an indemnity he would be glad to release the money to him. He stressed, catching something in Frank's expression, that when one bank manager telephoned another to check the bona fides of someone unknown to him – of course Frank's manager had not revealed Frank's financial position; he had simply indicated Frank's reliability.

Frank said that he would be pleased to sign. The money was ready in a drawer of the desk.

The manager was moving to open the door when Frank said, 'And I think there are a couple of things, notebooks, that he left for safe keeping.'

'Oh no,' said the manager at once, 'I would have been told.'

'I wonder if we could just check?'

'Yes, of course.' He spoke to someone on the internal phone.

It took some minutes for the lady to arrive with the ledger. She was slightly flustered.

'Here we are,' said the manager. 'Please stay, Miss Donald, would you, this won't take a moment.'

He was opening the ledger at a page marked by a slip of paper. 'It is true that your son deposited something with us but he also ... ' he opened the ledger at another page marked with a strip of paper, 'took it out again, despite the fact that we're computerised – when it comes to securities we use this, which is a bit Victorian, here we are. Miss Donald?'

The middle-aged lady said, 'It was a sealed envelope. Customers sometimes do this. They sign over the flaps and we put special sealing tape over the signature. Sellotape won't do.'

'Oh I see,' said Frank, 'you remember him doing that?'

'No. I remember the envelope.'

The manager pointed. 'He took it out, there – you see he signed.'

'I gave it to him,' said Miss Donald.

Frank looked at the entry. He looked at the signature and then the date. He put on his spectacles even though the morning light was excellent.

'When he was dead?'

The manager said, 'I don't understand,' and Miss Donald gasped.

'He was dead on Monday – this is Monday's date – the eighteenth.'

'Well I assure you it's his signature,' said Miss Donald.

'Did you know my son?'

'No, I ... we do have a very large number of customers, Mr Jones, and I – '

'Miss Donald', said the manager, 'has only been with us a month.'

146

'It was the first time your son had signed anything in or out since I've been here.'

'But', said Frank, 'you described the envelope.'

'Because I gave it to him.'

'I think', said the manager, 'that you have mistaken the eighteenth for the fifteenth, in fact – I'm sure you have! The fifteenth was last Friday and that was the day your son withdrew the envelope.'

'If you didn't know him,' said Frank to Miss Donald who was paler than when she had come in, 'how did you identify him?'

'We ask for a specimen signature and compare it with the one we hold. Or we can ask for the bank card.'

'I see – and you did that?'

'Certainly.'

'Which?' said Frank.

'The bank card, I think,' said Miss Donald.

'And', said the manager still looking at the ledger, 'he could easily have got the date wrong and written an eight for a five.'

'In a bank with the date on the wall?' said Frank.

There was a pause.

'I assure you', said the manager, 'that it would have been impossible for anyone other than your son to have taken the packet.'

'There was a small queue,' said Miss Donald. 'He had telephoned to say he would be in to collect it. So I was expecting him.'

'Expecting him?' said Frank. 'When?'

'Yes. He was tall,' said Miss Donald overlapping him.

'But you don't remember for certain which day?' said Frank.

After a slight hesitation Miss Donald said, 'It must have been Friday.'

'Have the security people been here?' asked Frank.

'Thank you, Miss Donald,' said the manager, and turned apparently to look out of his window at the pleasant view until the door closed behind her.

'Have they?'

'You don't really expect me to discuss confidential bank business.'

'Yes,' said Frank, 'in complete confidence.'

'As far as I'm concerned,' said the manager, 'the signature is genuine, the date could be an error. Incidentally, was your son's bank card among his belongings?'

'Yes.'

'Well that covers the only other possibility doesn't it?'

'The police', said Frank, 'gave it to me on Monday afternoon.' He did not stress 'afternoon'. There was no point. If you had the bank card you could do the signature. If you were about the right height and the right colouring and wore the gear that Bob usually wore you just stood in the queue, kept your head down and signed. It was obvious. Or it was ridiculous fantasy.

On the way out he stopped at a side window and Miss Donald, after trying not to catch his eye, came over.

'Was it', said Frank indicating the size of a Boots diary with his hands, 'about this size, about foolscap and thick enough to be a couple of diaries, Miss Donald?'

'That's it,' she said. Then she glanced at the manager's door and said, 'I'm sorry, Mr Jones.'

When he listened to it on the tape he could not make up his mind if she was sorry for him, or for not being more forthcoming.

2

He was early for Cynthia Goodburn. He drove to Imperial Gardens and cut under the nose of a fat man with a red face to get a parking place. There was a refreshment tent on the far side, pleasantly striped. The sun warmed his face and over to the left the flowers were beautiful in the morning light. It was the England which visitors paid thousands to visit. The feeling of real unreality was back shrouding him as if he were not so much a ghost as the invisible man.

He bought a beer at the tent, sat on a plastic chair and brushed away a wasp that tried to share it with him. People drifted by. Lovers even, at this time in the morning. In the Bob notebook he wrote: *Diaries taken from bank*. On the opposite page he wrote: *Diaries: Bob was dead. The signature was not right*.

148

Nobody was near. He put the tape recorder on the table, leaned his elbow close to it and played some of it back. It had been worth the money.

He walked to the other gardens which he thought of as the square. He was startled at how much he had not noticed on that Sunday with Bob. There was a bandstand with flowers round it. Beyond a hedge under a huge copper beech you could play giant chess with wooden chessmen. Had they been there in May?

He sat where they had sat on the other side of the hedge from the chessmen. The tarmac road which divided the square, up on his right, was empty. He closed his eyes to concentrate. There had been the distant sound of a silver band from the direction of Imperial Gardens. But no people up here. Except ... He opened his eyes. On the green in front of him, railed in, was a meteorological station with two white slatted cabinets like beehives and a metal pole ... someone had entered that while they talked. The man had something with him which he rested against the railings on their side. He was still there when they got up and walked towards the leprous statue of William IV against the old red wall and ... there had been some sort of official? ... corporation? ... van on the tarmac road near them.

And that TV detector van? It had been on the far side beyond the chestnuts and limes.

He considered it; which made him consider Bob's telephone; and what had been said both here and in Bob's room. He decided not to use his own telephone for sensitive calls. He was grateful to Matty, and the drunk – fake drunk? – for reinforcing the violently experienced sense of being observed, which had struck him at the moment of encountering the journalist Pickett on Monday. And which had never quite left him since.

He put on his sunglasses and returned to the car.

3

Although it was no more than five miles beyond the town it was completely rural. At the fork was a dirt road; further along, behind high hedges, some form of scrap dump and then the dog. It stood in the path of the car and barked as if it were insane. It raged. He pressed the horn.

A woman came from the house which was masked by trees and a hedge and ran calling. She took the dog by the collar and spoke to it, stroking its head and calming it. Then she put a lead on it and came to the car with it snarling.

'Mr Jones?'

'Yes.'

'I'll tie him up. I don't like to but since Allen ... he's behaved like this. He's out here day and night, I bring him food here sometimes rather than drag him in.'

Without considering Frank said, 'But where was he when it happened?'

She stroked the dog's head.

'I don't know,' she said, 'he should have been here but he'd wandered off somewhere. He came back the next day and ... '

'Yes.'

'He was sick, I nearly got the vet.'

She was a fair woman with wide clear eyes; about thirty, Frank thought, and out of the top drawer, the sort whose Daddy is an admiral. Pretty teeth and a decisive voice. Good hands soothing the dog. As he looked at her, for a second, there was a *frisson*; he could imagine the hands touching him.

'Please come in,' she said and turned, half dragging the dog. It was part Collie with a long snout and a thick coat which needed attention. It made distressed sounds and he waited until they were inside the gate before he drove the car carefully into the short drive.

The house was nondescript; two storeys with a garage added to one side. Painted white years ago, weathered to dullness with green window frames and a green door.

When he got out of the car he could see the child on the front lawn in a play-pen. The plastic toys looked very bright on the uncut grass. The child could manage two or three steps before falling. She stood now grasping the rails and making sounds in his direction. He went over and she began to throw the toys out for his attention. He was picking them up when Cynthia Goodburn returned. She came up to his shoulder. She shook hands and said, 'Would you like to come in?'

He hesitated.

150

'No,' he said, 'it's an intrusion anyway, I won't keep you, I don't even know why I'm here, really – it's pleasant outside.'

'All right.'

A few miles away he could hear the steady traffic noise feeding off and on to the M5. Trees everywhere, in town and out, an enormous sky with clouds spotting the blue far up. Blue above green below, England's green and pleasant ... this young, to him, woman ... like a Wren he used to know long ago.

'They used to play chess,' he said, 'Bob and your husband.'

'Yes.'

'Here?'

'No, not often; at Bob's place.'

'Were they in the same section at GCHQ?'

'Oh no. Allen was a mathematician.'

Frank knew this. He knew most of what he was asking. But he needed to find a way in, a way to unlock what was there, if anything. He did not want to speak of Dodgson too soon.

'Yes, of course he was.'

They walked to and fro on the grass; she watched the child, sometimes speaking to it, sometimes winding a toy which played a tune or chimes and the child laughed showing two small teeth in the lower gums.

'I couldn't believe it,' he said, 'I don't believe it.'

'Nor did I about Allen. He loved the baby. He doted on her.'

'Perhaps it was the work?' said Frank.

'Oh no,' she said at once, 'the work fascinated him, it was a tremendous challenge. Of course he was upset after the business with Ramsay.'

'Oh?'

'Dodgson.'

'Oh!'

'I felt so sorry for him, he always seemed so ... out of place. He used to play chess, too.'

'With Bob?'

'I don't think so, but with Allen. And sometimes he'd let his hair down. He used to recite "The Hunting of the Snark". He loved his namesake, you know.'

'No?' said Frank.

'*Alice*,' said Cynthia, 'you must have read it.'

151

'No,' said Frank.

'"The Walrus and the Carpenter" – '

'Oh that ... *in Wonderland.*'

'Yes.'

Frank remembered the reports from the Dodgson trial of the kiddy porn. He looked at the child in the play-pen with its nappy sliding down its plump legs and wondered at the tolerance of his race. Which he did not share.

'I loved *Alice* as a child,' said Cynthia. 'Do come in for a cup of coffee, she's quite safe out here.'

If she was not the admiral's daughter she was the daughter of someone with money because no GCHQ salary on its own would provide this table, that dresser – the crockery, the newly-tiled floor and ...

'I was his second wife,' she said abruptly, 'Allen ... perhaps it was my fault.'

'We all think that,' said Frank.

'You too?'

'Oh yes.'

When they sat at the handsome table drinking coffee she said, 'What I couldn't understand was that Allen wasn't very ... I don't know, he wasn't very practical. He was brilliant but not ... and the way the hose was fixed to the exhaust and – '

Frank was silent. He looked round to see if there was a telephone in the room. One of the books he had bought was *Tapping the Telephone* issued by the Post Office Engineering Union. More a pamphlet than a book but comprehensive on the subject.

'I liked Bob.' She looked down as she said it. 'He used to listen to me, one gets a bit stuck out here – and as for Cheltenham, well, I'm not exactly the literary type.'

He did not know what she meant.

'The police were very decent,' she said. 'I hated the press. I actually found one of them in here' – she indicated the door into the kitchen, 'he was reading a letter I'd left on the dresser.'

She poured more coffee. 'Allen didn't leave a note. Nothing. Bob was wonderful,' she said, 'he was terribly upset himself and he was wonderful ... wonderful!'

Oh Christ, thought Frank looking at her as she looked at a far corner of the room, were they at it, Bob and her? She's lost two of them.

'He wanted to do something about it,' she said, 'I didn't understand at all, he was going to resign.'

Then she wept.

'Sorry, so sorry – but it was so cruel of Allen, why did he? Why did he?'

He knew he could not possibly say, 'Perhaps he didn't.'

When she had recovered he said, 'Did Bob ever mention a chap called Matty Snelgrove?'

'No?'

'Or a chap called Bill Pickett? A journalist?'

'No.'

'Did he come to see you on – .' Frank opened the Bob notebook and gave the dates of the two weekends when Bob was away.

'No, I don't think so – I went to my parents, I'm going to sell this place, it won't be difficult.'

'Yes,' said Frank thinking, that's it.

Then she said, 'Wait a minute, that second weekend we met in London on the Sunday and came back together ... for company. Bob had been to see someone on the Kent coast ... Why?'

She did not say why she had been in London.

'Oh well,' said Frank, 'it's about the funeral, contacting people, we particularly want Bob's friends you see.'

She accepted the lie without question taking it as his reason for seeing her.

'I couldn't bear it, not so soon after Allen, but thank you for – '

'Oh, I understand,' he said at once, 'of course you can't, but I knew how fond of you both Bob was – '

'Yes, yes he was. In fact he was a truly good man. I've never met one before like that. Not a simpleton, not naive, but *good*, and prepared to take the consequences ... and loving. He spoke of you and Mrs Jones a lot. He very much respected you ... and your judgment.'

'Oh?'

'Yes. It's silly, I can't seem to remember some things or

153

perhaps they were never said and I just sensed them but I think he intended to get your advice.'

Frank looked at the beautiful plates and dishes and cups and hated all possessions and would have traded his life and accepted an eternity in hell to bring back his son.

She got up abruptly and went into the next room. She came back with a framed photograph. In it she sat at a table with her husband and in the near background was Bob. From the paper hat she was wearing it must have been Christmas.

'I'm wearing a wig,' she said, 'dark, and I'm tight. I look at that and I say "You thought you had problems" and then now . . . what wouldn't I give to have those problems back.'

'I was thinking something like that. You must have caught it.'

'Ah well,' she said, 'You're more like him than you think.'

'Did he mention which town on the Kent coast?'

'What? No.'

They went out again because the child was crying.

'Hungry,' she said and picked it up.

'Did anyone . . . on the security side from GCHQ come to see you?'

The dog started to bark behind the house because there was the sound of a car nearer than the main road. She kissed the child.

'She's all I've got,' she said. 'I must concentrate on her and put away the rest. Nothing can be done.'

She came over to him, tipped her face up and kissed him.

'The dog will never leave here,' she said. 'I'll have to have him put down. Can you imagine anything worse?'

4

He was dreaming when the click lifted him off the pillow gasping. The light was on; Margery stood in the doorway.

'What's the matter? Are you all right?'

'Yes, yes I am – stay there, Jay, I want to talk to you.'

'What time is it?'

'I don't know.'

154

'I can't find ... here it is.'

His watch had come off and lay on the crumpled sheet. He put it on. Four thirty. He had read until four. It was very hard to lose what was left of the night. The book lay face down and open. The alarm was set for six.

'I want you to leave it alone, Jay.'

'What?'

'I've been looking at your new books,' she said.

He smiled as if she were telling him something pleasurable, something in the family.

'Don't,' she said, 'you do that when you don't know what to say.'

He was silent.

She sat on the edge of the bed.

'You said nothing about the inquest.'

'I didn't want to upset you.'

'Not knowing upsets me more.'

'But Margie, I told you – accidental death.'

'Yes,' she said, 'but you see I know he wasn't happy.'

'No, you've got that wrong – I think like lots of people nowadays he didn't know what to do with his life, not really.'

'Is that what you talked about – that Sunday?'

'A bit.'

'I don't understand, Jay, you swore to me it wasn't suicide.'

'It wasn't, Margie – *it was not.*'

'Then you must think someone killed him,' she said.

It was shocking to hear it spoken aloud.

'Jay, you've always stuck things out, I've admired the way you've done it, and you've always looked after us – and you've always ... told me how things are. Now you've stopped.'

He took her hand. 'Listen M., you can't help thinking of every possibility when something like this happens, the police do as well – but they, and the pathologist, and the coroner are unanimous. Poor old Bob was out on that roof on a very dark night almost certainly because the cat was down in the garden yowling. Bob went to check he wasn't on the roof itself ... and he slipped. It's terrible, it makes no sense in the scheme of things, so we say there must be a reason, *there must* – but you see there isn't. It was dark, the roof isn't that big – he'd

155

been having a glass of beer and reading in the sitting room. He probably went straight out of the light on to the roof.'

'Is it true, Jay? Is it?'

'Yes,' he said, 'I'm sure it is.'

I'm sunk, he thought, I can't torment her by making a public fuss — I'd better drop it; God knows I've nothing much to go on. It wouldn't be unreasonable for the security people to get into the house to clear his room when the police told them he was dead — after the Dodgson business they must be jumpy, and just in case there was anything lying around that someone like me could pass to the press. It's possible he did get the stuff out of the bank on Friday. I don't believe it, but it *is* possible. And why should I believe our people behave like Boy Scouts just because this is England? If you're up against Dodgson's sort you have to do some dirty tricks. But they would never have touched old Bob.

Margery lay down beside him. He pulled the sheet over her. He held her tight.

'Oh God,' she said, 'it does hurt, it does hurt.'

It was like those pictures which show two different things if you look at them long enough: like the one which shows either a hideous old crone with a big hooked nose or a pretty girl with a tipped-up nose. When you get the knack you can see first the one then the other, at will.

She seemed to relax against him. How stupid of him to leave the books stacked up with the paper markers in them for her to see.

The picture shifted and the old crone was back: if they had heard what Bob said? If he had contacted suspect people and they knew? If he had written stuff in the diaries about his secret work and the people he worked with? And all this on top of the Dodgson scandal?

A new thought came into his mind and he went cold. Perhaps they couldn't stomach another trial and all that publicity. What would they do then?

Margery said, 'I'm truly sorry I woke you, I know you don't get much sleep.'

He kissed her face and tasted the tears.

'I'm so sorry,' she said, 'I know I'm not normal at the moment; I got the mad idea you thought someone killed him. I

thought it too. And that you were going to ... I don't know ...
it sounds ridiculous ... avenge him. It came over me strongly,
I'd been trying to pray, that's why I came up. But it isn't like
that, it's just the shock giving me mad ideas, isn't it?'

'Yes,' he said, 'it's called being paranoid, didn't you know?'

For the first time since Monday she smiled. 'That's you, not
me,' she said, 'it always was, that's what saved us through the
years – if you'd been a trusting idiot like me we'd have gone
bust wouldn't we?'

'Could be.'

'Shall I put out the light?'

'I'll do it.'

The Bob notebook was lying with the other contents of
Frank's pockets which he had cleared on to the top of the chest
of drawers. Near it was the small tape recorder. He eased them
both into the top drawer in the moment after he switched off
the light. Tomorrow he would use the office safe to keep things
clear of Margery.

She began to breathe evenly. He remained still until he was
sure she was asleep. He was wide awake. It ran again in his
mind.

Monday – the old brick mortuary behind the Cheltenham
General Hospital; Bob covered to the neck on a metal trolley; a
crucifix in a curtained window; chapel of rest next to the
three-tier refrigerators. Afterwards in the car, lacking the will
to start it, next to what looked like a jolly ice-cream van with
bright colours – in fact a white caravan with bright letters:
Cobalt Appeal Unit, Charity Sky Divers, Target £500,000. A
grey plastic sack. Small silver birches drooping over the
bonnet.

Tuesday – the police interview; Bristol for books, starting
in George's. The storm. The phone call in the night ... Mr X
wanting the diaries.

Wednesday – London, more books, the tape recorder. The
coroner's officer phoning: 'Number four court, the inquest,
two thirty Thursday. Will you be there? Will you be legally
represented? Magistrates' court.'

Thursday – Bob's bank, no diaries. Cynthia Goodburn and
the poor bloody dog condemned for loyalty. The entries in the
Bob notebook lengthening. Then the inquest: number four

court. A light room; not large, Venetian blinds at the street windows, reporters that side behind the witness box. 'More press than usual, Mr Jones, the *Sun*, the *Mirror*, the *Telegraph*, the *Gloucester Echo*, oh excuse me, I don't think the pathologist has got here yet.'

Small, square tables of light-coloured wood, chairs to them, all the way down this side. Blue patterned wallpaper behind the coroner; a bright painted coat of arms that end, *Dieu et mon droit*, and an electric clock on the wall.

In the inside pocket the tape turning. Two paces to the right the witness box with a view of profiles, sometimes three-quarter faces.

'Please rise for Her Majesty's coroner.'

Shuffle, scuff, scrape. And then settle.

'I am opening and intend to conclude this inquest into the death of Robert Arthur Jones. I understand there are no legal representatives present.'

It blurs away as he drifts across the border of sleep and back. Snatches of the oath ' ... shall be the truth ... '

'A well-nourished male in his late twenties to early thirties with no sign of disease ... injuries consistent with a fall of twenty to forty feet ... no evidence of another party being involved.'

He slept.

On the tape in the top drawer were recorded his questions to the pathologist.

'Was my son alive immediately before the fall?'

'Was he conscious?'

The pathologist, by reference to blood flow after impact, said that Bob had been alive and almost certainly conscious before the fall. The impact had rendered him unconscious. After that he lived for perhaps five minutes.

Frank did not speak of the three methods he had so far come across in his research by which professionals could render a victim helpless without it showing – prior to faking an accident or suicide. In this case holding him by the heels and dropping him.

It was not until he played the tape of the inquest back in the car that he was struck by something else. When the coroner's officer spoke of the cat, Frank realised how convincingly this

158

answered the question – why was the deceased out on the roof in the dark? It was so English, so acceptable in the land of animal lovers; a kind-hearted chap who used regularly to rescue a stupid but lovable pet. It was ideal for the local paper with a photograph of Tiger. There was even a neighbour, the little Welsh crow, who sat near Frank (she was not called because Frank did not query the police statements) making cawing noises to indicate grief and agreement when the subject came up.

If someone had killed Bob they would have done it that way rather than say, a hit and run or some other method, *knowing* the domestic arrangements. It was tailor-made. Knowing also he would be alone in the house. So who was most likely to tell them? Answer – Mark or Rose.

He expressed these thoughts on tape. Set against the light courtroom, the reasonable and courteous coroner, the quiet unemotional level of question and answer, the boredom of the reporter from the *Sun*, they seemed absurd and he erased them. But he did not forget them.

Dodgson's name was not mentioned in court but was prominent in those newspapers which published a version of the inquest.

This time there was no official comment on the veiled speculation about a third death at GCHQ in as many weeks. The press could find no connection between the deceased and the Soviet spy.

TEN

1

Two weeks after the Flutter Man returned to America Dodgson heard that Kedge and Goodburn were dead. He relaxed. The Interrogator had been seeing him daily, going over it, and over and over. Dodgson felt elated. His part of the deal was done. He had duped the black man, fooled the machine. Alice was safely in wonderland.

The Interrogator himself also seemed less concentrated than usual that day. They drank coffee. For the hundredth time they discussed his controller, that mythical father-figure whom he was supposed both to love and hate. It got closer to home. In imagination they strolled through the streets of Cheltenham and suddenly he had told the Interrogator of the visit from the member of the Russian Trade delegation, the meeting in the public lavatory of the town hall – neither acknowledging the other – the furtive exchange of cloakroom tickets so that each left with the other's coat; and in the lining of Dodgson's coat ...

'And the return visit?' said the Interrogator. 'To London? Just to clean up a few loose ends, using the flat keys he left you? When your controller came over, the only time, when was that? '82? September?'

'October,' said Dodgson, his mind halfway to Finland, or would it be Austria the route out?

'I got the impression you enjoyed the flat?'

'Yes I did,' said Dodgson, 'Russian territory in England, it appealed to me; their security is better than ours I can tell you.

They searched the flats twice *each* day. Even the special one I was in.'

The Interrogator said, 'Special – they're standard, you're boasting again.'

'The corner one,' said Dodgson, 'more windows.'

'But why take such a risk? We cover those flats twenty-four hours a day.'

'I went in and out in the bottom of a school bus,' said Dodgson, 'those Russian kids are marvellous.'

The Interrogator let it pass and said, 'More windows – more light. The better to see you with. They've squeezed you dry and now they've burned you. You do know? You do know the police would have had no idea to this day that you were anything but a filthy old man if some friendly soul hadn't telephoned to give them a little help.'

Dodgson smiled. 'I've been waiting for that, why has it taken you so many weeks to trot it out?'

'I'm being friendly. I don't want you to live in vain hope, Dodgson. It eats a man up. Accept it. They've ditched you.'

Dodgson continued to smile. The source of information about Kedge and Goodburn had passed something else. It was in a metal phial now comfortably above the sphincter with a nylon thread for extraction purposes. Not that he expected a body search at this stage. 'They never do that,' he said.

'You can see your wife next week.'

Dodgson stopped smiling and waited for the terms. The Interrogator put down his cup and saucer.

'And you will have seen the last of me by that time – I think we've got everything pretty straight by now.'

'How is she?' asked Dodgson.

'Well, I believe.'

'I know what you did to turn her against me,' said Dodgson; 'you showed her some of the videos. It had to be that. She would have been appalled. That was it, wasn't it?'

'I think', said the Interrogator, 'what appalled her was that you sold your country. By the way, now we've got nearly everything in the open – would you do it again? Do you really admire that system?'

'I'm like the gangster who becomes a born-again Christian. I repent personally, but I don't send all my former colleagues to gaol to celebrate my new salvation. The Russians didn't come to me – *I went to them.* Perhaps they have ditched me. In any case as we both know it's academic,' he tried not to smile, 'but even if I do not now support their system as I said in court – I *loathe* the hypocrisy of this one where people like you rule the roost. You don't imagine do you that someone like myself, who had access to a great deal, take the Falklands War for example, can be duped by the official rubbish obediently printed by the newspapers here?'

'Of course not,' said the Interrogator, 'but you're safely inside and the vast majority live happily outside in ignorance of such dangerous information. What is more I sincerely believe they *prefer* it that way.'

'And my son?' said Dodgson as if he had been mentioned.

'I don't see why not. Would a week today suit you?'

2

A few days later a dangerous gas leak was reported during the morning rush-hour in north London. Traffic was diverted and nearby buildings were ordered to be evacuated. The team which arrived to dig up the road filled the air with the sound of pneumatic drills. The owners of one block of flats protested and attempted to prevent the gas board detector team entering. The Foreign Office was called in to mediate. It was eventually agreed that each gas board official would be accompanied by an individual guard. The Russians even queried the equipment the gas men were using. The end flat on the first floor had extra windows.

The following day a set of photographs of its interior with many cross-referencing shots of the furniture and ornaments hung on clips in a bare room in a block of offices south of the Thames near Chelsea Bridge.

Another set of photographs showed the view from inside the flat through the windows.

Flecker waited until the Interrogator had examined them.

'Won't do,' he said.

'Yes it will. Curtains drawn and lights on is the answer. He'll

162

co-operate when he's told the place is under surveillance with long lens cameras. Is the specialist arranged?'

'Yes. Israeli.'

3

On the evening of the day he saw his wife and son Dodgson received the 'go' from his contact. He recovered the phial which was a habit by now, opened it, unwrapped the two small pills and swallowed them. In half an hour he was in a coma. They took him to the hospital wing. His pulse was barely discernible. It was decided to transfer him to Hammersmith Hospital for intensive care. The prison medical officer decided against an ambulance, the hospital being adjacent to the prison. It was past midnight when they put him in a car and drove out of the gates.

Almost outside the hospital the car was blocked by a van pulling across the road. Another car without lights stopped immediately behind the prison car. Four men in balaclavas got out. They pulled open the doors of the prison car, pushed sawn-off shot guns into the faces of the warders and dragged the unconscious Dodgson into their own car. It was later found abandoned. It had no recorded owner because it had previously been 'written off' after an auction in Manchester's disused central station.

The prison car returned the few hundred yards to the prison; as it approached and the guard at the gate raised the barrier before the main entrance one of them started to shout about calling the police.

The guard at the gate said, 'Shut up, and drive straight in.'

Inside they were taken to an office; a waiting official from the Home Office reminded them of the terms of the Official Secrets Act which they, like all civil servants, had signed. He forbade them to discuss what had happened with anyone and warned them that if there was a leak they would be held responsible and prosecuted. They would of course be sacked. He stressed that this was a matter of national security.

163

4

Dodgson woke slowly and took a long time to focus. There was something familiar about the room. The curtains were drawn and a single lamp was alight on the dressing table. He could vaguely remember taking the two pills. As he stirred so did someone else sitting in the shadows. Then a form bent over him and a concerned face gazed down at him. It was blurred. He fumbled for his spectacles and the figure handed them to him. He put them on. He could see the hairs in the man's nose, the lines on the face.

The man said something in Russian. Recognising the sound of the language Dodgson felt suddenly as if he had died and then woken in paradise. He tried to smile.

'Thirsty,' he said, 'terribly thirsty.'

The face above him smiled back and said in heavily accented English, 'Good. You are safe. There is water.'

He watched as the thick-set figure moved round the bed to pour water into a tumbler from a jug on the bedside table. The man had thinning hair brushed back and a heavy Slav face that was, to Dodgson, unmistakably Russian.

The man supported him to drink. There was a smell of pipe tobacco and a pleasant body smell of soap and food. Dodgson felt like a small child again being cradled by his stepfather; he could have wept for joy. He drank and drank spilling some while the man made encouraging noises. He lay back.

'Oh,' he said, 'I'm free, I'm free.'

'But you are not strong, comrade; you have to stay here a few days to get strong for the journey.'

'That's fine.'

'I am a doctor. You can call me Alex. Now let us see.'

Dodgson felt wonderfully drowsy in the bed. Utterly relaxed. He had stood weeks of interrogation following the arrest and trial and suddenly it was over.

Alex had large hands with dark hair on the back of the fingers. He held Dodgson's wrist and took his pulse. The feel of that hand on his wrist gave Dodgson a sense of extraordinary confidence. He closed his eyes. Alex took the pulse in the other wrist. Then with a stethoscope he listened to the chest saying, 'Breathe, breathe,' half supporting Dodgson as if he were an infant.

'I'm tired,' said Dodgson, 'I'm tired.'

'Of course, just relax.'

Dodgson lay back again. 'Where is this?'

Alex now had an ophthalmoscope in his hand testing the light. 'You have been here before,' he said, 'the last time was in the school bus.'

Dodgson smiled. Lying flat among those delicious little girls looking at their legs, catching glimpses of their knickers. 'Yes,' he said.

'Now, comrade, I will look at your eyes, just concentrate on the light for a moment and – '

Dodgson wanted to be obedient, to show his gratitude, to be a model patient. He began to drift away. Alex was saying something but his eyelids were so heavy.

When he woke again he was alone. The curtains were still drawn and the light on. He sat up slowly. He felt hungry. He began to get out of bed. He was in his underwear, the prison clothes were on a chair nearby. When he put his feet on the floor and sat erect he felt faint.

He heard the door and turned to see a woman enter. His first fleeting feeling was of dislike. She was middle-aged, dark-haired with it gathered tightly round her head. She looked dowdy and masculine. But then she smiled and said something in Russian and left to return almost immediately with a tray. On it was tea and toast. The doctor followed her in saying, 'Good morning, comrade, you have slept? You are hungry? Eat, eat – the woman will make you the eggs and bacon now you are awake.'

'Is it morning, Alex?'

'You remember my name, good. Yes, it is morning, to tell the truth it is afternoon!'

'The curtains?'

'You must not touch them, Ramsay – outside the British are like crazy men looking for you. There is enormous outcry.'

Dodgson was pouring tea, putting butter on toast, sitting propped against the bed head. The present was sharply clear but he could not remember what happened last night. Alex was saying, 'When you have eaten then the bath.'

The new clothes were waiting. After the bath Dodgson put them on; a coloured shirt, a sober tie, a dull suit with slightly baggy trousers. Alex said, 'And we shall change your appearance, comrade, you will have hair and a moustache, also I think, you will have a wheelchair.'

In the main room Dodgson recognised the furniture and the ornaments. Alex began to talk to him and again he began to feel so tired he could not keep his eyes open.

He woke in bed. He felt very happy. He dreamed that his father had talked to him about his whole life and somehow, not in words but somehow, had conveyed to him how proud he was of his son. He could not remember going to sleep. He could not remember getting undressed. But it did not matter because he was absolutely safe.

The door clicked and the middle-aged woman came in with a tray. He was terribly hungry. Afterwards he had a bath and put on his coloured shirt and suit and another man came in with Alex; an efficient, busy little man with a suitcase. He placed Dodgson on a chair in the middle of the room and fitted him with a wig which completely altered the shape of his face and took years off him. Then there was a moustache to match and they glued it on temporarily to show him the effect.

Dodgson was entranced. The hair, the moustache, the suit – it was wonderful, it was what he would expect of them with their ability for illusion.

They drank vodka together and joked. The small make-up man had brought a newspaper with him and Dodgson was delighted to find himself on the front page. 'Spy Escapes'. When the small man left he took the headlines with him. Once again Dodgson and Alex settled to talk, but within two sentences his eyes closed.

There was a telephone in the room. At some time Dodgson went to it and dialled a Cheltenham number. Later he dialled a London number. He spoke various short phrases.

5

Flecker explained to his wife that this weekend he had to be away. They lived in Greenwich in an Edwardian terraced house with a large back garden. It was an anonymous area, unlike Blackheath up the hill. Flecker liked the proximity to the river with the Royal Naval College and the Maritime Museum and the park. He liked the pubs. Mrs Flecker liked none of these things and, despite her resolute daily efficiency in the house and her part-time job, she was a woman who lived in quiet despair.

It was difficult to explain to your friends that you did not have a passport because your husband's was lodged somewhere secret, and you could never have the relief of sunshine and wine and beaches abroad and letting rip. She suddenly found herself saying, 'Take me with you.'

Flecker was astonished. 'Impossible.'

'Then *tell* me something about it.'

Two or three times in twenty years they had come to this point. Previously he had sidetracked her or browbeaten her away from the subject.

'You know I can't.'

'I have a lump on my breast,' she said.

Flecker said absurdly, 'Are you sure?'

'It's cancer. Most women who get it die of it.'

'But have you checked, I mean you never mentioned – '

He was appalled. He had gone pale.

She stood looking at him. He had a drink in his hand and he looked just like that actor in the cigar commercial on TV. Anything less like a ...

'No,' she said, 'I haven't checked because it's a lie.'

'But what ... ?'

'We're middle-aged,' she said, 'and I'm sick of it.'

She had not meant to say it. She was astonished to have said it.

'Go on,' she said, 'tell me – give me some idea why what you are doing is worth this sort of life?'

He finished the drink. He glanced towards his telephone. He said firmly, 'I can't tell you anything.' Then he put his fingers to his lips, led her from the room to the bathroom, turned on both taps with the plug out and closed the door. He sat her on the edge of the bath and put his face close to hers, which was averted.

'Listen,' he said softly, 'I love you, but you must *never* do

167

that again. It is dangerous. One is not forgiven. You must understand something – the intelligence world is accountable to *nobody* – not the politicians, not the courts – to *nobody*. If you think that you can achieve something by causing a stink you're wrong. The reason I don't talk to you is to protect us both. For example – it is very, very important that no one gets to know my profession and where I live. At the moment we're doing something of vital importance, that's all I can say. It has been very arduous and we're nearly at the end of it.'

It was the first serious conversation they had held for a decade. She looked at the familiar bathroom with its tiles and clutter and the two taps pouring away and the face of her middle-aged husband.

'Are you trying to tell me that something could happen, here in boring bloody Greenwich, if I kick up and your bosses find out?'

'Will you please lower your voice.'

'But you,' she said, 'are on our side or have I got it wrong?'

He took her hand and she pulled away. She wondered if he was suffering from some form of premature senility.

'Let me put it like this,' he said, 'since '45 we've lived with the bomb because you can't go back and undiscover it. We're stuck with it. It may finish us. Things look very bad at the moment but they have before. Now in my line it's the same. Since the war, since Philby and Blunt and all the rest it's got very, very rough. You see? We didn't start it but we're stuck with it. There's a war on. And it's exactly the same as the way Churchill *allowed* Coventry to be blitzed to buggery rather than let on – by intercepting the Luftwaffe – that we knew when they were coming: little people can't be allowed to get in the way of big issues. So if it was thought that someone in my position had become unreliable or vulnerable then something would have to be done about it.'

After a while she said, 'I didn't know that about Churchill, is it true?'

'Oh yes.'

'All those people.'

'Yes.'

'And then they made all that tremendous propaganda out of it and the bombed church and the cross and – '

168

'Yes.'

'And it needn't have happened?'

'Well, not to that extent.'

She considered it.

'And you work for people who do things like that?'

'Look,' he said, 'the war had to be won. That was a factor in winning it.'

'You can turn off the taps,' she said, 'I shall keep my voice down.'

Later that evening when they sat in silence opposite each other at dinner he said suddenly, 'It really wasn't true about the cancer was it?'

'You know,' she replied, 'the trouble is that I'm not the daughter of some admiral or colonel; you once told me that they fit in with all the things you do. You should have married one of them. And I should have married someone immoral who liked poetry.'

'I'm due for some leave, we'll have a holiday.'

She collected his plate and came back with the pudding. It was his favourite – jam roly-poly with custard. Long ago he had been a lower-middle-class little boy whose Mum made it for him.

He looked at it, he smelled the delicious familiar smell, he had a sense of emptiness and knew no way to express it.

'It's my job,' he said, 'it's what I do best.'

'I know,' she said, 'but what about me?'

6

The place was on the outskirts of Winchester. Sometimes the SAS came there to rehearse something violent. The empty huts stood in decrepit rows and the larger buildings occupied the centre. It was obvious to any passing motorist that a film company was on location. There was a coach, and lorries with words like 'Wardrobe' on their sides, and some lighting gear and generators. What was being shot could not be seen because it was in the centre of the camp. There were polite private security guards to prevent the public driving in. It was too far out of the city for pedestrians.

The Interrogator drove in, passed the inner security and went into a large caravan. Flecker was waiting for him. The caravan was curtained, with guards both sides.

'How is it?' he said.

Flecker showed him a piece of paper. On it were written two telephone numbers, one in Cheltenham and one in London. Against each number was a name.

'Well well,' he said. 'One' and 'Two' were identified at last.

There was a knock on the door. Alex the doctor entered.

'Ah,' said Flecker, 'welcome, well done, excellent.'

'He was a very good subject,' said Alex, 'it took five days to reach the necessary level.'

'What will he remember?'

'Nothing. In dreams perhaps, but nothing.'

'Is it all on tape?' asked the Interrogator. 'Video?'

'Of course.'

Outside the film crew appeared to be wrapping up. An ambulance drove away. Then a private car with Alex to Heathrow to catch an El Al flight.

The Interrogator and Flecker went into a building which had once been a gymnasium. In the centre was a stage set; curiously it was completely enclosed, not, as normal, open on one side.

Flecker was proud of it.

'Listen,' he said and flicked his fingers. From speakers all round the set came the sound of north London traffic. Then lights came on to shine against the curtained windows.

Flecker opened a door and led the Interrogator inside. They toured the 'flat' with its bedroom, bathroom, kitchen and sitting room.

The heavy-faced woman was there. In the bedroom on a chair was a suit, a coloured shirt, a plain tie.

The Interrogator sat in an armchair. There was a pleasant smell of pipe tobacco in the air. On the head-shaped wooden block on the sideboard was a man's wig and lying beside it a matching moustache.

He went into the bathroom and turned on the hot tap – it ran hot. In the kitchen a kettle was boiling.

'Cup of tea?' asked Flecker.

The Interrogator had never seen him so animated. Usually a dull pudding of a man, he was exuberant.

170

'One of my better productions,' said Flecker, 'they made a wonderful job of the furniture.'

Recollecting the photographs the Interrogator said, 'They did indeed. And our Israeli friend, was he as good as he seemed?'

'He had to use drugs as well. We were prepared to use ECT if necessary.'

'Oh?'

'Under anaesthetic. It weakens the will and makes control considerably easier, but at the same time it may affect memory in a way that is counter-productive. But Dodgson was highly susceptible, fortunately.'

'I'm afraid I don't believe that there will be complete amnesia,' said the Interrogator, 'but in the circumstances what does it matter?'

'What indeed,' smiled Flecker as the woman brought them tea. The Interrogator opened one of the curtains and looked out at the lighting gear and cables and the decaying wall of the old gym.

'Well well,' he said, 'a special flat with more windows! What would we have done if he'd believed me when I told him our friends on the other side burned him. Incidentally, what's happening to Dodgson's contact? The one who passed him the pills and so on?'

'He's getting ten years off his sentence. And then he's going to Northern Ireland for us.'

There was a knock on the door.

'Come in.'

A cheerful lean man in jeans and sweatshirt entered.

'Can we strike, guvnor?'

'Ten minutes.'

'Right you are.'

7

Dodgson woke slowly. For over an hour he seemed to drift through a substance like heavy cloud. There were short bursts of light which hurt his eyes. Finally when he became conscious he could remember nothing. The prison smell which he detested was in his nostrils, the bare bulb hurt his eyes, he struggled to sit up and felt so sick he thought he would vomit on the floor.

Outside the barred window it was dark.

He called out. There was stirring in other beds. Nobody came. He lay down again in a state of despair which he had not experienced in all the years since his mother told him that his American stepfather whom he had adored would never be coming back. Never. He had been abandoned.

In the morning the medical officer told him that he had been very ill for five days. In a coma. Part of the time he had been in hospital until out of danger. When he was a little better they would do tests on him to see what had caused him to become unconscious. Perhaps something was pressing on the brain?

The medical officer had been in the Army. He was matter-of-fact. Chin up – you might be dead.

When they returned him to D Block there was something that nagged him. Some vague elusive recollection. Someone who wasn't there. He found it difficult to concentrate on mathematical problems.

After a week or so he felt more normal. He enjoyed the television news reports of American reverses in the Middle East and various South American states. He comforted himself that alone he had beaten the spooks. His two colleagues were safe and deeply dug in. They would carry on the work. It hurt him that his wife did not come again and that the letters from his son were so childish and ill-written. But soon, next year, or next month or even next week his comrades would find a way to get him out and then they would bring his son afterwards. They always did everything in their power to bring the families.

When he had this thought a shadow seemed to cross his mind and for a second the faintest sense of something having happened touched him. But it passed.

Someone anonymous sent him an edition of *Alice in Wonderland* and *Alice Through the Looking Glass* illustrated and in one volume. Printed on the title-page in black Letraset was: *With reference to the chess problem – the capture of the red knight and the final checkmate of the red king is strictly in accordance with the laws of the game.*

PART FOUR

ELEVEN

1

Small Japanese gentlemen with enormous suitcases came up the single escalator in a tight line like paratroopers waiting for the pat on the shoulder to go. Up and over with cameras round their necks and their fathomless eyes fixed on some objective beyond Frank's view. They marched briskly across the lobby with the No Entry doors to Level 2 of the car-park. They ran their cases on small wheels without having to stoop to do it. Perhaps they were a martial arts squad en route to chop their way into some building with their bare hands.

Frank passed them to go on to the balcony above Terminal 3 Arrivals. He glanced over to see a fat Sikh in the brown uniform of Heathrow security topped by a turban. Sikhs and Japs, an old association from World War Two.

Three of the four television monitors were blank. The fourth told him that the flight from Los Angeles had landed and its baggage was in the hall. He went past the long rows of seats and down the staircase facing the coffee shop and bar. No sign of her there; and nothing stirred in the passage formed by portable barriers making a wide exit from the screened customs area. A notice on the opposite wall said that it took sixty minutes after landing for passengers to emerge.

The sound level of voices and announcements had a muffling effect and he ignored what could have been someone calling because nobody at Heathrow could possibly be calling his name.

'Hey Frankie!'

175

The impression of someone coming at him from behind; he side-stepped and turned.

'Good God!'

'No – not him, Frankie – me!'

'Charlie Ricco.'

'The same. I couldn't believe it when I spotted you just now. It was the walk. How are you, Frankie, long time no see.'

Charlie had aged very well. He was tanned, and standing there in the tropical suit holding the American Express luggage he looked like an only-just-over-the-hill tennis star. The moustache was a surprise. You're not allowed the moustache in the Navy – only a full set – and Frank had not seen Charlie since those days. He still grinned. He had big flat teeth in front and his fair hair – sun-bleached was it or something out of a bottle? – still flopped on his brow giving him a boyish look and as if that wasn't enough he had blue eyes that the bints went dotty over.

They were shaking hands.

'Well, how's it go?'

Charlie put a hand on his arm. Charlie always touched. He touched and he looked you in the eye and he was always easy, relaxed. He was the only one who really enjoyed the take-off with the rockets when the steam catapult failed and they cleared the flight deck. Others said it. Charlie meant it. For a moment Frank wondered if Charlie was still flying and a stab of envy went through him.

He eased away from the hand and said, 'Fine, fine.'

Charlie had never really been his mate, his oppo, but they had got on, had runs ashore together, flown together.

'Meeting my daughter,' said Frank. The envy persisted, the bloody man didn't look a day over forty.

'I've just come back from the Gulf,' said Charlie, 'bit different from our day – you been?'

'No.'

'Come and have a drink.'

'Can't, she's due, in fact overdue, she's in there somewhere, mustn't miss her.'

'Well, how are things, Frank – you look good.'

'My son just died.'

176

Charlie stopped smiling and said, 'I'm sorry to hear that, I'm bloody sorry, Frankie, that's rough. How old was he?'

'Twenty-eight.'

'I never had any kids.'

'Yes ... well, it cheers me up to see you — you flying, Charlie?'

'Never! That's like driving a bus nowadays. I did some crop spraying after I came out but ... '

From the customs hall the first passengers emerged; one of them had a leg in plaster and a fat companion who puffed and complained.

'I'm sorry about that drink.'

'Some other time. Where are you nowadays, Frank?'

'I don't come to London much,' said Frank, 'but I'm not far out, Reading, here,' he fumbled his wallet from his jacket to find a business card, 'look here's where you could find me if you ever go West, my son. You can't miss it, I'm a few streets away from a sort of underpass called the Inner Distribution Road, they just built a big new hotel in red brick the other side. The Ramada.'

'Ah,' said Charlie, 'like America, they have Ramada motels there.'

'That's it.

'Do you know,' said Charlie, 'I might drop in. I'm in the oil business would you believe? Not exactly *in*, but you might say, a sort of sucker fish among the sharks.'

'What do you do?'

'Run a company of divers.'

'You would,' said Frank. It fitted Charlie exactly.

He had one eye on the thickening stream of passengers emerging. Charlie was tucking away the business card. Something very faint, a wisp of memory, something about Charlie touched his mind and then was gone.

'I'll ring you', said Charlie, 'when I'm your way and we'll have a night out.'

'Great. And you really do look prosperous.'

'Well wouldn't you? With all those wogs in Rolls-Royces? Talk about the Golden Goose.'

Frank chuckled. 'Drinks on you, then?'

'Right you are, chief, and mind how you go.'

177

Charlie sloped off. Long legs, very slightly hunched in the shoulders. He had brought with him the days of sailing in company with the Yank carrier, competing to see who could get the most airborne and fly the most sorties. Frank could almost smell the bread baking between decks, the high-octane fuel and feel the bump as the long-gone-to-the-knackers carrier put her bow into it. For the first time in years he thought of his dead oppo Vic.

'Dad!'

She rushed across to the barrier and he embraced her over it. He took her case and they walked with the barrier between them until the opening when he put his arms round her and hugged her and thought, 'God, she's thin this girl.'

He patted her and said, 'There, there, it's all right, it's all right,' and she tried not to cry.

'Where's Mum?'

'Getting things ready at home.'

'Poor Mum, she sounded so terrible on the phone.'

'Tell you what,' he said, 'there's a motorway caff just down the road, let's have a spot of breakfast.'

They went past luggage trolleys, oblivious to the ticket sales, car hire, hotel booking under the big yellow signs, and up the single escalator.

Some weeks earlier a man in a chauffeur's uniform accompanied by what looked like a black Olympic shot putter had gone the same route, driven away from Level 2 as they were doing – out through the tunnel and on to the M4.

Frank – like the liaison man – had to remind his passenger that seat belts are obligatory in England.

2

In the entrance hall they avoided the lads playing the machines. They negotiated a group in filthy leather, heavy with studs. Others, cropped to the skull and wearing fake para boots, drifted between the machines and the shop. In a corner were two with made-up zombie faces whose green and orange hair stood like tropical plumage.

The lads kept on zapping the aliens and monsters from space while the machines kept on bleeping and eating their money.

Inside were their natural prey – Asians. Serving conscientiously they never looked up, or spoke, unless it was essential: composed in attitudes of non-aggression as near as possible to non-being they endured the endless repetition of white faces being filled.

Frank and Helen sat as far as they could from everyone else.

'Has it got worse here, Dad?'

'What?'

'Here. England.'

'Did those yobs out there bother you?'

'No – you should see the freaks in Los Angeles.'

'Yes, I suppose so.'

They could not talk to each other, it was too soon.

'You look a bit tired, are you all right, Dad?'

He was tempted to tell her about the short nights and the cold showers and coffee in the mornings.

'Fine, fine,' he said.

Antigone again came to mind. He had now read it and found it tedious. He could imagine she would be thin and quick like the one facing him; when she smiled she would look mischievous and sixteen instead of solemn and twenty-six, that's why the king's son wanted her. She was unpredictable. She had long dark hair which lifted when she ran. It would not do for her, the one drinking coffee opposite, to fix upon her brother's cause. All the same the joy and relief of her company almost made him confide in her.

Then it jumped into his mind. Bogey Knight! Good old reliable Bogey. Meeting Bogey years ago after they were both out of the Andrew and he was working for that old rogue. In the city. A bitter day with the wind driving between the buildings. A coffee shop. Bogey saying, 'I bumped into Charlie Ricco the other day; you'll never believe what he's been up to, Frankie.'

'What's the matter, Dad?'

'Nothing.'

He could see Bogey's admiring expression as he told him what Charlie Ricco had been up to. He knew then, sitting opposite his daughter, that everything Bob had said was right.

They had taken all that trouble so that Charlie Ricco could bump into his old shipmate. They knew where and what time. Well! Well! And when would he turn up again?

Helen had said something which he missed. He said, 'Sorry, I didn't – '

'I still can't believe it about Bob.'

'I know.'

'I was only talking to him last week.'

Frank stopped eating. 'He phoned you?'

'Yes. It was lovely, he was so cheerful.'

'Did he often do that?'

'No, of course not, it's too expensive.'

'Yes, of course it is – why was he so cheerful?'

'Did he tell you he was changing his job or anything?'

'Well,' said Frank, 'we did talk a few weeks ago.'

He watched a coach party tumble on to the forecourt beyond the window; a few elderly gentlemen and many elderly ladies in search of coffee and cakes and lavatories. They were remarkable shapes, many of them as broad as they were tall, wrapped in cardigans, their heads topped with what looked like twists and wads of cotton wool. They laughed and their National Health choppers gleamed. They all talked at once and pointed and gave shrieks of laughter; some tried to force their way back into the coach for forgotten holdalls and auntie bags. Like a disorganised flock of birds which responds to some mysterious signal to act as one they suddenly turned and bore down on the yobs in the entrance hall and went through them like a Roman phalanx. Their cries and laughter preceded them. They rushed for the trays.

They were plump, knobbly, angular, they suffered from arthritis, flat feet, piles, bad eyesight, varicose veins, bronchitis and many other unspeakable ailments for which they took thousands and thousands of drugs a year – but they had the breath of life in them and would keep going to the last gasp.

Frank knew them, and they, if there had been time to talk, would have known him. They were the England he understood and used to believe in – knew they were free and lived in the best country in the world and they proved it when they took a package holiday to Spain or Yugoslavia and made comparisons. They knew red from blue and if someone who was

180

stark naked went by talking about the lovely suit he was wearing they were very polite to his face and when he'd gone they made jokes about his little Willie.

And they *were* free, the way he had been before the copper pressed the doorbell six days ago. Then he understood why, in Orwell's *Nineteen Eighty-Four*, only the proles and the animals were free.

The whole atmosphere of the place cheered up; even the Asian apologetically wiping the table smiled.

Helen waited until he had gone then she said, 'Being Bob he'd got the time wrong – I mean the time difference between here and there – so he woke me up and I was a bit hazy because it's a shock in the night. He was so cheerful I thought he might be tight or at a party or something.'

'You don't remember the day do you?'

'Er ... yes ... I think it would have been Sunday here.'

'Which Sunday?'

'Just a minute.'

She took a small diary from her bag and flicked back. 'There.' She pointed. 'The Sunday before last. It would have been about midday here when he phoned.'

'But Bob wouldn't have been at a party in the middle of the day would he?'

'Well, I don't know. Drinks on Sunday before lunch?'

'Dinner,' said Frank straight-faced.

'Now you know it isn't,' she said, 'and I don't want your working-man act which you never were – now were you?'

'Definitely not.'

'I feel a bit better,' she said, 'it's always a shock, you look forward to it too much, and then ... '

'I know,' he said.

'I don't mean I looked forward to – '

'I know,' he said, 'I know exactly.'

After a moment she said, 'When's the funeral, Dad?'

'Monday.'

'I'll be able to help Mum.'

'That's right ... what else did he say? Bob?'

'He made jokes about starting a new life, that's why he phoned, and he said something about blowing the whistle.'

For six days Frank had turned over the facts concerning

Bob's death. For five weeks before that he had been filled with unease by the conversation they'd had about the secret world. He had already skimmed twenty books focusing on the areas they had discussed. In particular American secret actions.

As Helen said 'blowing the whistle' he understood exactly what Bob's intention had been. He heard the voice of 'Mr X' gasping down the telephone in the middle of the night saying, 'Sea Air Dowry'. It had been under his nose: the book with big red letters on its spine – *CIA Diary*. The author was Philip Agee. A whistle blower. 'Whistle blower' was American for those who blew the secrets of organisations with which they had become disillusioned. Bob intended to blow the whistle on whatever he knew about GCHQ.

But Bob was no mug. Nor, as he had said, was he the stuff of which martyrs were made. He knew that if he tried it in England they'd have him inside, and even if it were written and reached a publisher it would not see the light of day. What did Agee do? He stayed out of America to write his book. What therefore would Bob do?

'Dad,' said Helen, 'are you all right?'

'Fine, fine – I've just remembered something,' lied Frank. 'When we last talked, Bob and me, he said something about wanting to visit you before your time was up in the States, did he mention that?'

'That's what's so awful,' she said, 'he *did*. He said he wouldn't tell me any more on the phone except it was the best decision of his life, he'd come and sleep on my floor if he could raise the fare and he was sure he could and we'd have time to talk about everything.'

'Yes,' said Frank, 'yes I see.'

'He was so happy – it came right across the six thousand miles on that line which has a funny echo, you know? Sometimes even as you're saying "goodbye" over it you still get the echo of your last word – it was the middle of the night and the echo, and the happiness rolled off him. I sort of thought he'd got a new girl as well, do you know? There was something in the background of the call.'

'A child?'

Helen looked surprised. 'Yes! I think it was, how did you know that. It was, now you say it.'

'Oh,' said Frank, 'he had a chum who was married. Bloke he used to play chess with. They have a small girl. It'd be a likely place for him to be on a Sunday.'

She would never find out how long before last Sunday Goodburn had been dead.

'Excuse me a moment, too much coffee.'

He made sure she could not see the telephones in the entrance hall before he went in and dialled.

When Cynthia replied he said, 'Hello, this is Frank Jones.'

'Oh hello,' she said, and sounded pleased.

'Look, I need something confirmed, it's very important to me – was Bob going to take you to America?'

There was a long silence.

'Yes,' she said in a small voice.

'And were you going to support him while he wrote it?'

'Yes,' she said, 'nothing would have stopped him – and I loved him, I couldn't help it. How did you know?'

'I worked it out,' he said, 'I've just worked it out.'

'What happens now?'

'I don't know,' he said. 'I have to go – thank you.'

He pressed the hook to cut the connection. Among the Space Invaders behind him was a single pinball machine. He could hear the chonk chonk chonk as the big metal balls hit and registered the way they did when he was that age and he hung around arcades on leave, sometimes even seeing what the butler saw.

He still held the phone in his hand. 'Oh you fool,' he said, 'oh you bloody, bloody fool.'

He went back through the animals playing the machines and then inside past the proles laughing and eating cake.

He wondered why they had not killed Agee. The fact that he was well known and had many friends in the press did not quite cover it. Perhaps if you balanced the public effect of the book against the public outcry if he suddenly had an accident – you decided to settle for the former because in time such books are forgotten. In the West there is always another sensation. But if your target is unknown and you balance his death against another GCHQ secrets trial and scandal … ? Particularly after Dodgson?

He sat down. He managed to smile.

'Well,' he said, 'you're a sight for sore eyes, girl.'

Is it really possible? Here? In England? With all these cheerful old buggers stuffing their faces and talking at the top of their voices. After all, that bloke Agee even *named names*: columns of them; I know they pushed him about and even kicked him out of the UK – *but* it all got published. And he's not the only one. So why Bob? I don't have a single speck of proof.

He had read that both the KGB assassination and sabotage squad stationed in London, and DI5, and the counter-espionage section of DI6, used criminals – particularly when it came to murder. The Americans trained their own assassins often recruiting out of military prisons.

3

Frank looked past the flapping white surplice at the dishes and aerials in the grounds of a country house. He had always been aware it was there – the BBC monitoring station, Caversham – but the sharp contrast between it and the huge stone garden where he stood shocked him. He had his arm round Margery. His son was lowered into the geometrically-dug slit trench. The others were a huddle of dark suits and dresses and solemn faces. Margery and Helen had their heads bowed.

BBC Caversham seemed a modest version of GCHQ. On the day of the inquest he had driven slowly past GCHQ, turned the car and driven back, driven past again identifying the flat roofed pre-fabs with barred windows to which Bob had referred when he spoke of his interviews for the job. There it was. Also on the town map for all to see. And here too, just beyond the cemetery railings – without a guard or electric fence in sight – a similar place serving a related purpose.

The earth to cover his son was a mound on a wooden platform with two wooden sides supported by metal stakes to contain it. It was the only raw and temporary thing among the rows of headstones, the green marble chips, the fresh and fading flowers, the carved banalities of the bereaved. Like the place beyond the railings the crude earth was shocking as was the bedraggled nylon grass which did not cover it.

Better a pyre and the clean flames: in the open, not the underground business of cremation and a wretched urn.

On the far side of the place, near the entrance, a modest car: near it a woman doing something at a grave; in it a man with a pair of binoculars.

4

Frank left the sitting room with a tray of dirty glasses. Margie and Helen were doing wonders. The guests were still eating. Frank ran the tap aware of a movement behind him and someone coming into the kitchen.

Mark said, 'I was very relieved about the verdict, Mr Jones.' Although he was quietly standing there, his head slightly averted, Frank had the impression he was both shuffling and wringing his hands. He was flushed; perhaps he had been drinking before he arrived; perhaps it was his usual left-footed approach due to embarrassment.

'Oh?'

Mark took two paces into the kitchen, started to speak, and then turned back to close the door. He lowered his voice and said, 'I expect you know we were all questioned?'

Frank recollected what the inspector had said.

'Who by?'

'A sergeant.'

That checked.

'And', said Mark, 'like an idiot I said Bob had been depressed.'

He let out a long breath of relief as if to say, 'There – now I've said it.'

Frank remembered the mother with the diffident little boy clinging to her in the photograph.

'I didn't know that.' He was busy with the clinking glasses. 'We had a chat, you remember, Rose's birthday? – and Bob was very cheerful then – not a care in the world, he was always like that, very steady. What was he depressed about, Mark?'

'Oh, well . . . you see, you probably didn't know but a friend of his committed suicide.'

'Really?'

'Yes ... er nice fellow, not that I knew him, I just met him once or twice, chap named Goodburn – Allen?'

'And Bob was upset was he?'

Frank moved round the kitchen to find a glass cloth.

'Yes.'

'Well,' said Frank in a friendly voice, standing close to Mark, 'you can't blame yourself for telling the truth, Mark.'

Mark began to say something, stammered and was silent.

'Don't worry about it,' said Frank, 'I know you were his friend and you certainly wouldn't let him down. I'd never have let them bring in a verdict of suicide, you know.'

'No,' said Mark, 'no, of course not, I just sort of, it's ridiculous but I wanted to apologise to you and er,' he glanced at the door, 'sorry to be so conspiratorial but, I mean there's nothing to be conspiratorial about – but since Dodgson' – He tailed off.

'I understand that all right,' said Frank firmly, 'I was in the Navy – twelve years. Flew in the Korean War – United Nations markings on the wings and all the rest of it – I know who the enemy is, believe me.'

He hoped he had not overdone it.

'I didn't know, I knew you'd been in the Navy but – '

'Oh yes. Lost a lot of chums.'

'I wanted to get it off my chest,' said Mark and laughed. 'The police sergeant went on about it for a bit after I said it, and about the other chap, Goodburn; what upset Bob was he'd been to the birthday party of the little girl a week before it happened – he showed us the present because it amused him – it was a telephone you wound up and it not only marched about the place but it did a voice which sang.'

'Sit down,' said Frank, 'have a drink.'

They sat opposite each other at the kitchen table and Frank poured two Scotches from a new bottle.

'Water?'

'No thanks.'

'I appreciate you telling me, cheers.'

'Cheers.'

'Of course,' said Frank, 'it was rather tricky for you because you had to take the police round the house on the Monday – I suppose you were first back?'

186

'Yes, yes I was. They were already in the house, they'd borrowed a ladder and come in by the roof. It was a terrible shock. I couldn't believe it. So ... yes ... I took them round.'

'All the rooms?'

'Oh yes – they were very thorough.'

'I expect Rose told you,' said Frank, sipping his whisky, 'I was grateful the way Bob's room had been cleared up. Did you do that?'

'Oh no,' said Mark, 'Bob must have done it himself.'

'Really?'

'Oh yes – it was very neat when I went in with the police – not its usual state at all.'

Frank regarded him with friendly eyes and made a smiling noise to encourage him.

Mark said, 'There's been a terrible feeling ... where we work ... and every kind of rumour. I know I can't imagine how bad it must be for you and Mrs Jones. I wanted to get it off my chest, and I'm very, very sorry about everything.'

'I know,' said Frank, 'but it's not your fault, Mark, it was an accident. Did you know any other friends of Bob?'

'No, not really. We were in different sections.'

'You don't know one that boozes and likes his comfort do you?'

'What does he look like, Mr Jones? I might, I suppose.'

'Well,' said Frank, 'I think he looks like a man who knows something very bad, that he can't prove, and ... like you ... he wanted to tell me about it ... and get it off his chest because he has a bad conscience.'

Mark began to tremble.

'I don't understand.'

Frank said, 'No. *I* don't understand. You tell me, Mark.'

Mark got up from the table and started to say something. Frank came round, put a hand on his shoulder and said, 'I think he was murdered, you see – '

'Oh Christ!' said Mark. 'No, that's impossible, I didn't mean to – '

He crossed to the sink and threw up. He made unpleasant sounds. Frank put a chair under the door handle and waited. Mark ran the tap to clear it then he splashed water on his face. When he turned he was a terrible colour and tears were

187

running from his eyes from the effort of vomiting. Frank stood by the door.

'Who would?' said Mark. 'It's impossible.'

'They did,' said Frank, 'then they cleared his room and took his diaries and letters and books. But what did you do?'

Mark drank some water. 'I can't say it,' he said. 'I can't say it to you.'

'Yes you can — you'll feel better.'

'Look,' said Mark, 'we were all told to do it. After Dodgson. And my position, I mean when they PVed me I kept something back — '

'I'll bet you did,' said Frank, 'something to do with Mummy — and Daddy — and Mummy's first husband.'

Mark straightened. 'I informed on Bob. He was saying things and writing . . . things; they told us it helped keep people on the rails. The worst that happens is a transfer to another part of the service. There was one chap left a wad of Top Secret stuff in a restaurant, all they did was transfer and promote. know for sure — '

'Writing things? Bob?'

'Yes. After all, you don't have to take stuff out to remember and record its contents do you?'

'No,' said Frank, 'no — and what else did you do?'

'I gave them the negative.'

'What?'

'I stole it when Rose got the photos back. They needed a photograph. Also, I let in the man to fix the telephone.'

Frank shook his head. 'All that?' he said. 'All that for the red, white and blue?'

'Once you start,' said Mark.

He drank some more water. Someone tried to open the door.

'Hang on,' said Frank in a cheerful voice, 'we're a bit jammed in here, won't be a sec.'

'I'd better go.'

'Yes,' said Frank, 'then you can tell them about our chat and what I think.'

'No,' said Mark, 'no, I'd never do that, but I don't believe he was murdered.'

'Yes, you do,' said Frank, 'when I said it you believed it. You

188

felt it like I do. One more thing — was there any sign of an intruder in the place when you went through with the police?'

'No.'

'Then why did you think it?'

Mark poured himself some whisky. 'The people on the other side,' he said, 'not the Welsh woman, the other side, they said something.'

'What?'

'I don't know. They had Rose in for a cup of tea, and they pulled the blinds and they told her something and said that a plain clothes man had told them to tell nobody.'

'Plain clothes?'

'I think Special Branch. Not the ones who went through the house.'

'And Rose didn't tell you.'

In a whisper Mark said, 'That righteous cow! Do you know what she is? Some kind of Christian bigot, some fundamentalist sect, her appalling father, the doctor, used to invite his neurotic *women* patients for sessions of *exorcism*. Do you wonder he had to emigrate? She wouldn't tell you anything. Neither, I must admit, would she lie. She simply told me they'd been forbidden to speak.'

There was a pause and then he said, 'She's like my bloody mother and I *loathe* her.'

He got up.

'And your son was like Dostoevsky's Idiot. No help to anybody. All the same I loved him. I'm not gay but I loved him because he had this quality. I don't know why I betrayed him. I think the quality he had was to show you what you are. I don't know. If it was I'm a sort of natural Judas. I did it in a dream, almost. I never meant to, right up to the moment I knocked on the HEO's door. The same as now. I never knew I was going to betray them to you today. It wasn't you. I don't like you any more than you can stand me. It was your wife. Her expression at the graveside, and the people next door pulling the curtains and having Rose to tea. And what good will it do? To anyone?'

Frank took the chair from under the door handle. Mark went out, down the stairs and out of the house.

Frank found the disinfectant and a scrubbing brush. He had

scrubbed the sink, the table top and was methodically scrubbing the chair in which Mark had sat when a short, bulky young man with a large head came into the kitchen. Frank did not look up. The man's face seemed to vibrate with intelligence, he seemed also on the verge of smiling all the time and he had a glittering eye.

'I brought this,' he said and put a large manila envelope on the damp table top.

'Thank you.'

'Accident?'

'Hmm, something got spilled.'

'Ah.'

A silence. Frank finished and went to the sink with the bowl to clean it. He knew he was going to have to deal with Matty but resented the fact that simply by his presence he seemed to demand that you wake up, concentrate, give your entire attention because so much was going on in his brain that if you didn't you got left behind.

'We ought to chat,' said Matty.

'Not here.'

'No, of course!'

Helen came in with plates and sniffed and said, 'Golly it smells hygienic in here.'

'Hmm.'

'Where's Mark?'

'No idea,' said Frank, 'isn't he in there with you?'

He took the manila envelope down to the office and shut himself in. It contained three consecutive copies of the *Senator* from the previous year. In each was an article by Bill Pickett. The overall title of the three was: 'The Whistle Blowers'. Frank looked at the small, blurred photographs of Agee and Ellsberg and Marchetti and Marks and Prouty. Pickett's list was all-American except two who had published in England: Bloch and Fitzgerald — one South African, the other, by name if not by place of birth, Irish. Neither had been career members of secret organisations like Agee, or Bob.

The light in the office came through a frosted window with bars outside and the frosted glass on the door. Frank turned off the overhead light. It always felt private and secure in there. He could faintly hear sounds from the shop where Anne was dealing with customers. He switched off the telephone. Then he opened the safe and took out the Bob notebook. He brought it up to date, facts on the left-hand pages in continuing sequences; opinion, based on fact, on the right-hand pages. When he finished he glanced again at the Pickett articles and wrote on the right-hand page : *Perhaps they only kill their own if they turn?* and then *Who cares while there's telly and bingo and James Bond and the oil lasts out to pay the dole? I didn't until last week.*

He took the tape recorder from the inside pocket of his suit and ran it back to check that the conversation with Mark was all there. Then he put on an ident and date and removed the tape to put it in the safe with the tapes of the inquest and the bank interview. He regretted he had not bought it in time for the police interview. He put the Bob notebook back in the safe and locked it.

He sat with his feet on the desk in the dim light. He had slept all night last night for the first time since the day the doorbell rang. This time last week he had been in the place known locally as Rose Cottage – identifying Bob. Now Bob lay in the shadow of Caversham Park which, like GCHQ Cheltenham, runs in double harness with the Americans, in this case the Foreign Broadcasting Information Service which is run by the CIA.

He had never given a damn about do-gooders and bleeding hearts: the conditions in prison, the fact that every now and again the Old Bill killed someone in custody, the clamour concerning women's rights, racial equality, the anti-nuclear protesters ... on it went, daily, weekly, monthly and yearly and on he had gone doing what made sense which was to look after his family and pay the bills.

If the majority were told that a bloke called Jones had been about to blow the whistle on GCHQ when he fell off a roof and was killed they would have said, 'Serve him right'; if they had been told he might have been pushed they would have said, 'That's a bit much,' or 'What do you expect?' and ordered the other half. As would he; being, until a week ago, in the majority.

You don't, he would have said, sign up for something like that and then break your word.

He considered all this. It hurt him to think it. He groaned and pressed his hands hard against his chest under his ribs as if to hold it in. He began to yawn with his lower jaw dropping on its hinge as if he could not get in enough air. He shook and could not control it. It was like a fever; he felt cold and the sweat broke out making him clammy. Slowly it passed.

He remembered, with shame, his attitude in the angriest moment with Bob in the square: they were walking the tarmac road, passing the bandstand, and Bob had said something about only taking the job in the first place because it seemed secure as well as interesting.

'Well what's wrong with that?'

'It's conniving to stay on if you feel as I do now, knowing what I know now. Do you see?'

'No I don't – I bloody well don't, Bob.'

Bob stopped, shoved his hands in his pockets, hunched his shoulders and said, 'You could go on to say – as they do to justify anything that's profitable but disgusting – that if I don't do it someone else will.'

'*That's right!*'

Frank was raging. He glared at Bob. Bob looked unhappy.

'I'm sorry, Dad, I didn't mean to get you going, just hear this bit and then we'll drop it – when I was still at Bristol and drunk one night someone told me a story. She was the daughter of a refugee, you know, and she said that before the war in Nazi Germany there was an executive with a firm which made fertilisers – perhaps it was one of her relations, perhaps I don't even have the small details correct but I do remember *exactly* the implications – so: this firm made a particular insecticide to which no one paid much attention until one of the Nazi ministries started to buy it in bulk. Really huge quantities. By chance this executive found out why ... '

Frank remembered this moment with particular clarity because Bob, looking inwards as he recollected, put a hand out to hold his shoulder. He remembered the warmth of the contact.

' ... being on the inside and being an executive. He was decent enough, a well-educated chemist, married, and of course he had taken the oath – '

'What oath?'

'They all had to take it in 1935 if they wanted to stay in business – the Oath of Fidelity . . . like the Official Secrets Act. Well, this executive thought, "Even if I say something it will make no difference, *except* I'll be out of a job – and marked. Besides," he thought, "no one will believe it, because it is so unlikely that I can't really believe it myself – "'

Frank with his feet on the desk, alone in the half light, understood – as he had not on the day Bob said it – exactly how the Nazi executive felt . . . no one will believe it because it is so unlikely that I can't *really* believe it myself . . .

'He thought,' said Bob, ' "Perhaps I've got it wrong. After all *there is nothing in writing.*" So he shut up. The insecticide was a gas called Zyklon-B. They didn't actually use it on the Jews until a few years later in 1943. These things creep up a little bit at a time. Each time the liars in authority give their reasons, like the national interest, until one day the smoke starts to come out of the chimneys – and then those doing the job say to each other in the evening after a hard day's work, "Well, if I didn't do it someone else would – and I've got my pension to look after." '

They had reached the mouldy statue of William IV who stood against an old blank wall.

Frank looked at the wall of his office in the dim light.

'How do I do it, Bob?' he said. 'How the hell do I do it? – I can't write your book.'

5

When the guests had gone he walked with Matty.

Round the shopping centre with the metal boy cartwheeling on the red wall; down and under it with the water falling from the two chutes; not seeing nor hearing but hammering away at the problem.

In the end, after rejecting the idea of an appeal to an MP or the use of a solicitor, it came back to Bill Pickett.

Matty had recently talked to Pickett. Pickett was on holiday for two weeks at the moment.

'What's the most I can hope for?' said Frank. 'I'll tell you because I've read the stuff now, the most I can hope for is a few weeks' notoriety if Pickett can get past the Official Secrets Act and the libel laws.'

'No, no,' said Matty, 'if we could dig enough up you could get published in the States – and then perhaps here.'

'But I don't have any contacts,' said Frank and stopped ...

'Yes?'

'One of the ways you prove your phone is tapped is to ring up a few friends and tell them that there's going to be a subversive meeting somewhere, and lo and behold the Special Branch turn up but you don't!'

Matty chuckled.

'What's so funny?'

'Nothing – it's just that people who do that don't usually look, if you'll forgive me, like you look.'

'Yes,' said Frank, 'well, perhaps I should get a T-shirt and jeans and a ring in my ear ... anyway I'll try a variation on the phone routine just described.'

They made some practical arrangements if the phone call worked. Some time later Matty said, 'When you audit computer accounts particularly if you're working late, on your own, you sometimes get the impression that you are playing chess with an unknown opponent. Somebody like you has programmed the thing, before that a number of people like you have designed it, so it is all in terms of logic, engineering, mathematics – practical. But in another sense it isn't. There are a lot of games you can play. People like me are always suspect incidentally, because we're the ones who know how to cheat the system. Creative theft, you might say, do it right and you make your fortune ... which makes me think that what happened to Bob might have been a mistake.'

They were sitting on a concrete-backed bench. A few yards away a wino lay on the small patch of grass on his side with his cap between his hand and his head. Sometimes he farted topping the sound of the water dropping from the pool above to the pool below.

'A mistake?'

'Yes. Even the Russians have given up killing their dissidents.'

'How do you know?'

'It gets out nowadays.'

'I can't deal with the theory,' said Frank, 'I can only do what's in front of me. Let's go home, I'm going to make the call.'

Matty still irritated him. He got up and walked, the small man came springing after him.

'What do you want, Mr Jones,' he said, 'I mean – what?'

'I can't let it lie,' said Frank.

'But you can't win,' said Matty, 'and as you said yourself – you can't stand out there and yell because your wife would suffer, and they'd have the excuse to clobber you.'

Frank stopped and turned on him. 'You listened to him, you put him on to Pickett, you encouraged him – you made the bullets and he fired, or intended to.'

'No,' said Matty, 'I listened and I told him the odds, he'd have tried it anyway. But I don't think that's got anything to do with it.'

'It must,' said Frank, 'it *must* have.'

'You have to consider everything,' said Matty, 'every possibility, no matter how unlikely. Consider that it was simply a-causal – '

'What the hell does that mean?'

'It means that two things happen which are totally unconnected, but because they happen close to each other – in space, in time, in the actions of one person – they *appear* to be connected, the one *appears* to lead to the other. You say – my son was discontented, my son intended to be a whistle blower, my son was murdered. I say – Bob was discontented, Bob intended to be a whistle blower – but at the same time for some quite different reason he was murdered. *If* he was murdered. You say – the security people must have done it. I say – it could have been someone else.'

'All right – if it was murder who else could possibly have done it?'

'An intruder, burglars are *always* hyped up, like muggers – everything racing, and if caught in the act you're best to open the front door and say "this way". Or – something to do with Dodgson. Those other two died. Bob knew one of them well. There was a government statement. Getting warm? Related to that – the Americans.'

'The Americans!'

'Yes. They're the senior partners, aren't they?'

'That's typical,' said Frank, 'because you're like Pickett, you're a Leftie, you've got yourself to the state where you think the Americans are the enemy.'

'And you think', said Matty, 'that the present so-called liberal democratic system only needs a bit of tinkering to get things right.'

They glared at each other.

'Don't get the idea', said Frank, 'I'd ever join your lot: I know a little Stalin when I see one.'

'Do you? – Well, what you've missed is that if it's coming it won't be a little Stalin, it'll be a little Hitler – Germany was full of people like you minding their own business and grateful that somebody had stopped the inflation. Not being a Jew, like me, or a black like him,' he pointed at a passing man who looked startled and increased his pace, 'you'll be all right, won't you?'

Frank raised his hand, stopped and then put both hands in his pockets.

'That was true about me', he said slowly, 'until recently. It will never be true again. But you'd better understand – I'm a non-joiner. Don't tell me I have to take sides – I don't have to . . . anything.'

Matty looked round. He pushed his hand through his black curly hair. He was breathing heavily.

'Did someone actually *design* this – ?'

'Took two years,' said Frank.

They both appeared to be absorbed in the three-sided black plastic obelisk which rose from the waters of the upper pool with its metal clock faces. They continued to walk.

'Better out than in,' said Matty once again on the verge of smiling.

'Yes,' said Frank, 'you could say that.'

'I just have,' said Matty. 'Do you enjoy Monty Python?'

'Why?'

'Bob did.'

'I heard that Dodgson enjoyed *Alice in Wonderland*.'

After that Matty drove to Manchester and Frank left a message on Pickett's answerphone.

TWELVE

1

Charlie Ricco walked into the shop making the bell ping and smiled at Anne. Anne stopped typing and smiled back. She was thirty-five and unmarried. She did not look after her mother but she was a terrible picker of men.

'Hello,' said Charlie, 'is Frank about?'

Anne was so dazzled she did not ask his name.

'I'll see,' she said.

Charlie looked round. A small operation, definitely a small operation.

When Frank came through Charlie noticed that he was even more preoccupied than he had been at Heathrow. He seemed to have shrunk and to lack spirit.

'Frankie,' he said, opening his arms, 'good to see you.'

Frank cheered up at the sight of him, 'Chasser, my boy – what're you doing here?'

'Well, I have to meet some fellers so why not the Ramada? Direct connections to Heathrow and Gatwick from here.'

'Come on up,' said Frank, 'I'm on my own; Margie, that's my wife, has gone to stay with my daughter in the States for a month – there may not be much food in the house but there's booze!'

'No, no, no – can't have that, I'm in the chair.'

Frank looked at his watch. 'Tell you what, I'm expecting a call – half an hour and I'm yours.'

'OK,' said Charlie and gave him the room number.

He left behind a scent of aftershave. When he was gone Anne said, 'Are you all right, Mr Jones?'

'Fine,' said Frank cheerfully, 'why?'

'You looked poorly when you came down.'

The glow of Charlie was in Anne's eyes. Frank smiled. 'Not like my old buddy,' he said; 'now he's a real bobby dazzler, always was.'

Charlie had been wearing a bomber jacket of fine leather, a snug polo-neck jumper, Italian slacks and handmade shoes to match the jacket. When he smiled his big teeth under the moustache were as white as the polo-neck and his fair hair flopped charmingly over his brow.

'He's like Robert Redford,' said Anne, 'he really is.'

'And my age even,' said Frank still smiling.

'No!'

'Hmm – some people have all the luck wouldn't you say? – he may be three years younger.'

'I didn't mean,' said Anne quickly, 'that you – '

'Of course you didn't, you see Charlie always believed in exercise, he was always very physical being your natural athlete.'

Frank looked at his watch. Give it thirty-five minutes. He went to the kitchen, put sliced bread under the grill and opened the fridge for milk and butter. He watched the toast while taking the two gold tops off the milk and pouring the cream from each into a cup. This he sipped very slowly. When the toast was done he buttered it thickly and ate it slowly. He noticed that his hands shook.

He had already chosen the gear: an old pair of trousers with flares which had been in fashion over ten years earlier and a wide-lapelled sports jacket of the same vintage. They came from the Oxfam shop the day after he telephoned Pickett. The jacket was slightly but not absurdly too large. It had two inside pockets: painstakingly, in the locked office, Frank had sewn a press stud to each so that even when the jacket swung open the inside pockets did not gape.

The hip pocket of the trousers had a zip. It would just close over the hip flask. He put on an old shirt with a slightly crumpled collar and a dull tie which someone had given him years ago and he never wore.

He stood in front of the long mirror in the bathroom. He turned both ways with the jacket undone and used a hand mirror to check the back view. Nothing bulged. He deliberately put his keys, wallet and handkerchief into the side pockets of the jacket. He put his specs case into the breast pocket so that it bulged over the top.

He walked. Then he ran up and down the last flight of stairs – all secure. He sat on a chair in the bedroom. He lounged back on the bed. There was one other item. He took it from the bedroom drawer where he had hidden it after removing it from Helen's handbag. In a sense it was the only risk. The rest, as the actress remarked, you can take two ways. He put it under the handkerchief in the side pocket. He took a last look. In contrast to dashing Charlie here was middle-aged, ill-dressed Frank, looking ten years older, and no threat to anyone. Poor old bugger. As his first employer used to say, 'Never waste time on the ones whose minds are in the pence column, Frank, little men are born that way.' He definitely looked like a man in the pence column.

He could have walked there in five minutes. He made himself take ten. He paused on the bridge over the Inner Distribution Road clearing his mind, his eyes seeing but not noticing the traffic underneath. The flags outside the red-brick complex of hotel and offices were, suitably, the Jack and the Stars and Stripes side by side next to the house flag. Even the fittings in the main foyer made him look suitably shoddy and he was surprised no one asked him where he was going. He took the lift.

Charlie was delighted to see him.

'Come in, come in – look at this, they must have been expecting us.'

The drinks cabinet was a chest with a brown candlewick cover on its lid. Charlie opened it with a key: a lovely light, a fine arrangement of bottles.

'Sit you down,' said Charlie as Frank appeared to admire the decor – rich brown, delicate fawn, the pictures on the wall, the bottle of champagne in the ice bucket, the real pineapple and other fruit in a bowl nearby. This was definitely Ricco country.

Frank took out his spectacle case and put them on.

'Bloody things,' he said apologetically, 'but in artificial light, not that this is, it's easier to see – you must be glad you don't need them, Charlie.'

199

'No, not me,' said Charlie, 'what'll it be – they've got the lot and if we run out I'll have 'em re-stock.'

'Vodka,' said Frank, 'and anything really, tonic?'

Charlie was very deft. 'I'll join you – it's not the real stuff so we don't have to be too frugal do we, chief? Well! How long's it been? I was really chuffed to see you again the other day, Frankie, it made me remember all sorts of things. I hadn't thought about Korea for years – you remember we were in company with that Yank carrier, *Valley Forge*, was it? Here, put in your own tonic. Ice? Fine. You remember the time the old man went bananas and came out on to the key flat and said to the marine corporal, "Get that horse out of my cabin"? He used to lower a bottle of gin a night . . . Hmmm, well cheers!'

'Cheers.'

Charlie spread himself over one of the two large beds balancing his drink, lighting a very long cigarette. 'Nobody here remembers any of that do they? Korea? By God! if we'd had the publicity they gave the Falklands, eh? All those smart-arses saying it wouldn't work, then when it did, saying it shouldn't have happened! How many pilots did we lose in those two years? And that was just us. Flying piston-engined aircraft against MiGS. We did it though.'

'Yes we did.'

It was less stilted after the first drink. Talk of rest and recuperation in Australia, in Japan; talk of ship's concerts and turning out at three a.m. Swing the lamp, Jack. After four drinks it was jovial and easy because Charlie had the knack of making you feel the centre of attention even as he spread his own jewels for you to admire. Every now and again it came round to current affairs; Charlie made funny and obscene comments about politics and politicians and Frank laughed but failed to take his cue, so Charlie changed tack and made funny and obscene comments about the Yanks with the same result which brought Charlie round to making funny and obscene comments about the Arabs. Which brought them to their fifth drink.

'Remember Vic?' said Charlie.

'Sure.'

'A good hand, Vic.'

'Yes,' said Frank, 'yes he was.'

'I really admired what you did, Frankie, over Vic. I couldn't have done it. Not even if he'd been my closest oppo.'

'He was mine, you see.'

'Oh I know, I know,' smiled Charlie kneeling across the bed to hand Frank his glass, 'but I couldn't have spent all my savings.'

Frank seemed embarrassed. 'What's money, Charlie?'

'Essential', smiled Charlie, 'to my style of life – so don't knock it.'

'I watched him go down,' said Frank, 'he bloody nearly made it but his cooling system blew and that was it. His Mum was a widow, I'd met her, decent woman. His old man bought it in the war like mine.'

'I know,' said Charlie, 'but it often bugs me – I mean it brought out the fanatic in you. We all knew that when you got an idea in your head it took a bit of shifting. And you were pretty bolshie, weren't you?'

He chuckled at some recollection.

'Was I?' Frank adjusted his spectacles. His hair was slightly ruffled. Charlie lounged, adjusting his slacks, drawing on his long cigarette, watching Frank who still sat awkwardly as if out of place in this hotel.

'Yeah,' said Charlie, 'you were, and at the same time you were very straight-up and by the book. We never knew which way you'd jump.'

'Oh?' said Frank. This was not quite the old, easy Charlie.

'I mean after Vic, for example.'

'I suppose', said Frank, 'I used to get a bit closer to those North Korean bastards.'

'Yeah! Don't you remember when you ditched on a beach and the Yanks picked you up and gave you fried chicken? We never had fried chicken and they never had, what was it, bully beef? No, tinned ham! So when we came to fetch you in a chopper I swopped my sandwiches for the chicken, you remember? And I said to you on the quiet, "You're not the Lone Ranger, Frankie – it's just a job."'

'Just a job,' echoed Frank finishing his drink. 'This may not be the real thing, Charlie, but it warms the cockles.'

'Help yourself.'

'You?'

'Sure.'

Frank became busy with miniature bottles and unscrewing tonics. Between the beds were rows of buttons for the radio and the big colour television. Charlie pressed the radio switches until he found some musical wallpaper and switched on some shaded lights.

'I don't think I'm like that now,' said Frank with his back to Charlie, 'you can't exactly apply all that to selling business machines.'

'How is it? I mean how is it now, it must have been very tough ... your son I mean.'

They drank. Frank wandered about the room but was seldom far from Charlie who settled in a chair with his legs on one of the beds.

'Bob? Well the funeral was ten days ago. I'm working. Bite on the bullet time. Margie was shattered; Helen, that's my daughter, said her Mum should stay with her for a bit – so I dug into the building society ... '

'What happened, Frankie? Do you want to talk about it?'

'If you like. It was daft – he fell off a roof where he lived. Just like that.'

'What did he do? I mean work.'

'He was a linguist at GCHQ Cheltenham.'

'Oh?'

'That's Signals Intelligence.'

'Must have been a bright boy.'

'Yes,' said Frank, finishing his drink and stretching his hand for Charlie's glass. Charlie shook his head.

'Shave off!' said Frank. 'You used to drink the rest of us under the table.'

'Quite right, chief – and then walk the line,' he finished his drink and handed over the glass, 'on my hands.'

They both laughed.

Frank said, 'Do you want to turn over to gin or whisky or – '

'Why?'

'Running out.'

Charlie reached a long arm for the telephone and told room service to bring up a bottle of vodka, the best, and bottles of tonic by you-know-who – oh yes, and ice.

'Vic', said Frank, 'used to do the best Carmen Miranda I

202

ever saw in a ship's concert.' Charlie glanced at him. Frank was steady. He was unflushed, but something about the way he said it and then laughed told Charlie that Frankie was feeling the effect.

'And you', said Frank, 'were the best bloody pilot I ever met, fixed wing as they say now, you were a definite natural, my boy – so cheers.'

They drank.

'You were saying about Bob?'

'Was I?'

'Yes – a bright boy.'

'Oh yes,' said Frank, 'but not happy.'

'Oh?'

'Nope.'

'What was the trouble?'

'I', said Frank, 'couldn't understand it. You see, Charlie, when these kids go to university, and they learn all that ... theory ... that's another world. Not practical. Well, anyway I did my utmost to stop him.'

'To stop him what?'

'Resigning. Chucking it. Good job, pension.' Frank slurred on 'pension'.

'Oh,' said Charlie. He seemed to be considering something. He was no longer smiling.

The room service waiter knocked on the door. Charlie smiled again, took the tray, gave him a huge tip. He looked at the bottle.

'This is better,' he said, 'you're going to like this – the Russians take it neat, very cold, pinch of salt and a big bite of pickled cucumber and some black bread.'

'Sounds good – you tried it?'

'Not in Russia, Frankie.'

They both laughed. Frank laughed for quite a long time then recovered and said, 'Sorry, it's been ... er ... difficult – I really miss the silly bugger.'

'"Course you do. So would I. I get the impression there's a bit more to it than that – am I right?'

'I need to pump ship,' said Frank, 'the old bladder seems to have shrunk lately.'

'You want to watch that,' said Charlie, 'that's the first sign.'

Frank left the bathroom door slightly ajar, he ran one of the taps in the basin, he took his time; after he washed his hands he left the tap still running. When he came back its sound mixed pleasantly with the musical wallpaper.

'I topped them up,' said Charlie.

'Oh yes ... more to it ... yes,' said Frank, taking his glass. He seemed uncertain about saying more.

'You don't have to tell me,' said Charlie.

'I want to,' replied Frank, 'but ... you know ... Official Secrets. I signed that when I came out — did you?'

'Of course, Frankie, also, after I came out, I was a bit involved myself.'

'Involved?'

Charlie smiled. 'Yeah — you remember I got a commission? The white cap band, HMS *Hawke*, don't eat peas off your knife — all that?'

'So you did. You did and I didn't!'

'Because you were bloody bolshie, right?'

'Right!'

They both laughed and Charlie slapped Frank on the arm, shaking his head.

'Well,' said Charlie sitting down opposite Frank, shifting the chair so they were almost knee to knee, 'part of that was going to Greenwich, the Royal Naval College. I met a bloke there, not naval ... they used to have all sorts of civilian VIPs to lecture us, anyway I met this bloke. I was really gung-ho at the time — the little sports car, Korean veteran, you know. He was next to me at a guest night in the Painted Hall. Not by chance I found out afterwards. Well, a year or two later I resigned, quite unconnected with him, it just happened to be golden bowler time. Not long after I met this bloke again. He offered to give me a leg up.'

'Yes?' said Frank in a baffled way.

'Well, I was recruited, you see. And then I did one or two things for auld lang syne — and cash in the hand!'

'What things?'

'Finland, for example. I went there a couple of times. Once as a tourist and once as a seaman and I brought something back each time. You know, Frankie, things they didn't want to put in the post.'

He chuckled. Frank was looking at him in amazement. 'You mean you did a James Bond?'

'I should be so lucky. No birds, nothing shaken and not much stirred. Just a postman.'

'Like that bloke er ... Glynn?'

'Wynne.'

'Bloody hell, Charlie – you could have been caught and shut up in the – '

'Never,' said Charlie, 'not me, you know me, try anything. Anyway, you can trust me. See.'

'That's a relief. You see about Bob ... I couldn't tell the police, but he'd *never* have fallen because well, he just wouldn't. Wonderful head for heights.'

Charlie was silent.

'No,' said Frank, 'and then there was his mother, it was bad enough him being dead without upsetting her more so ...' He tailed off.

'Go on,' said Charlie, 'spit it out, you'll feel better.'

'Well,' said Frank violently, 'he was bloody miserable, we had a row. I think he was drunk. The pathologist didn't say anything but it took very little with Bob. I think he'd be here today if I hadn't got stuck into him and he hadn't had a jar too many.'

Charlie got up. The tap was still running. 'Now it's my bladder,' he said. As he went into the bathroom Frank moved as fast as he had ever done in his life. When Charlie came back he was standing by the ice bucket with the champagne in it. Their two drinks were still by the bed.

'So you don't run a diving company,' said Frank, 'I just worked it out!'

'Oh Christ, yes,' replied Charlie, 'very useful it is. I'm not a regular. I'm not your civil servant. It doesn't work like that.'

He drank and winced slightly. Then he took the nearest tonic and topped up his tumbler. Frank did not appear to notice. Instead he took the vodka bottle and filled his own glass.

'Cheers,' he said and his speech was more slurred but his legs were steady, 'here's to double oh Ricco.'

They laughed and drank. Frank became reckless. 'Bottoms up, wingsy-bash, it's tot time, gulpers not sippers.'

He whistled like a bosun's pipe and yelled 'Uuuuuuuup spirits.'

Charlie laughed, he was now slightly unsteady.

'Stand fast the holy ghost,' he shouted and they both drained their tumblers.

'More,' said Frank, 'for Bob's Dad and his old oppo, the man of steel.'

'I'll pour,' said Charlie firmly.

'You pour, skipper.'

Charlie poured himself a small vodka and topped it with a tumbler of tonic. For Frank he poured three fingers but when he lifted the tonic Frank said, 'No, no – neaters, my boy – you only die once.'

Although Charlie had all his days been a ladies' man he had forgotten the one when you bring her to the flat and she drinks gin and orange. You water the gin and spike the orange. In Frank's hip flask there had been pure alcohol innocent-looking as water. It was now in the two tonics. In the vodka was fifty per cent water from the ice bucket which contained, now, the displaced vodka.

Frank watched Charlie who went red and then eased back across the bed holding his glass. 'You know what, Charlie,' he said deliberately lurching, 'I am definitely unfit to drive.' Then he roared with laughter and dropped on to the other bed.

Charlie was having difficulty in focusing.

'You're a really decent hand', said Frank, 'to tell me about the secret stuff. I expect you still do it?'

'Yeah, course I do. Once you're in, you know, Frankie, you're in for life.' He tried to sit up and clutched the bed. 'Jesus,' he said, 'I think I better – '

'What you want, Charlie – some water? I'll get you ... '

Frank went into the bathroom, poured the balance of the pure alcohol into the tumbler and topped it with water. When he returned, he said, 'Ice, must give it some ice,' and dropped ice cubes into it, splashing, and letting some fall on the floor.

Charlie took it and drained it. He fell back again on the bed.

'Listen,' he said, 'they telephoned me ... 'bout you.'

'About me,' said Frank, pulling a chair to sit near the head of the bed so that the two recorders in the inside pockets would get it all.

206

'They always telephone,' said Charlie, 'I never met one of the buggers in all the years – except ol' J.B.'

'J.B.?'

'Told you about J.B. Wake up, that man!'

'Oh, Greenwich.'

'Been a good friend, J.B., got me out of a few spots of bother with the law, you know?'

'No – tell us!'

'Can't do that – well, let's just say ... you get nicked y'see an' then you say "Pardon me, officer – if you would kindly ring this number, my ol' son."'

They both roared with laughter and Frank repeated, 'Ring this number!'

To Frank, Charlie's face blurred in and out of focus. He put down his glass and took the soft flesh on the inside of one wrist and dug in his nails.

He said, 'They telephoned you about me – why was that, Charlie?'

'Pickett,' said Charlie. He had his eyes closed.

'Don't go to sleep,' shouted Frank and shook him.

Charlie started up. Frank just ducked the punch. Charlie stared round shaking his head. His fair hair flopped and he no longer looked at ease.

'What the hell?' he said.

Frank waited.

'Frankie?'

'Yes Charlie?'

'I've got to tell you something. I'm here to ... '

He flopped back on the bed.

'I'm here to', he said again, 'warn you.'

'Charlie Ricco', said Frank clearly, 'is in Reading to warn Frank Jones – what about, Charlie?'

'You see, Frankie, they keep in touch.'

'Who?'

'DI5.'

'DI5,' said Frank, 'I thought they were MI – '

'No, no, no,' said Charlie, 'Jimmy Flecker always calls them DI5.'

'And Jimmy Flecker is your mate, Charlie, the one you met at Greenwich? I want to get it right.'

207

'Course he is,' said Charlie, 'he's the only one I ever see. He's the one I bring stuff back to. You know what — ' he said and lurched across the bed towards Frank. The whites of his eyes were bloodshot round the blue and the capillaries in his cheeks burned. 'It was ten years before he invited me home — ten years! And can you believe he was jus' roun' the corner from the college all the time. His wife doesn't like it. She should never have married into it. Jimmy doesn't understand women, thas the trouble, Frankie, the job comes first with Jim.'

'Of course it does,' said Frank, 'Queen and country.'

'Now lissen. Keep away from the journalist.'

'Pickett.'

Charlie was making a tremendous effort to speak clearly.

'Him. There's an H and S file on him. You realise that? You realise he's on their side, Frank?'

'I didn't know that.'

'Oh yes.'

'Good job you tol' me.'

'I wanted to keep you ... out of trouble y'see ... I mean when they phoned and they said there's this old shipmate of yours I tol' them you were bloody bolshie but dead loyal.'

'I am.'

'I know that.'

'What would have happened if you hadn't told me in time, Charlie. Charlie, wake up, it's important, what would have happened?'

'They ruin you, ol' pal, it's easy; they'd fit you up. You'd be banged up in a cell or better still ... '

'Come on, tell me, I want to do the right thing, Charlie — what else would they have done?'

'Put you in a loony bin, plenny of doctors on the payroll get you certified, my ol' lad — Frank Jones gone bananas, strain of son's death, certified ... '

'Not make me have an accident then.'

'Wha'?'

Charlie started to laugh. 'Wha'? Accident? Why bother? Eh?'

'*Listen*, you're here to tell me. You have orders to tell me — so tell me. Would they have fixed me up with an accident?'

'No, no — they don' have to do that. *We* don' do that! ... oh

208

yeah ... nearly forgot ... they said, "Remind him tha' America's a dangerous place." So ... Frankie, America's a dangerous place. Enn it? Always was.'

'You mean if I don't do as I'm told something could happen to Helen? *Charlie* – is that what you mean?'

'It's wha' they *said to say* ... if you were fanat ... fanatical an' bolshie like you were after Vic went in the 'oggin. You know what, Frank?'

'No – tell me.'

'You should ... get rid of ... those bloody awful clothes an' make the mos' of life.'

'I will.'

'Thas good. I wanna keep you out of trouble, see?'

'And you, Charlie, you'll go back to J.B., right?'

'Right.'

'In Greenwich?'

'Right.'

'J. B. Flecker, and you'll tell him that the only reason I contacted – '

'You did,' said Charlie, sitting up trying to focus, 'you definitely did contact by phone ... very stupid, my boy ... they'll use you ... '

'I know. I'm very sorry. I only wanted to tell him that as far as I was concerned I wanted nothing written about Bob.'

'Good lad ... I'm ... I'm bloody smashed, Frankie ... used to be able to ... '

He closed his eyes again. His jaw dropped and he breathed as if he were gagging on something. Frank wondered if he would die of alcohol poisoning.

He got up carefully and looked round. It took all his will-power. Then one by one he emptied the tonic bottles, the vodka bottle and the champagne bucket into the lavatory in the bathroom and flushed it.

He refilled the bucket with water and put in the remaining ice cubes. He took all but Charlie's glass and washed them and dried them carefully. Then he used a towel to wipe everything he could remember touching. He polished the wood on chairs, the taps, the lavatory seat, the lifting edge of the drinks cabinet lid and the doors where he might have touched them. All this in case Charlie died or choked on his own vomit later.

He considered whether the room service waiter had noticed him. Charlie had taken the tray at the door.

Using the towel to hold things he squared off the room. When he left he used a handkerchief to open and close the door. Instead of the lifts he took the stairs which were for emergency only. They had bright yellow paint on the hand rail supports.

He came out opposite a kitchen, turned through a door into the foyer and then left by the side door. At home he took off the trousers, jacket, shirt and tie, put them in a plastic bag and after dressing drove to the tip and ditched them. All the way he prayed he would not be breathalysed.

Then he went to a public call-box, dialled Matty's number, let it ring three times and hung up. He left and went to another call-box and waited outside. It would take Matty five minutes to reach his call-box in Manchester.

The phone rang in his box. He picked it up, heard Matty say 'Computers here,' and replied, 'He came to warn me.'

'Right.'

'But it's worse. He threatened Helen in America if I do anything. Margie's out there too.'

'Did you believe him?'

'Yes.'

'Let me think about it, there's a few days before Bill Pickett's back.'

His head ached and he was parched. He locked up carefully, drank a pink of water and fell into bed. He woke to the phone ringing. He staggered down to it.

'Yes?'

'Frankie?'

He froze.

'Frankie?'

'Charlie,' he said slowly, 'I've got the worst hangover I ever had in my life. Speak softly ... and thank you for seeing me home.'

Charlie did not speak for a moment then he said, 'It was a great evening.'

'You're right,' said Frank. 'And I really appreciate the advice you gave me, it was good to speak to an old oppo and I'd been worried about old Bob.'

Charlie chuckled, he sounded relieved. 'Any time, ol' pal. See you again soon ... and mind how you go.'

'And you,' said Frank, 'an' you, ol' pal.'

2

He drove to Greenwich and parked in the station car-park. It was still the tourist season and the place was lively with people come to look at the *Cutty Sark* and the Painted Hall. He went through the electoral register street by street until he found the address of J. B. Flecker whose wife, M. E. Flecker, was not understood by him.

He drove to the street. A dull, grey street – some kids about both white and black. The house had railings and a red front door. Close as it was to its neighbours it was a detached house and, he thought, big inside.

He had considered many things since last night. Now he felt empty, isolated. He knew only two facts: they had sent Charlie to warn him off, no boat-rocking; and Charlie reported to the man in the house across the road. Suddenly he got out of the car, ran across the road and up three steps to the front door. Afterwards he could not remember moving; he was simply there, listening to the bell ringing in the house. All that mattered was to stand face to face with the man who ran Charlie Ricco and get the truth out of him. He heard feet coming; the door opened and a woman said, 'Yes?' She was tall and had white hair which was arranged elegantly round her head. His impression was that she was well dressed. She had a friendly expression which took him by surprise.

'Mrs Flecker?'

'Yes.'

'I'm a friend of Charlie Ricco and he suggested that – '

'Charlie Ricco?'

'Yes. He's a colleague of your husband's and – '

She had become cautious. 'I'm sorry,' she said, 'you've made a mistake, I don't know anyone called Charlie Ricco.'

'But I was only speaking to him last night,' said Frank. 'Your husband is James Flecker, J. B. Flecker?'

'Yes he is – perhaps you should speak to him.'

She turned and called, 'Jim, could you come a moment.'

There was a sound in the room beyond the hall on the left and then a tall man came through the door. He used a stick to support himself because one leg was badly crippled. He had the expression of someone interrupted in work and impatient to return to it.

'What is it?'

'This gentleman wants to talk to you.'

'Oh?'

'My name is Frank Jones, an old friend of mine, Charlie Ricco, gave me your name and suggested – '

'I've never heard of Charlie Ricco – what do you want?'

'Are you J. B. Flecker?'

'Yes.'

'And you don't know me? You've never seen my photograph for example.'

'Why should I – are you on television or something – is it to do with that?'

They stood there side by side in the hall, the handsome crippled man and the elegant woman.

'He was at the college,' said Frank.

'Oh,' said the man, 'was he? Well, well, so was I at one time, I went into submarines – it was the time they couldn't get enough volunteers so they simply drafted us – was he in subs?'

'No,' said Frank, 'he flew.'

'Ah.'

There was a silence. Frank thought they must hear his heart banging.

'But I fear', said the man, 'I don't recollect him. What did he suggest I might do for you?'

'Nothing,' said Frank, 'it's a mistake. Sorry.'

They closed the door.

All the way across the road Frank said, 'You bastard, Ricco, you bloody sly bastard.' He bitterly regretted his loss of control.

He drove up on to the heath. Then he took out Charlie Ricco's business card. Before leaving the hotel room he had gone through his wallet. He looked up the address in the A–Z.

It was in the Ladbroke Grove area. He parked a street away

212

and walked. There were steps from the pavement to the front doors; two storeys of peeling façades above that and a smell of dustbins. When he found the house there were no plates on the street door, only a battery of small bell-pushes and slots for name cards. Some had them but they had weathered and were indecipherable.

He pressed the bells one at a time until a voice rasped out of the grille, 'Yes?'

'Electricity Board,' said Frank grimly.

The buzzer went. He pushed the door and went in.

Brown lino on the floor, worn treads on the stairs: coin telephone and a table littered with junk mail, bills, final demands. He read some of the names. He went to the telephone and checked the number against Charlie's card. It was the same number. Whatever else this was it was not the headquarters of the Full Fathom Diving Company.

Someone came down the stairs, looked at the mail on the table and went out.

Frank left the building. He walked slowly until he came to a telephone box. Perhaps even Matty was in it and lying? There were no directories and he had to ask the operator for the number. When he got through to the *Senator* they told him, yes, Bill Pickett was on holiday. He dialled again. This time the tone was unobtainable. He checked with the operator. Disconnected. Cynthia Goodburn had gone. He had realised too late that she was the only one who might know Mr X because if Bob and she had been lovers, and if they had come back together from London that weekend then Bob would have told her where he'd been.

As he approached his car he saw something and swore. Of all things a bloody ticket and this wasn't a restricted parking ...

It was a white envelope under the wiper. He took it and looked at it. It was sealed. He opened it. Typed on a plain sheet in capitals was a single word:

AMERICA

3

When it was dark he left the house and drove out towards Caversham. The main gates of the cemetery were closed. On one side of the huge place was a housing estate and a school and no way in. He drove to the other and found a narrow path with bollards either end. Off this was a lane which had the peeling green railings on one side. It led to a playing field. Halfway along, making sure he was alone in the place – no lovers, no burglars – he put the old blanket folded over the spikes and hauled his way over.

He was trembling when he got to the other side. It took him ten minutes to find the grave in the dark. He put the blanket down and sat on the cold earth at Bob's feet.

For it to be real it had to be spoken aloud. In the days of the Newbolt book, the days of praying for his Dad, that had always been the understanding between himself and God. Pray aloud even if you only whisper.

'I can't do any more, Bob – I can't risk Helen. If I asked her, and I never would, she'd say "Go to the limit." I never understood revolutionaries, I mean Northern Ireland – for example – but I do now. I haven't the stomach for it. I thought I had, but if I was faced with the ones that did it and given a gun I'm not sure I'd pull the trigger in cold blood. It was different in Korea and after Vic it was personal. I never ever thought I'd be licked. I mean in my ordinary life I always knew I'd have to fight for it but I always reckoned to win. That's the worst of it. I've let you down.'

The noises of the night, the solitude, the half moon and over there the dishes sucking voices round the globe down on to the spinning tapes of Caversham.

Bob had said, just before they got into the taxi to catch the train, 'You know I really did believe it ... about the Americans,' he was laughing at himself, 'I thought I knew all about them from the films, and do you remember, Dad, how we used to be glued to the telly when I was a kid watching them go to the moon – *and walk on it*! Wasn't that bloody *marvellous*? Do you know I even bought the idea – for years – that the man in the white hat always wins in the end. I did!'

214

'So did I,' said Frank to the earth mound, the temporary cross, 'I suppose that's really the opium of the people.'

4

When he got back to the house it was after midnight. He locked his car, looked round – no muggers – and went to the door. As he put the key into the lock the door opened quietly inwards. The hairs on the back of his head seemed to lift.

He went back to the car, opened the boot and took out the foot-long wheel bolt spanner. Then he went back through the door and deliberately freed the latch to lock it behind him. He listened. Nothing. He put on the light. Nothing. He moved fast to the door from the passage into the shop. It was locked.

Taking a breath he ran at the stairs and went up them faster than he had ever done in his life. He banged the sitting room door open and put on the light. Nothing. He did the same with the kitchen. Then he took the next two flights hitting each door in turn going through with the spanner ready in his sweating hand.

Every light in the house was on. He was panting. He came into the bedroom, his and Margie's bedroom, last.

He looked round. Saw something and could not believe what his senses told him, looked again.

Laid out neatly on the top of the chest of drawers was money. Ten and five-pound notes, cheques, silver and copper. The latter were bagged up for the bank. Beside them was the paying-in book.

Then he got it.

He ran full pelt down all the stairs, sweated and swore as he fumbled the key into the door. He went into the shop and switched on the strip lights. The place was neat and clear. The street door was still double-locked and bolted. His office door was locked. He unlocked it and went in. Like Bob's room it was exceptionally neat. Laid out on the flat table he used as a desk were the other contents of the safe.

He unlocked the safe which was bolted to floor and wall. The heavy door swung open. The tapes, the Bob notebook had

215

gone. It contained only one thing. He took it out and unfolded it. Los Angeles is an enormous, sprawling city. On this map one section was shown in detail. And one place was marked with a red-ink circle: the avenue where Helen lived.

He went round the desk and sat in his chair. He looked at the building society passbooks, the insurance policies, his will, his and Margery's birth certificates, their marriage certificate ... forms, documents ... and he remembered something else he had read: if the State does not give protection to its citizens they no longer owe it allegiance.

As he replaced the documents it did not occur to him to call the police because, in the new reality, he understood that there would be nothing for the forensic people to find; inevitably they would suggest that he had done it himself because, following the death of his son and their contact with the police at Cheltenham, his mental stability was in question – and what, they would ask, was he doing taping conversations and did he really expect them to believe that funny story about his old shipmate Charlie Ricco, not to mention the LA map.

He waited twenty-four hours before ringing Matty's number from a call-box and receiving the answer from another. Matty's duplicates of the tapes and a photocopy of pages from the Bob notebook were safe. As Bob might have said, and often did when he was a boy in the 1960s admiring the astronauts – 'one small step for man.'

THIRTEEN

The Interrogator had a new sports car, Japanese, low slung, which he took round the lanes like a silver bullet until he came to the high wall, a mile long, abutting the road.

The gates, not the original gates but special gates placed in the most remote part of the wall, were locked. The Interrogator hooted; a door in the gates opened; a man in country clothes, English and tweedy despite the heat, came through and ducked to look at him and examine the pass.

Inside, the last rhododendrons, azaleas and camellias had died two months before; what had been exotic and scented was now an oppressive green; the whole place dense and the drive meandering. When the house came into view he found it ugly: a heavy granite affair, late Victorian, made more oppressive because all curtains were drawn at the ground-floor windows: nothing gracious or stately about this home, merely something elephantine.

The drive widened to a gravel square; he braked carefully not only to spare the tyres but to prevent the least scratch on the low silver body.

As he approached the steps at the entrance two men came casually from opposite sides to confront him. Polite men in country clothes, each with a walkie-talkie.

He entered. The main hall and wide staircase were empty. As instructed he crossed to a door opposite and entered. It was a place a gentleman could feel at ease in: the chairs, the pictures on the wall, the very smell of it was right; behind the bar stood an ex-Guards sergeant-major in a glazed white jacket ready to serve and to keep both his ears and his trap shut.

Lord was standing, leaning on his stick, looking out of the French windows at the sunken garden.

He turned, smiled, extended his hand and said, 'My dear fellow.'

'Good morning!'

'Drink? We have your favourite, I believe.'

'Perhaps a little later.'

'Yes. Shall we?'

Lord indicated the glass doors; they went out past the dried-up lily pond and the stone urns into the semi-jungle effect of thick green which rose to over a hundred feet in places. The path was very narrow.

'Years since I was here,' said Lord, 'I'm glad we keep it up. Good for morale in the service, there's a pool you know, over there somewhere, for swimming.'

'Really?'

'Oh yes, and a stream, you can just hear it, very well arranged with waterfalls, largish pools, bridges, all artificial in the first place, done to the lie of the ground. Fished, I remember.'

'Ah.'

'Yes,' said Lord, 'yes, takes patience, fishing – I agree with your solution to "One" and "Two".'

'Thank you. It does avoid the courts on the one hand and er ... on the other it avoids ...' He did not like the phrase, 'termination with extreme prejudice,' so implied it.

Lord nodded. 'With regard to "One" there have been talks with the Attorney-General, and he has agreed; *but*, since Blunt, these sort of people, senior people like "One", are very, very cagey; they don't want their old age ruined by some journalist writing a book and some prime minister making a statement so that they're publicly blown, lose their K and all that.'

'Of course.'

'One can understand it,' said Lord. 'We are not, when it comes to "One" dealing with the grocer – immunity should mean immunity, wouldn't you say?'

'Absolutely.'

'My view is that we let him get on with it until we have him dead to rights, which we do not at the moment, legally. Then we'll turf out all his Soviet contacts and give him the choice.'

'Our good friends have finished clearing up I believe,' said the Interrogator.

'Oh yes. And Dodgson has taken the ghost train.'

The Interrogator looked puzzled.

'Prison jargon. They come in very early, catch the chap sleepy and undressed in his cell and ship him off to another prison before anybody else is awake. Not that he's been awkward but you can never tell if the opposition might put some IRA man up to sticking something lethal into him. We don't want any headlines. As for "Two" – now he *is* in the grocer class.'

They were in a place that seemed, except for the trace of a path, impenetrable. Lord stopped and leaned on his stick.

'I'm leaving him to Flecker,' he said. 'Flecker has a very creative bent. Of course it's extraordinarily useful to have the two of them in our sights in the meantime.'

The Interrogator looked at the handsome and ravaged features of Lord reflecting a greenish hue from the surroundings.

'Will our good friends be told about "One" and "Two"?'

'Do they need to know?'

'I'm not in a position to judge.'

'No,' said Lord, 'but effectively the operation is complete – come in, and have some lunch, do you know Greenwich at all?'

'No? Just passing.'

'I was there the other day. Wren was a master. I went down by river. Fine sight.'

'Yes?'

'Hmm. Wonder what the original palace was like? Elizabeth the First was born there I seem to remember; had a wonderful spy-master in Walsingham – I think we have a knack for it, don't you? It goes with the sort of mind which produces Emmet and Beachcomber, wouldn't you say?'

'I've never considered it.'

'Hmm – not quite the same as the chess mind or the computer mind, related of course, but not quite the same otherwise our good friends on one hand and the opposition on the other would have the edge.'

'Yes.'

'Take this place,' said Lord, 'just over there we let the public in – it all seems entirely open, they walk about in the spring and early summer and it delights them – it is, in fact, ravishing to the senses; they can take tea and ice-cream, there is even a coach park. They can sit by clear flowing water and see fish move in it. It refreshes them.'

He smiled at the Interrogator.

'All we do is keep for ourselves a small inviolable area – in it we are, as some foolish socialist politician said in 1945, the masters.'

FOURTEEN

1

In the late summer of that year a civil servant was posted from GCHQ to the British base in Cyprus. Not long after he arrived he strayed, while drunk on the local wine, into the Turkish sector. Frank read that he had been found in Famagusta, the city of the dead, where every shop and house remains as it was left in 1974 when the Turks took it. Sand has risen and sifts through the goods which survive the looting in the shop windows, so said the report picturing the ' ... still unsunburned civil servant wandering stupefied until a patrol found him hooked to the wire which protects a beach where East Germans come for a holiday; presumably the guns, the no-man's-land and the barbed barriers make them feel at home in the same way that tea like mother makes and fish and chips solace the British on the Costa Brava.' Frank was not interested in the journalist's opinions. He kept a file of anything which touched on Bob's death.

This item went on to say that when arrested the civil servant was carrying heroin of a street value in excess of fifty thousand pounds. The article cast doubts on the efforts of the Foreign Office to repatriate the man who, after all, knew some of the secrets of GCHQ. At the trial it was said that the drug came from Lebanon, by yacht, and was en route to Italy. The civil servant was sent to one of Turkey's notorious prisons although at the trial he protested that he had been drugged at a party on the British base. His relations were not allowed to visit him.

Some weeks later, and still in that season of the year when parliament is in recess and a third of the nation on holiday, eight Soviet diplomats and officials were expelled from Britain. They were seen for forty-five seconds on television denying the charges and smiling while their wives carried bouquets and smiled and said nothing at all.

Frank did not notice this item which had become a commonplace; nor was he interested in the report, at the same time, that a junior minister had to resign and give up politics for health reasons. Pickett noticed because the *Daily Mail* ran the two stories in adjacent columns for those who had eyes to see. There were odd rumours in the man's constituency among the local faithful who had selected and supported him over the years but these were stilled when, after a period of recuperation on a yacht in the Bahamas, the man was appointed to teach in a distinguished establishment. He even served on the boards of one or two companies. Pickett noted that although previously the man had been a frequent visitor to America he now never applied for a visa.

On the rare clandestine occasions when Pickett and Matty and Frank met to get up to date such matters were discussed.

In Soho the building which had been A. J. Ball Builder and Decorator became a wine bar.

Without appearing to exert pressure Frank encouraged Margery to write to Helen in LA two or three times a week. Obsessed with 'justifying' – as he put it to himself – Bob's beliefs and at the same time keeping the business going he waited with a terrible patience for Helen to come home. He had already decided the method by which Bob would be justified. Matty and Pickett agreed and quietly pursued the right man to see it through.

Just before Christmas Helen came home. She had decided to complete her thesis in the UK even though it meant giving up the American firm which had financed her Ph.D. so far and intended to employ her when she had completed it.

When he met her at Heathrow he wondered which of the passing crowd might be Charlie Ricco's replacement. He told her his plans for Christmas. He said that to be at home with an empty chair at the table would be a dreadful thing and he had a better idea. He did not tell her that, as with everything now, there was another strand, a secret undertow.

Matty once said to him, 'What happened to Bob, and in a way to you, Frank, doesn't affect ninety-eight per cent of the population – but it could hit any of them, like a car crash: so the least we can do is tell them the odds. The truth is that it's far too late for simple beliefs, things like unqualified honesty, or decency if you like, the worm's in the bud and as soon as you know about it – it's in you. The simplest parallel is infidelity, isn't it? That's what it is after all – and all those subtle justifications when you're sticking it into your best friend's wife or your wife's best friend. If you go through with this you're stuck with a secret life lying to your wife and daughter to protect them, not trusting Pickett or me, always looking behind the statement and the face for the real motive.'

'No,' Frank had replied, 'no, no, bloody no – Bob wanted the truth in the open. Freedom of information, isn't that it?'

'Oh true,' said Matty almost smiling, 'all that of course – but you want to feel righteous with it.'

'I'll tell you what I want,' said Frank, 'and there are a lot like me – I want to believe in England again.'

Matty laughed and said, 'Oh dear, oh dear me – I haven't laughed so much since Ma caught her tits in the mangle.'

'I thought it might embarrass you,' said Frank, 'you clever little chap.'

2

Among Frank's clients was a man who owned a gite in the Loire valley. Frank rented it for Christmas. They closed the shop a week before the twenty-fifth and went by car. In France they drove nearly four hundred miles, found the place, opened it, filled the big fireplace with logs and lit them, got in food and wine and endured the beds.

Frank went for walks on his own along the paths between the vineyards. The vines, pruned and bare, waited for the year to turn over. Margery said they were twisted as if in torment, also that they felt evil. Sometimes, nowadays, she said things like that looking ahead of her, speaking in a quiet, matter-of-fact way.

On his walks, further and further from the gite, the freezing damp air made him hunch and swing his arms as he had not done since the days of Whale Island. The village was two miles one way, the rising ground like inland cliffs, clothed in trees, undergrowth, weeds, three miles the other.

When he climbed in among the trees and pushed through along muddy tracks with brambles hooking his trousers he found clearings only half overgrown. In each was the mouth of a cave hacked into the soft rock to store wine in the old days. Then he found the house. It had two storeys with outside steps to the first floor and a garden. Every inch of it was overgrown. The creepers were as thick as ropes and the garden grew chest-high. On one side was a sheer drop. You could not see it until you were on it. He carried a pocket compass. With it he sited the direction of the main road between Chinon and Saumur. He found the paths which led to it and when he reached it he made a note of the best place to turn off and hide a car.

He had already discovered that in rural France you cannot receive a call by public telephone, there being no number to dial. As with certain modern architecture at such places as universities, designed to permit armoured vehicles and riot police a clear run to the centre of the trouble he deduced that this system was, in part, a security measure making the timed call impossible. This thought came so naturally he did not connect it with the worm in the bud.

There was a phone in the gite but he decided not to risk it. From the box in the village he made a call, let it ring twice and then put it down. He went to the café checking his watch. He drank bad coffee and good cognac and twenty minutes later called a box in Manchester. He talked for ten minutes as the coins in the glass fronted sections fell from sight.

The next day he went back to the shrouded house and broke into it, avoiding rotting floorboards. He spent an hour arranging lines of sight.

Then it was Christmas Eve, dull and lowering and the fire smoking. No one said that last year on Christmas Eve Bob came home in a borrowed car with a crate of wine from

Avery's in Bristol and bags which bulged and would not close and new records which he played in his room until the walls trembled. No one said it, and Margery smiled with every remark.

When the light started to go at about ten to five French time Frank said, 'Come on, let's get out of here for a bit – Chinon, it won't take twenty minutes and we'll see other people even if they are French.'

Coming to Faubourg, the false town, under the huge plane trees was like driving down the aisle of a gigantic cathedral, the rain started and when they reached the bridge it was hammering the car but Margery said, 'Oh how wonderful,' because high above the old town on the edge of the sheer drop the battlements of the huge shell of a castle were floodlit. The waters of the Vienne were high enough to flood the campsite this side and reach the terraces of the houses on the island supporting the centre of the bridge. They came over slowly with the rain twisting down the windscreen round the wipers and the garlands of lights on the far side smearing like melted gold on the glass.

They turned right off the bridge under lights and stars strung from the trees on the river walk to the shops opposite. The left turn into the square was blocked; they waited with the winker going by the Christmas tree and the statue of Rabelais for a gap in the oncoming traffic.

Margery said, 'That's the first tree this year,' and then was silent.

They parked under the plane trees whose branches were full of lights. The windows misted as they watched people in every direction, almost an umbrella'd mob, doggedly shopping. The owner of the gite told Frank that the French did all their shopping on Christmas Eve, went to Mass at ten, ate a huge meal beginning with oysters and *pâté de foie gras* and opened the presents at midnight. All the shops were decorated and in the street parallel to the one they had left the people tripped along on duckboards because it was lower in places than the river which seeped through.

None of this, told self-consciously by Frank, seemed to bring Margery back from some place in her head although she smiled and said, 'Yes? Yes, do they really?'

The oyster sellers were undercover when they ran for a patisserie to buy cakes to take home. In the back room there was a tea shop, neat and silent with poor lights because, as Frank said, 'They always save on electricity, the frogs, must have special eyesight.'

'This is genteel,' said Helen, 'fancy – tea.'

'Oh lovely,' said Margery, 'tea, what a good idea.' She ordered it in careful French and Frank was alert, fearing the woman would patronise her.

Then they sat like exiles. Frank hoped that Margery had not seen a gypsy woman lying deliberately on the pavement under the feet of the shoppers, a long skirt to her shoes, a padded jacket and her head covered with a piece of cloth whose green sheen made him think of the ducks in Regent's Park. By her was a tin for money, and a baby in a basket with a plastic umbrella balanced over it. The woman's clothes were sodden black. He had got between her and Margery to block the view. The thing had shocked him.

Margery poured the tea and said, 'I must give her something.' She left the table. Helen watched her go over Frank's shoulder.

'What was it, Dad?'

'A beggar. On the pavement.'

'I didn't see.'

'No. Never mind.'

Margery did not come back. Frank went into the shop and looked out at the square. He could see the gypsy on the pavement.

He turned abruptly into the back room and said, 'You stay here, would you, won't be long.'

He ran through the rain to the car. He thought she might have gone there to hide. It was empty. He ran down to the river dodging among the cars with them hooting at him and mouthing behind glass. He stood by the Christmas tree. He made himself think. If she had done it there would almost certainly be some commotion, the place was thick with people. He turned to look up at the castle. Then he remembered that last year Bob and Margery had decorated the tree and that her mood changed when she saw the tree he was standing beside.

He ran back through the square and began the long climb up

the twisting causeway of stone stairs towards the battlements. The rain ran into his mouth from his face as he gasped for air, by halfway he could hardly force one leg to move in front of the other. The rain soaked his hair to the skull, it soaked through the shoulders of his coat and through his trousers to his socks. There was a metal hand rail in the centre of the steps. To keep going he hauled himself up by it.

The gate in the keep was still open. He ignored the ticket booth. The area was like a dreary municipal garden with the parapet sharp against the upward glare of the floodlights from the town below. He could see her standing by the edge. He ran again as the man in the booth started to shout. As he got closer he made himself walk and when he reached her he carefully put an arm round her but did not pull her back. It was a fearsome drop into that rain-filled light.

She said without looking at him, 'After you climb all those stairs and think about things – it would be silly, wouldn't it?'

He had a violent stitch. He could hardly speak.

'Yes it would,' he managed to say.

On the way back he paid the man who shut the gates behind them.

'Don't upset Helen, will you?'

'Course not, M. – I'm not daft.'

In the patisserie they had fresh tea and Margery said, 'The bridge was beautiful from up there, and the lights on the water.'

In the night when she stirred he said, 'M.?'

'I thought of phoning my Compassionate Friend.'

'Oh?'

'Don't put on the light, Frank.'

'All right.'

'We've stopped talking.'

'I'm sorry, I find it a bit difficult.'

'Can we talk about Bob? Properly?'

'Yes, yes, of course.'

Then she talked for an hour without stopping while he lay by her in the darkness and held her hand and fought down the temptation to tell her his side.

227

3

On Christmas Day at three in the afternoon the telephone rang twice and then stopped. Frank made no move to pick it up leaving it to Margery.

'No one there,' she said.

'Father Christmas,' said Frank pointlessly.

Three days later he persuaded them to take the car and visit Richelieu while he stayed to work out some business matters for the New Year.

When they were clear he locked up and left. He had an hour. When he reached the overgrown house he checked the area before going inside. The cold seeped into him and the small rustling noises did not seem friendly. He heard them two minutes before they appeared and for no reason remembered an English-speaking Jap saying to him when he was on leave there in '51, 'At first we always heard your men coming, they wore boots, and we could smell them because they used some anti-mosquito liquid.' The Jap was smiling and healthy.

Matty appeared first, stepping jauntily in fur boots with his trousers tucked into the tops; he also wore fur mittens and a fur hat and could have defected from the Bolshoi at Charles de Gaulle the night before. As usual the motor of his intelligence seemed to be at maximum revs as he saw the house, looked sharply round, signalled to the others and moved this way and that on his short legs looking for Frank. He was at the mouth of the cave on the far side calling Frank's name when Pickett came into view. He wore old jeans and a bomber jacket, a long scarf was wound round his neck. He had cut his blond hair and looked like a depressed choirboy. With him was the other man, the one they had told Frank about, the one whose name was known for, as *Time Out* put it recently, his 'radical chic'.

Frank was surprised. He had expected a younger man wearing the sort of gear you see in the King's Road, possibly homosexual and certainly not Frank's cup of tea. This one was short and thick-chested with a gut on him and a beard that looked gun-metal in the winter light through the evergreens. He walked like a sailor. He wore a suit that was undistinguished enough to have been Frank's with a chain-store anorak over his bulk. His hair was cropped fairly close to his skull, going grey and on his aggressive nose were a pair of spectacles in National Health frames.

When he spoke saying, 'Not half bad, this,' looking round and smiling, 'I'd have chosen it myself,' the voice was deep, resonant and had grown up not far from Salford.

Frank did not know what radical chic meant but he knew a man when he saw one.

Frank left them to congeal for five minutes. He moved cautiously checking from his lines of sight that no one else had followed them and there was little chance of long-distance photographs of their meeting. He came out silently on the blind side and was standing in the open watching them before Pickett saw him.

'Brass monkeys,' said Pickett. He was smoking and the smell of it was heavy as if in a room.

'Well done,' said Matty cheerfully.

'Good journey?' asked Frank.

They were all moving slightly with the cold and the feeling of animals in a closed place circling.

'Owen,' said the other man sticking his hand out and smiling, looking carefully at Frank through his spectacles. Frank wondered if it was his surname.

They shook hands.

Matty grinning with excitement said, 'First the good news and then the good news – we found Mr X, Frank.'

Pickett also became animated and they competed to tell him like two children out of the playground, 'Guess what we did today, Dad, we ... '

Frank in his world of unreal reality, never unconscious of his dead son, had a feeling of violent revulsion – to them it was a *game*. He stood still as he had learned to in the last months, detaching himself from the violent upsurge inside him, this recurring sense of savagery wanting to break out from reason and restraint, wanting to smash, obliterate, maim – die. He concentrated outside himself on the words, the pictures made by the words. When it came to Mr X, that slurred, harsh voice on the phone in the small hours, he knew exactly the questions.

The contrast between Matty's sardonic tone, over-inflected for effect, and Pickett's nasal sub-cockney, even their differences in pace, made an irritating chorus as Owen, as still as Frank, watched from a few paces away.

'Bill found Cynthia Goodburn, what a lovely lady, and you were right, Bob had told her where he went that weekend – '

'She wouldn't talk to me at first, hates journalists – some prick had got into her house when her husband died and she caught him reading a letter – '

'I went to see her and told her it was for you, she spoke warmly of you, God knows why when one considers your unappealing character but she did, she told us and – '

'Did you tape it?'

Matty looked surprised at Frank's tone. 'No. Not with her. Bill took – '

'I took notes, I do shorthand you know and – '

'So we went down to the Garden of England and found him and he talked – '

'He liked a drink – '

'And he liked used fivers, he was disaffected, washed up and wanted someone "to put a bomb up their arses" as long as it couldn't be traced back to him so – '

'Named Greenwood. Proper name, I checked the register. Reginald Stanley Greenwood. German wife. No children.'

'A real old thug with a brutal sort of face, could have been a GBH merchant or the Old Bill, heavy and with back trouble because he'd been one of those Slam! Blatt! Thud! merchants who – '

'What,' said Frank sharply, 'what?'

'Matty means he was a martial arts expert of some sort – not judo, one of the others. He said that was a reason for recruiting him – '

'Recruiting?'

'Yes, Frank. Why?'

'I was remembering what Charlie Ricco said. About being recruited and then something else he said – '

'I loved his background, it was probably all lies but his story was that he was a real tearaway, used to take the tops off bottles with his teeth, worked as a racing car mechanic on a top team, that's where somebody contacted him first.'

'Don't tell me,' said Frank, 'he brought a few packets home.'

'That's it. And it accounts for the German wife.'

230

'So,' said Pickett, 'he became a career officer in DI5 – '

'He did a lot of nasty things and finally they put him out to grass, recruiting. By that time the martial arts business was booming in all directions, what with Bruce Lee and the general decline into brutalism. He said a lot of recruiting was done in those circles, and that was the connection with Bob. Apparently someone whom Greenwood had tried to recruit worked in Bob's section at GCHQ – '

'Who?'

'I don't know.'

'Which one told you that, Cynthia or Greenwood?'

'Cynthia.'

Frank walked away banging his hands hard together. His face was pale and he kept his back to them. Pickett remembered the day in the road outside Bob's house.

Frank turned and said quietly, 'Are you telling me that an ex DI5 man under the Official Secrets Act and dependent on his pension welcomed you with open arms and told you the story of his life. Are you?'

'But he's retired, Frank, and – '

'They *never* retire. Never. Ricco told me. Ricco was blind drunk. Ricco was only a part-timer. I *know* Ricco. I knew him through to the backbone. I *flew* with Ricco. Ricco was giving an old oppo his last chance. Ricco knew me. Ricco said two things: 'We don't kill people,' and he stressed the word *we* because a nod's as good as a wink to a blind donkey. I conned Ricco just long enough. Second – they never retire. Greenwood was under orders. Whatever he said to Bob, whatever he said to you – they know and they approve.'

'Whatever you say, Frank,' said Pickett, 'he hated the guts of some of his old colleagues and he wants them shat upon. It could be both things. He carries out his orders but he gets a bit done on his own. How do you think all these revelatory books get written about the security services? It's because individuals and groups inside them have an axe to grind – they want their version of the story out in the open.'

Owen said, 'Perhaps we could walk up and down a bit before I freeze to the ground?'

'The answer to that,' said Frank over his shoulder as he strode away into the undergrowth with Owen forcing along beside him, 'as Bob would have said, is it's the secret world putting out the story they want believed. It's called disinformation and – get to Bob, would you, I'm sick of this rubbish Greenwood fed you.'

Owen said, 'I could summarise if you like, I know it all. When this woman Cynthia's husband was found dead, apparently suicide, Bob did not believe it and was very uptight. He had a chum in whom he confided. The chum obviously couldn't give an opinion but thought he knew someone who could because a few years earlier a man named Greenwood had tried, and failed, to recruit him. There had been no hard feelings and they sometimes saw each other because this chum kept up his martial arts stuff and went to competitions. Greenwood was a respected coach. Bob went to see Greenwood. That much from Cynthia. From Greenwood himself. He liked Bob. He did not give a direct reply. But he did tell him about a very nasty operation outside this country carried out by some of his colleagues – '

'Which meant by him, I thought,' said Matty from behind.

'Possibly. He said it took place in Malta but Matty got the impression it was somewhere else, possibly Italy – '

'They killed people? Yes?'

'Yes.'

'Foreigners?'

'British. A whole family. A fake accident.'

'I see,' said Frank, 'and you are telling me that this helpful chum, whom we don't know, in Bob's section at GCHQ is exactly what he seems? That after Bob was stupid enough to confide in him he did not go to his supervisor and then get his orders from someone else?'

They were silent. They marched on until they came to another clearing and there they stopped and separated. An observer would have thought them confused and without purpose. They became aware of the distant sound of hunting rifles and Owen chuckled and said, 'They shoot anything that moves here.'

Suddenly Frank said, 'Greenwood was supposed to warn him off. Bob that is. Whatever he actually said to Bob – that story, or some other more likely, was to choke him off – he weighed up Bob as a blundering, timid sort of bloke not like all those stroppy lads doing judo or whatever it was. Instead Bob decided to go the other way because he was so shocked. And because Cynthia's husband was dead – and because he loved her and the child – got it?'

Owen said, 'I wasn't told that.'

'Nor were they,' said Frank looking at the other two. 'I didn't want any preconceived ideas when they went looking.'

'That makes it worse,' said Matty. 'Somehow that's so much worse.'

Frank said to Owen, 'Did you take Greenwood at face value?'

'I haven't had your practice.'

'No,' said Frank, 'and no one has told me the key thing.' He pointed at Pickett. 'Bob was supposed to meet you on the Monday he was found dead.'

'Yes.'

'They must have known that. Bob, being simple, was expecting Greenwood to give him permission to tell you about the family murder story. Yes?'

'Yes!'

'Well,' shouted Frank unable to control it, 'did he, for God's sake? Did Greenwood contact Bob that weekend? What did Greenwood say when you asked him? You did ask him?'

'I don't know,' said Matty interrupting, 'we don't know, he gave the impression that he phoned but he went all round it.'

'Of course he did,' shouted Frank and then stopped. He felt as if he had been stabbed. He now knew. Rather than say it because he feared he would not control himself he said instead, still shouting which was the nearest he dared come to violence, 'Wasn't it convenient that weekend, Bob alone in the house, waiting for Greenwood to call – can you believe such stupidity and he was my son, my son, my son … expecting a murderous old thug to permit him to tell a terrible story against the security services to a smart-arse, left-wing journalist … I mean, wasn't that brilliant?'

Owen did a surprising thing. He came over to Frank and said, 'In the merchant navy we used to cycle round the deck of the tanker to get rid of it – you fancy a trot, skipper?'

He was smiling. He did not stand too close. He and Frank began to jog up and down the clearing until Owen was puffing and muttering about his gut and the effect of fags. They stopped. He had a briefcase with him. It was very old and battered. He contemplated it.

'Old friend,' he said, 'something in there for you in a minute, but tell me what you want. I've read the cuttings, heard the tapes, heard what Bill and Matty know . . . but what about you?'

'I want', said Frank, 'a documentary like *Death of a Princess*. I want something that hits them and that they *hate* just like *Death of a Princess*. I want outrage, and questions in parliament and I want millions to see it.'

Owen considered his briefcase. Matty and Pickett looked anxious.

'You don't have a prayer,' said Owen, 'not a prayer.'

Frank stood with the feeling of life draining out of him. Finally he said, 'Why make the journey? Why bother? What are you doing here? They told me – ' he indicated the other two, 'they told me that you . . . ' All the rage had gone out of him. He felt sick.

'I worked it out,' he said. 'I'm an ordinary bloke, reliable and God Save the Queen, that's what I was – I have no power, no posh friends. It was useless to go to my MP or a lawyer once the inquest verdict was in. I worked out that the only way to tell people, other ordinary people, was over their heads. Over the heads of the lawyers and the police and politicians. Only one way to do that. Television. So I got Matty and Bill to find you. I've risked my family and lied to them. I didn't expect to change the system because I don't have the stomach for putting bombs under cars. I just wanted it said. I thought you – ' he looked at Matty and Pickett, 'both agreed.'

'We do,' said Matty, 'with the exception of bombs under cars, possibly.'

'You're still right,' said Pickett, 'you're right about everything except a documentary. We've been into it with Owen.'

Owen said, 'Would you glance at this?' He took a handsome, glossy folder from his briefcase and handed it to Frank. On the front was a red logo combining the letters AVMA. Frank held it stupidly looking from one to the other. He could not make his eyes read the words properly, but he registered the word Victims. He dropped it on the grass and Owen grunted as he bent to retrieve it.

'This is the report of a society called Action for the Victims of Medical Accidents,' he said as if at a board meeting. 'From your point of view the important fact is that the society did not exist until a man named Peter Ransley wrote a television play called *Minor Complications* about a girl called Stella Burnett. As a result of the screening the society was formed. In its first year it dealt with – twelve – thousand – cases. Also in its first year it raised over thirty-three thousand pounds. The GLC alone kicked in twenty-nine thousand pounds.'

He put the brochure into his old case which hung awkwardly open.

'A single play,' he said, 'and I think your story would make a four-part serial – four plays on, say four consecutive Thursdays.'

'Plays,' said Frank, 'plays! You mean soap opera. You'd turn my son and – '

'No. You know my record. But fiction. Seven-eighths of your story is deduction, out of sight, no company would touch it as a documentary.'

The sound of the hunters' guns seemed nearer and the sky was changing through the trees, darkening for more rain. There was no shift in the wind but the cold damp air seemed freezing on his face. He jumped up and down banging his hands and swinging his arms. He felt outmanoeuvred. The worm had all but consumed the bud. He knew himself to be beyond what all his life had been normal in his case. The monitoring intelligence seemed to separate slightly from the body which would take action.

He turned away saying, 'You can forget it. I shall visit Mr Greenwood.'

'He's dead,' said Owen.

Frank laughed involuntarily.

'Heart attack,' said Pickett wiping his nose. 'I went to the inquest.'

Frank could not stop laughing. 'Did anyone see it? Him dropping dead?'

'No. He was on his allotment.'

'Oh my God!' laughed Frank. 'His allotment, all this drama and he digs an allotment.'

'His wife did usually,' said Matty, 'to get away from the house.'

'How old was he?'

'Fifty-seven.'

'And how long', said Frank not laughing any more, 'after he was good enough to tell you the story of his life?'

'A week.'

'Look,' said Matty, mistaking the reason Frank intended to visit Greenwood, 'you shouldn't worry now, about your family. I don't think anyone's at risk, I'm sure it was the truth when Greenwood told us that *our* side seldom resort – '

Frank raised an arm as if to strike him. 'You stupid bastard,' he said, 'don't you realise what happened? Can't you put it together? There was no struggle, no break-in that Sunday, the police were telling the truth. Greenwood didn't telephone – he called. Bob was expecting him. I don't know how many ways there are to fix an accident but I know three. And one is a jab to a point which renders the victim unconscious without a mark. Then you can do what you like with him. That was Greenwood's job. He did it. Then he went leaving the door unlocked and the others whom he would never have seen, watched him go, went in, took Bob on to the roof, held him by the ankles and dropped him. Got it? Or shall I write it down so you can study it. There's more. Someone next door, on the other side from the Welsh woman, either heard or saw something and they were shut up by the Special Branch next day – but they did speak to Rose who also shut up except she mentioned it to Mark.

'They did not kill Bob because he intended to blow the whistle – you put me on to that, Matty, with your a-causal remarks on the day of the funeral – they didn't because none of the other whistle blowers came to a sticky end. They were harassed all right, but not hurt. So it had to be something else. The only other thing was Bob's association with Allen Goodburn, Cynthia's husband. He was a friend of Dodgson's. It boils down to this – either I'm mad and my son tripped and fell or they thought he was a spy, him of all people, and they weren't having another trial.

'And *that* is why Greenwood telephoned me in the night,

Tuesday or rather the small hours of Wednesday, forty-eight hours after Bob died. He was drunk the way Ricco got drunk, he told lies and truth like Ricco told lies and truth, like they all do, I expect, until they can't tell the one from the other. It was *not* conscience that got him on the blower, it was orders; it was *not* about the diaries, they had them already from the bank. It was because that morning, Tuesday, I had the police interview and it was clear I thought Bob might have been murdered. There was another bloke with the inspector. Bloke in a suit who never opened his trap. They made Greenwood phone to see if I'd come across something they'd missed. And Greenwood, like Ricco, put in a bit of his own. Now he's dead too.' Frank drifted towards Owen as if preoccupied with his reconstruction of events.

'I had a word with the German widow,' said Pickett, 'after the inquest, bought her a drink. She told me that three men came in a van and cleared Greenwood's room of all papers. They told her not to talk about it. She was used to that. She's going back to Deutschland, never liked the UK.'

Frank took Owen by the lapel with one hand. In the other he held a small object. It could have been a spray can.

'Keep still, please,' he said quietly and they were all still. 'This is a CS gas canister, compliments of my daughter from America. She never knew I nicked it from her bag.' He put it close to Owen's face. 'I nearly used it on Charlie Ricco when he took a swing at me. It couldn't kill you, but would put you down. Then I might. I was going to use it on Greenwood. Are you his replacement? I want to be sure you're not on their team, Owen. I don't know how to find out. So tell me.'

Owen was silent.

'You can't. And I can't be sure. These people poison the air. I want you to know I have made legal arrangements – everything is in my wife's name now, and after her, my daughter and after her if she has no children the daughter of Cynthia. I have nothing to lose. So if you undertake this and betray me I shall kill you. The publicity of what I shall say at the trial will go round the world and serve the purpose. When I was a pilot I killed a number of enemy pilots and people on the ground. After my best oppo died I did it with satisfaction.'

He let go and stepped away. Owen made a gesture of disgust

and lit a cigarette. Frank threw the canister into the trees. He took a flask from his coat pocket and offered it.

'Duty free,' he said, 'off the ferry, best in the shop – want some?'

'No,' said Owen. He picked up his old briefcase and walked away. Frank watched him carefully. He disappeared into the trees. Frank laughed and ran after him, calling. Owen kept walking. Frank caught up forcing his way through brambles.

'That's the answer,' he said, 'you've answered me. I didn't know any other way. Their man would have bullshitted and stayed. Come off your high horse, Owen, I want the bloody plays.'

Owen stopped and faced him. 'I nearly put my knee into your bollocks, old friend,' he said and his face above the beard was red.

'I know,' said Frank, 'I'd have felt the same.'

The other two caught up with them, panting, expecting violence.

'A drink,' said Frank, 'no chat – a drink.'

They passed the flask round and Matty sighed. 'Is it on?'

'Yes,' said Owen. 'I mean all I have to do is sell it to someone with a budget of one point three million, all on film! We already have the denouement of the fourth episode, in a place in France.'

He took a small tape recorder from his pocket. Frank regarded it for a moment and then produced his own. They began to laugh, and then laughed until they were helpless and the tears flowed.

'It's a farce,' said Matty, 'dear God, it's one of those black farces.that went out at the end of the 1960s.'

'Life,' said Owen, and then he stopped laughing and said, 'I shall want a document from you promising me all you know and protecting me if we fall out and you try to sue.'

Frank stopped smiling. 'No. Nothing on paper. I still think it's only a fifty-fifty chance with fiction, whatever you say.'

'No, no,' said Pickett, 'not quite fiction. For example Dodgson will be in it. Another name and other habits but people will catch on. They're not stupid, and the press will get more than a hint.'

'How do you know?' asked Frank.

Owen said, 'Bill will write the story for me, perhaps someone else will dramatise it. He and I have many contacts and sources. Also we'll protect you.'

They all began to walk, forcing their way back towards the direction in which Frank would return to the gite. The rain started, hitting the trees, making a swishing sound.

'You're right,' said Frank, 'most people are fair-minded and decent given half a chance. They'll make up their own minds. What would you call it?'

'I don't know,' said Owen, 'start with a working title, something to do with the way the secret world functions ... discreetly. We have to convey that impression, that they're just in the corner of your eye, and when you turn ... !'

'I thought, *Wonderland*,' said Pickett, 'to go on with.'

Matty laughed, stopped, raised an arm dramatically and declaimed:

> 'Long has paled that sunny sky
> Echoes fade and memories die
> Autumn frosts have slain July

'Do you like that? It's part of the original Dodgson's lament for the real Alice in the punt. Did you ever see the photographs he took of her. A right little Lolita was Alice. I suppose our Dodgson feels something of the same for the videos which used to turn him on. Do you think he's writing a poem in solitary?'

'I'll write the scene,' said Pickett. 'We have a few contacts on the prison circuit.'

Frank said, 'No pieces of paper' to Owen.

'Money?' said Owen.

'No money.'

'Anything?'

For the briefest moment Bob spoke in his head of Antigone.

'Make it good enough to last,' Frank said, 'try that.'

It was the best an ordinary man could do.